Régis B(

Back to Buenos Aires

A story loosely inspired by real, totally unrelated events.

Translated from French by

Jason Kavett

To Murche, Ato, Juju, and Raphou

A fetid, heady, unbreathable odor forces Major Roucaud to shield his nose in his folded arm. The deputy and the plainclothes cop accompanying him imitate him, pawing with impatience around the decomposing cadaver. Henriette is keeping them waiting. Henriette is always late—it is exasperating. A forensic pathologist by trade, her only appointment is with the dead, as she always says. The corpses are in no hurry, there is no rush, you might say. She's seen and cut up thousands of bodies in her long career. There is no vision of horror from which she's been spared, not really any kind of situation that could make her emotional, especially since the death of her only son over ten years ago. Henriette always takes her time, in every situation. That they have been waiting here, in Beaumont, in this little attic hole filled with damp heat and an odious mustiness, amidst flies, for over an hour—she couldn't care less. Roucaud finally sees her step out of her navy blue Renault 4L, a Gauloise hanging from her mouth. Filterless. She makes a little sign to him with her hand in a knowing way. Despite her clumsy gait, her excess forty pounds, her short brush-like hair, and the deep trenches dug by her wrinkles into her sagging face, Henriette has kept her old charm. Her sculpted beauty vanished with the years, the cigarettes have lowered her voice by an octave, her hips have thickened, her breasts have become heavier, her skin has withered, but the major still recognizes the sparkle of the woman who had been his wife for over thirty years, until the death of their son led them to separate, because it was impossible for them to share their grief. Each their own, each alone, that was more tolerable. But Roucaud still loves the young girl with azure eyes hiding behind the grumpy, portly old woman—Roucaud will always love her.

She takes almost three minutes to climb the creaking stairs that lead up to the second floor. She is out of breath when the major greets her in the doorway. She kisses him and immediately lights another cigarette. "Say, Jacques, doesn't it reek a bit of rotten meat here?" She laughs. Roucaud is irritated by her peculiar habit, her strange passion for de-dramatizing the most horrible situations with indecent, insane talk. He raises his eyes to the sky. She asks: "So where's the meat?" He leads her through the short hallway towards the room where the two cops and the gendarme are waiting, each of their mouths and noses covered with a makeshift handkerchief that they apply rigorously, in front of the cadaver lying in a sea of dried blood. Without seeing them, Henriette stops a moment in front of the body and raises her eyebrows dubiously. "It's been two, three days, let's say." She writes down in her notebook: *probable death on July 21 or 22, 1987.* Roucaud, one hand on his face, the other in his uniform's pocket, nods in agreement, as though to say he had guessed as much. Pointing at the other man in plainclothes, Henriette asks him; "And this guy, is he from work or did he show up here randomly?" "This is Police Inspector David Rosenberg." Henriette flicks her chin upward to nod at him, and puts on the glasses hanging from her neck on a chain. Supporting herself with the side of an armchair, she kneels with difficulty before the bloodied head of the poor devil. "He took a hard blow on the back of his head. A single one was all it took. He was caught by surprise. There was no fight." She opens the checkered shirt of the man lying before her, undoes his pants and removes them, reveals his thighs and his forearms. She pinches, raises, draws nearer, seeming absolutely unbothered by the intolerable stench of the place. "No trace of bruising, no fracture. The blow was not preceded by a struggle. I'd say that this guy did not expect to be attacked." She gets up effortlessly, steps back, walks around the body for the first time, observes the angle with respect to the window and the door. The others remain in silence, their mouths and noses covered, squinting out of their scrunched-up eyelids. They are awaiting the verdict of the *boss,* as she is called in the underworld, because of her

6

shrewdness. When they give her a cadaver, she unearths a murderer. For killers, if they don't want to get caught, it's in their interest to prevent the bodies of their victims from falling into the expert hands of the forensic pathologist. Henriette reflects once again, then declares finally: "They were interrupted. The death is accidental, in a manner of speaking. This guy," (she points to the cadaver), "was about to go looking for something in this piece of furniture."
The top drawer of a grayish Formica cabinet is open. Henriette points it out. Roucaud walks over and picks up a large spiral notebook. He opens it. "It's a manuscript," he says.
"Well it must have something in it that was not supposed to have been read. The guy kicked the bucket there. Boom. He collapsed. I think he didn't die right away but he did immediately lose consciousness and the hemorrhaging did the rest. The attacker left in a hurry and so didn't manage to take the notebook you're holding, Jacques." The major is absorbed by the title of the text he is holding in his hands. He has not yet opened it. On the first page is written: "Rodrigo Ganos – Autobiography in the Form of a Confession." The cop and the deputy draw near, curious. Roucaud begins reading aloud: "My name is Rodrigo. Rodrigo Ganos. I was born on May 15, 1945 in Buenos Aires…"

My name is Rodrigo. Rodrigo Ganos. I was born on May 15, 1945 in Buenos Aires. Of my childhood, I can remember only books, equations, classes. Mathematics, physics, chemistry, biology, Latin, French, Spanish, a bit of English, my father's native language. My parents spared nothing on my education. They wanted to get the best out of me, for me. An only child, I was their joy, their alpha and omega. My mother taught tango to the children of the bourgeois who had the means to give dance lessons to their progeny, as well as the higher-ups in Péron's government. My father was a waiter in a bar in the city. He worked a lot, came home exhausted in the middle of the night, but never neglected to come to my bed to give me a kiss before going to sleep. Sometimes, I awoke to the sound of the creaking of the door's hinges, or to the feeling of his breath on my neck. But I did not open my eyes, out of fear that he would give up this habit, if perchance he noticed that he disturbed my sleep. I can avow that no child on earth loved his father as I cherished mine. He was nothing but gentleness and tenderness. If sometimes it proved necessary to reprimand me, which was rare in any case, it was my mother who undertook this painful task. She liked correcting me no more than he did, but she resolved herself to do it when it was truly necessary. My father, never. I adored both of them. I was a child at once joyous and serious. I believe we never had anything to reproach ourselves with, neither they nor I. Not that I can remember, in any case before having sought to find out the truth about my father's history. And even afterwards, what did that change, essentially? I wonder if I did not love him even more in his weakness.

I was an obedient, brilliant, ambitious student. I could not stand not winning first prize in every subject. I also did not have many school-friends. Almost none. My parents sufficed to satisfy my affective needs. I was their *Rodri*, as they called me. They were my gods. We were happy. Life was eternal, punctuated by the suffocating heat of January, ruled like music paper by the dictatorship and the military parades, tango, and the peaceful sound of string instruments. I practiced the violin for long hours, diligently. On Sunday evenings, when everything was closed, my father would give me a lesson. He himself had once played a lot, had been in an orchestra, he said, a long time ago, when he lived in Ohio with his parents. We lived very modestly, in a small apartment on the third floor of a rundown building. In my first years, our situation seemed normal to me. Nothing shocked me, neither the odor of fried food that pervaded our little hole, nor the insufferable heat of the summers that left us immobilized in an overwhelming mugginess, nor going to get water every morning. As I became older, I began to compare myself with the other students in the local school. If it is true that some of them came from shanty towns, it must also be acknowledged that they were only sporadically present in class. Most ended up disappearing entirely. The children who persevered, on the contrary, were from a different social milieu from my own. Their parents were teachers, doctors, functionaries, bourgeois in any case. I finally realized, belatedly, that my parents were relatively poor, déclassés. It was then that I began to wonder. Secretly at first. Then, finding no logical answer to my legitimate questioning, I eventually asked my mother what had happened in their life. Why was her husband, Juan—the Spanish translation of his first name, John—why had this man, of whom I intuitively understood that his learning and knowledge were very wide-ranging, been unable to extricate himself from his condition of being a barman? Mama detested this question. She shrugged her shoulders, sent me to buy oil in the grocery store, returned to her cooking. I'd better take care of my homework if I didn't want to find myself in this situation, instead of needling her with my questions! I objected that Papa seemed, precisely, to have done his homework well as a child, since he was a fount of science, of culture, and a very good violinist, but that he had not been rewarded for that since he ultimately wound up a barman in a squalid city bar; he worked like a condemned man for a starvation wage and seemed to accept his situation without trying to change his miserable destiny. "Be quiet then! Have you no shame to speak like that of your poor father who bleeds from his veins for you?" she concluded. The conversation was over.

All the same, there was a mystery. Why did we accept this state of affairs? Why did Juan, my father, show this obstinate fatalism about his sad fate? That did not seem like him. Why didn't he seek to pull himself out of this condition, if only out of love for me, to offer me a better life, to allow us to flee the hovel that served as our nest?

His answers were rare and obscure. He stressed his limited Spanish. He had left Ohio at the age of twenty, when his parents died suddenly in an accident. He had roamed more or less all over the southern United States, had left the country during the war, had stayed some time in Mexico, had finally departed for Buenos Aires, where he had met my mother in a cabaret, and had never left her since. They had danced tango, it was she who guided him, initiated him. She was so beautiful in her red dress. She had introduced him to the city, its wide boulevards, to La Boca, the neighborhood where we still lived, to Café Totoni, to Plazza Dorrego and its innumerable antiques. And then I had come into the world… In short, the subject was quickly abandoned. I did not have the answer to my question: why did a cultivated man, who I sensed had been trained as an engineer, limit himself to serving *cervezas* to old alcoholics in a dingy bistro reeking of sweat and of piss, instead of seeking to raise himself to a more honorable station? Why did my mother, Soledad, accept that?

On May 15, 1960, on my fifteenth birthday, I planted myself in front of our little hole and demanded an explanation from my father. If he gave me no clear justification, I would not let him leave. I had chosen my day poorly. Since the day before, indeed, Papa had been in a state of extreme anxiety. He had woken up his wife in the middle of the night as he came home from work, which normally never happened to him. They had whispered for a long time behind the flowered curtain separating their bed from the kitchen. I had not heard their conversation but upon waking, I understood from the defeated face of my father that something was wrong. Another reason to receive a clear response, finally. It was a grave mistake. After having ever so calmly attempted to bring me to reason, Papa got angry. It was a black anger, a state of rage he had never been in before in my presence. He shouted, ordered me to let him leave immediately! I resisted firmly. His enormous fist came down on my face and sent me sprawling. I lost consciousness for an instant and a molar forever. For the first time, the only time in all my life, my father had struck me. It was a terrible aberration, for both him and me! He immediately kneeled before me in tears. "Forgive me, forgive me, forgive me." He did not want to, he should not have done that, but he could not give me an answer. For me, for all of us, I must never again ask him about this. I would do well to continue my work as best as I could, without asking myself – and especially without asking him – questions. I was a good kid, I was the boy every father in the world dreamed of having. He was going to go break open his piggy bank and buy me a present to be forgiven for his brutality, as sudden as it was unrestrained – a scale model of a Pontiac or Chevrolet Corvette, ok? But he beseeched me not to bother him again with my questions. In his light blue eyes, I read his fear. Worse than that, terror. Pale, with an elusive gaze, he smoothed his long hair turned white by the years with a trembling hand, with these same fingers that had just been balled together in his palm to come crashing down

11

on my scrawny jaw. At the moment, my mouth was filled with an unmistakable aroma: that of the iron released by the pasty blood spreading over my tongue. The bleeding was the result of the loss of my bottom tooth wandering now beneath my palate. Papa stepped over me and ran down the stairs in long strides.

It is in this metallic taste, this inimitable iodine flavor, that I am submerged in again today, twenty-five years later. Exactly the same taste, along with the same sharp pain running through my lower maxillary. But this time, the attacker is not my papa who gave in to a brief access of rage. The man who has just struck me does not regret his action. My torturer congratulates himself, on the contrary, and is preparing to begin again if I don't confess quickly. The police here have muscular methods, as they put it discreetly in the press. Yet my adopted country is reputed to be democratic. I left the Argentinian dictatorship a long time ago. I was arrested by a loyal police force, subject to international monitoring. The only thing is that the intensive smear campaign, of which I have recently been the target, has gotten the better of the most philosophical minds. I deserve no indulgence, no pity. I have been on the front page of all the newspapers for weeks. The pharmaceutical magnate that I have become cleared off after having pocketed the goods and stashed the money. Fishy, rotten, corrupt, abject, there is no adjective strong enough to characterize me. I am an authoritarian, an autocrat full of himself, a megalomaniac, and above all, endlessly greedy. What, I couldn't leave any crumbs to those who had worked for me all these years, from the highest-ranking to the humblest? So I had to scrape the bottom of the barrel of the empire I had founded, giving preference, still and always, to my personal enrichment? The photos of me that appeared in the papers during my forty-two days as a fugitive were not without raciness either. With or without a mustache, depending on the period, I systematically looked odious, troubling, immoral and lawless. They showed me only leaving a yacht, at the wheel of a luxury car, or leaving Cartier. Whereas I have always had the feeling that I exhibited a certain sobriety, they presented me everywhere as an incorrigible showoff, driven by my supposed pathological greed. The contrast with the poor journalists was striking—Marcel Carton, Marcel Fontaine, Jean-Paul Kauffmann, and Michel Seurat, held hostage in Lebanon, whose days of detention were counted off every night on the 8 o'clock news. While these brave reporters whose courage inspired everyone's admiration, who had left for Beirut for a noble mission, were rotting somewhere in the hands of their dreadful abductors, I, Europe's medicine magnate, had absconded with a fortune. The extremely wealthy Franco-Argentinian had vanished into thin air to avoid facing justice and answering for his crimes. Heroes on one side, cynical huckster on the other. Good, evil. It was extremely urgent that I be caught. That is what they managed to do yesterday, Tuesday, September 3, 1985, at the Bourget airport. I was preparing to pass through customs, I was almost through. I was going to get into the private plane that I had managed to unearth to reach Geneva, in order to then take a commercial flight back to my native Buenos Aires. From there, I would organize my defense. I would take apart one by one all the lies spread about me to the good people avid for gossip and I would prove my innocence. I advanced with steady steps towards the guy behind his counter and I gave him the false Argentinian passport that my mysterious protectors had made for me, they who had watched over me in the shadows since my arrival in France twenty years ago, without my ever really knowing why. The customs agent looked at me. Lowered his eyes to look at the official document, then rested them on me again. My papers were in order. He was going to give me the sign to advance, but just when he was about to return my papers to me, he suddenly changed his mind, brusquely withdrew his arm, and

13

began rummaging around in his desk. He finally took out a list of photos. He selected the photo of Rodrigo-Juan-Henrique Ganos and he stared at me for a long time. Even if I had disguised myself as best as I could, the resemblance must have been striking enough for the agent to linger over my features, to approach me and ask me finally to follow him. Evidently, he had recognized Rodrigo Ganos, whose photo had been displayed in the papers for many months, the odious character whose success had for a long time been just as dazzling as his recent fall. He recognized the founder of Rodrigo Chemicals, the king of anti-inflammatories, of sleeping pills and other analgesics as well as anesthetics. A large international pharmaceutical group, built from scratch in less than fifteen years and in which I still have a two-thirds ownership stake.

I should have no illusions, no one will feel sorry for me. No one will run the risk of raising a finger for a guy like me. Even less so given what people have learned about me over the past few days. People are happy when filth of my ilk is brought under control. If the world is still unaware of what precisely I am guilty of, I certainly know it. I should not be surprised. They will retrospectively justify my bad treatment. They will eventually bring my schemes to light. With a mug like mine and millions in my bank account, in any case I will have a hard time making people believe in my total innocence in this affair. I've got quite a record, as they say. The best proof, indeed, if they needed any, is that I disappeared as soon as the first bit of information was divulged, and that I attempted to flee to Argentina. Why would I have wanted to leave France secretly if I had had nothing to reproach myself with?

Everything went very quickly for me. I had no choice, I had anticipated how the process would unfold by the first days of the affair. As soon as my file was transferred to an investigating judge, I was quickly summoned. I knew in advance what would follow: they would charge me and throw me in pre-trial detention. I would not come close to being able to speak to a lawyer. With the reputation they had fashioned for me over the last few weeks, there would be few voices raised in indignation against the iniquitous treatment I was being made to undergo. On the contrary, people would lament the fact that there were two justice systems: one, for the powerful like me, and the other, hostile, severe, for the plebs. My fate would inspire no pity. So I saw only one solution: to hide, then flee to a country where I could work to reestablish my reputation. I believed in that, I really believed in that. I saw myself as free. I was convinced that I was going to get past the border police, until that damned customs agent recognized me. I was going to be able to return to my country and defend myself from there. The new Argentinian government, even if it has normalized its international relations since it has been reputed to be democratic, would certainly not turn over one of its children. From Buenos Aires, I would prove my innocence. Returned in full glory, I would take revenge on these dogs who wanted to have my skin. I would denounce the ignoble campaign of defamation of which I had been victim. I could almost see myself there already. But instead of that, last night I ended up in a black and white Renault 18 Break, with tinted and opaque windows. It took me here, that is to say, I don't know where. After forcing me into the car, they blindfolded me for the entire trip. I didn't see anything. Nor am I sure about how long the journey took, because they made me swallow something that put me to sleep for an uncertain amount of time. All I know is that it was a winding road at the end, when I woke up. The windows closed, a damp heat reigned in the car. The rolling of the turns together with the smell of sweat coming from the three cops – yes, they were cops – gave me a nausea that I had the hardest time holding in. To calm my body and spirit, I tried to organize my ideas in order to understand what was happening to me. Without much success. Only one thing was certain: I am not a "normal" pre-trial detainee; I do not have the same rights. In fact, I have no rights. I cannot, moreover, truly be considered a "pre-trial detainee," since I sense that we are totally outside the law. I did not even have the right to make a phone call, neither to a family member, nor to a lawyer. I have entered a world of lawlessness.

For many hours, I have been locked in a windowless room with decrepit walls, covered in faded, peeling blue paint. I have had nothing to eat. They gave me only a little to drink and they let me go to the toilet twice. A squatting toilet, without a door to preserve a bit of privacy. The three fellows observe me constantly. I think of my fiancée, Noura, of her olive complexion and her sweet skin, of her silver smile. Mine must be less winning at the current moment: I think they chipped one of my front teeth. My cracked lips have become swollen under the effect of the hematoma. The pain is sharp. Yes, I was hurt under the rain of blows. But above all, I was afraid. I really thought that I would not catch my breath and that I would die before being able to breathe a word. Just when I was going to lose consciousness, as I was beginning to let myself be carried away in the limbo where my mother's comforting face appeared to me, covered in her long brown hair falling over her frail shoulders, just when death was about to deliver me, the thrashing abruptly stopped. They suddenly comforted me, gave me a drink, helped me to breathe. They assured me that I was really wrong to be stubborn. All they asked of me was to confess. They would leave me alone. I should confess? But to what? Because I swear to them that I didn't know anything. Yes, I sold a few shares of Rodrigo Chemicals before the bad news came in. But that was only because I needed cash. I had no special information, I swear. I was totally ignorant of what would happen afterward. I was not familiar with the results of the study—those that had led to the collapse of the stock a few days after my sale. I affirm that to them once again, with all the sincerity that I try to communicate to them. Unfortunately for me, far from convincing them, I have the impression that my stubborn denial of the facts I am reproached for galvanizes their zeal, kindles their annoyance. Just as I am catching my breath, just as I am beginning to recover my spirits, I receive a monumental smack that pierces my eardrum. And I realize suddenly: these guys have taken no precautions. I have a chipped tooth, my face must be horribly puffed up, my lips swollen, gashed, oozing blood. There are probably already large bruises. If someone from the outside were to see me in this state, despite my bad reputation, they might be indignant. But despite that, it would no doubt be rather difficult to make myself heard. A smooth-talker like me, whose treachery is equaled only by his greed—you would expect him to make up stories, to try to inspire pity that he does not at all deserve. All the same, I would manage things so that my version of the facts would be broadly diffused. In France in 1985, people would not accept cops putting a guy into such a state, even if he was as detestable as me. So, these three individuals would not run this risk unless they thought it was negligible. If they don't hold back their blows and are not worried about the possible traces they could leave, it's because they have their own little idea in mind. They are sure that I will never be able to speak, simply because I will not leave this hole alive. If death does not intervene during the interrogation, it is surely waiting for me just afterward. No one will see me again, no one will interrogate me. They will not have to explain themselves. There is no other possible outcome. But then why do they need my avowals so much? What will a detailed confession be worth, even if it were signed by me, if I am dead by the time it is made public and if people know nothing about the conditions under which it was obtained? Not much, certainly. And then, once the guilty man is dead, the affair loses its interest, including for the police. No, in all reason, if they want to make me speak, it is because they are convinced that I have information. Either they obtain it and they get rid of me, or they don't succeed and they must pursue their business "all the way to the end," with the same method. The longer I remain silent, the longer I will stay alive. But in a few hours, or at the most in a few days, my fate is the same: to die here. I realize that, whatever happens, I will finish my life in this insalubrious basement. It is too stupid. I start to cry.

The guy who is looking at me right now with a malicious smile is David. It is not because he kindly introduced himself to me that I know that. I learned it when the two others addressed him, two or three times, when he hit me, and encouraged him to calm his passions. "Take it easy David, don't get carried away, let him breathe once in a while…" "Hey there, David, a little softer, you're gonna kill him before he can speak." So his name is David. He is blond, with light blue, greenish, eyes, an angular face, a wide jaw, prominent eyebrows and close-set eyes. His medium-length hair closes around his cheeks, enveloping his face like a wizard's hood. Even before he had put a hand on me, he terrified me already. His shoulders are broad, his arms thick, his fists massive. His white t-shirt stretched against his pectorals and abdominals is covered by a jean jacket that he has still not taken off, proof that the first blows have not really warmed him up. A boundless animosity for me emanates from his entire being, the reason for which is still totally obscure to me. As his associates seem to have realized also, I sense that he takes real personal satisfaction in beating me, going beyond the necessities of what must still be called, at this stage, an inquiry. And so here I am sobbing in front of this brute. Not that I am doing it on purpose and that I hope to inspire his pity or his benevolence. The truth is simply that I cannot hold back my tears. Unfortunately, the lamentable spectacle of the weakling crybaby that I am only increases his rage, if that were possible. He takes me by both ears, which he crushes in his enormous fingers, and shakes my head, grumbling at me through his teeth to stop blubbering immediately, or else he'll bump me off straight away.

"Got it?"

Curiously, his unrelenting hatred tends to make him seem more human than his two colleagues. As he continues to beat me, I grow less afraid of him. His anger is neither feigned nor cold. He hates me in earnest and for a specific reason, maybe for several reasons. He hold it against me personally, as opposed to his associates, whose torture, I foresee, will be more technical, methodical, professional. Inhuman. I sense that they left the first hours to David, as though to be nice to him. But time is passing, and the two other henchmen will soon take care of me. That will be worse, I am certain of it. If only I could understand what exactly David has to reproach me with, perhaps there would be a glimmer of hope. Only, I have no idea. I have no idea what it is they hold against me, what they mean to make me admit, what they believe they know about me. They insist that I confess to a financial crime, to Machiavellian embezzlement, of which I know nothing. Behind David, the two others stand up and stamp their feet with impatience. In the ceiling, the lightbulb, the only thing illuminating this gloomy room, gives signs of weakness. It flickers occasionally, casting terrifying flashes on the dripping walls and on these Cerberus faces. One of the two cops in the background silently lights a cigarette. With my still valiant eye, I cast envious glances at him. He gets up, approaches, puts his hand on David's shoulder and pulls him towards himself to make him back away. David takes a step backward and leaves a clear path. The guy moves forward again and hands me the pack of Rothmans Bleues. I take one out with difficulty, activating my swollen hands as best as I can. He watches me with his globular eyes. The man is heavy-set, taciturn. His gate steady, he roles his hips like a

19

cowboy getting down from his horse, his arms alongside his body, slightly separated from his thighs. His black hair is cut very short, but still brushed in a perfectly straight line. Despite the long hours we have spent stuck in this damp atmosphere, his dark gray shirt is still buttoned all the way up. He gives me a light, then softly puts the pack back in his pocket, puts the gold-plated lighter right next to it, perfectly aligned. This man is most certainly well organized, maybe even a tiny bit fanatical. I inhale a long mouthful, my first for a long time, The smoke sweeping through my lungs makes me reel a bit, at the same time that it briefly relieves my pain. The guy looks at me and smiles coldly.

"My name is Stéphane," he says in a longtime smoker's voice. I nod.
"Rodrigo – I can call you Rodrigo, right? – you are going to have to be more cooperative. David is hot-headed, as you've noticed, and you will see your face… Sorry but I am telling you honestly, you are not much to look at."
Without looking away from me, but addressing David, who is behind him, he adds:
"You've got to learn to control yourself, David. Look what state you've put us in."
The sturdy man, furious, is leaning against the wall, his arms crossed. He looks daggers at his associate and does not respond. Stéphane continues:
"Rodrigo, I will reformulate the question that we have been asking you since you've been here, and which you don't seem to have understood, given your obstinate silence for three hours already. We should have finished a long time ago, you understand? We are all a little exhausted now and we need a break. So I'll ask you one more time: who informed you about the results of the clinical study called AIDOS?"

In the guise of reformulating, he repeats the question that they have been drumming into me since I've been locked up here. If I tell him again that I was not in the know, that nobody gave me the faintest hint, he will really blow his top. Yet, if I did sell shares of Rodrigo Chemicals before the results of this study were made public and before the stock market price plummeted, it was not because I was informed illicitly, it was because I needed the money, that's all. AIDOS was a randomized blind study on over three thousand patients about the efficacy of a new anti-inflammatory medicine, in totally new therapeutic class, for arthritis of the knee in post-menopausal women. The study was entitled AIDOS for Arthritic Inflammatory Disease in blind Osteoporotic Subjects. The molecule that Rodrigo Chemicals had developed was a new-generation anti-inflammatory that was supposed to make possible a long-term treatment that would avoid the well-known side-effects of existing products -stomach ulcers in particular. Our miracle remedy was harmless to the digestive system, a small revolution. Alas! Just as the study was reaching its end, in the third and final phase, I received a call from the scientific director of Rodrigo Chemicals. He informed me that an abnormal number of cardiovascular incidents in patients receiving the real product and not the placebo would oblige us to suspend the clinical study. The events were statistically significant: not only would we have to end the study, but – and this was even more serious – it was more or less certain that the product would never be put on the market. The next morning, Rodrigo Chemicals sent out a detailed press release. The stock market shares would plummet in a few days. As I had sold a portion of my shares two weeks earlier, I was immediately accused – if not by the law at first, then by rumor – of having been informed of the results in advance.

The three torturers I have before me, and who have no doubt about my guilt, want to know who gave me this crucial information and for what purpose. I remain speechless. Famished, thirsty, morally and physically exhausted, crippled with pain, I would accept just coming straight out with what they are asking of me. Unfortunately, I don't know what to tell them. I knew nothing. Nobody gave me the scoop in advance. There was no conspiracy at all. I wonder where exactly their certainty comes from. Stéphane smokes as he gazes at me with a kind of pity. He seems to want to say to me: "What you've been through so far is nothing compared to what is waiting for you. Come clean and let's be done with it." I would be thrilled to follow his plan, even if "being done with it" means my getting bumped off, let's be clear. I have nothing to "come clean" about. Not even a crumb of a fact, I have to say. Nothing. Stéphane, who had sat down on a stool, crushes his cigarette until the last glow dies away and no more smoke emanates from it, then he gives me the ashtray so that I can do the same thing. He stands up to go chat with the third sinister fellow. The man in question is taller than the others, thin as a rake, his face emaciated, his cheeks hollow, his bald head covered by a single tuft of black hair plastered on his white skin. His deep wrinkles attest to the fact that he is much older than the two others. Who knows, perhaps he is in charge of the group. I wouldn't be surprised, judging by Stéphane's posture with respect to him, or the tone in which he speaks to him. He whispers. I have a hard time understanding what they say to each other. I put out my cigarette in turn and stand up with difficulty to place the ashtray on the desk. David straightens up all of a sudden, like a feline about to spring at its prey. What does he imagine? That I will flee? That I will lunge at them, chuck the object at his face? My hands are cuffed and all my muscles numb—I am not about to become a worthy adversary. With a single gesture, Stéphane orders David to calm down. When I sit down, I hear the nasal voice of the third man.

"You are a real tough guy, Mr. Ganos. I congratulate you on your courage. But your obstinateness will not lead you very far, believe me. No one will ever bear witness to your unfailing endurance in the face of adversity, to your ability to overcome physical suffering. You will not appear in the pages of History, Mr. Ganos. Because if you persist, I fear that you will not appear anywhere, you follow me?"

With a flick of his chin, he orders Stéphane and David to do what they have to do. Intuitively, I suspect that this is not going to be the pleasantest part of my stay spent in this terrifying place, even if what came before was not very cheerful. The two strapping fellows walk towards me now together. They stick themselves very close to my face. Their breath bothers me, and reminds me that I am also totally dehydrated, even more than them, of course. I ask them by a kind of borborygmic gargling that means: "Can I have something to drink?"

They look at one another in hesitation. Stéphane finally shrugs his shoulders and turns around to grab from the table a half-full plastic bottle. He gives it to me with a half-smile. A mysterious expression, the reflection of a regret, appears on his face. I ask myself if it is having to give me water that annoys him, or on the contrary, seeing me in this state. I don't think that this guy is very endowed with feelings or empathy. So I opt for the first hypothesis. His having given me something to drink will no doubt allow me to survive the following ordeals and to speak, but that could also delay the moment they will be able to get rid of me. I guess that he is starting to have enough, himself, of rotting in here, even if his position is – we can agree – clearly more enviable than mine. I hurl myself at the bottle that I hold directly against my mutilated lips. Despite the pain I am inflicting on myself, I swallow the lukewarm liquid as fast as I can, fearing that my torturer will tear it out of my hands at any moment.

However, posted in front of me with his arms crossed, Stéphane does not make a move as long as I drink, and lets me empty the bottle to the last drop. The water goes down the wrong way and I cough profusely as I give it back to him. David scrutinizes me with a fiery gaze. His teeth are clenched. I see his jawbones vibrating. I suddenly wonder if he is going to bite me. Stéphane insists one last time:

"You are sure that you have nothing to tell us, Mr. Ganos? I am asking you once more before we move on to serious things. And I will not exactly be happy about it. Who?" He screams: "Who gave you the information? You understand when you're spoken to? Who, for fuck's sake!?"

Since I still do not respond, Stéphane gives me a smack. Not very hard, but enough to make me lose my balance. Then he murmurs: "Absolute idiot."

Turning back towards the tall skinny man, he raises his arms in a sign of abdication. This candidate is stubborn as a mule, clearly. They won't get anything out of him unless they use other means. So, the tall man straightens up, in turn, and approaches. The two others move away. It's as though they are afraid of him, too. Almost as much as I am. As though they don't feel like bearing witness again to what the torturer is about to carry out. They foresee the scenario that is going to play out before them and, frankly, it can be sensed that they have seen better, more pleasant things. As detestable as I am, you would not wish on your worst enemy having to undergo the fate reserved for me. For my part, I imagine, I invent scenes, but unfortunately for me, my imagination falls well short of the reality. While I do anticipate that what awaits me has not the slightest bit of pleasure, I have no inkling of the degree of sophistication of the guy who will henceforth deal with me. More than an artist, the man is a virtuoso of torture.

I was not wrong about the abilities of the third man, the tall thin man with an emaciated face. Sometimes, not always, but sometimes, people bear in their visage the mark of what they really are. The timid seem timid, the gentle seem gentle, the wily seem cunning, the bastards seem honest. Regarding the abhorrent creature who tortured me for hours, his features betray everything about him, represent his profound personality with precision. His hollow cheeks, shadowed by deep wrinkles, his prominent chin, his sunken face, his close-set, piercing little black eyes, his almost bald skull on his long, blade-shaped head, and his straight neck, his slender torso, set on his long stilt-like legs, gave to this man the allure of the boogieman, as I had always imagined him. But the fantastic monster who threatened children was certainly more tender than my torturer today. Several times, I thought I would faint, suffocate, pass out from the electric violence of his treatments, but the silver-fingered man could always stop his action before it was too late. He kept me alive. Soon, moreover, he didn't even need to act anymore to tear cries of pain from me. It sufficed to brandish the instrument he had just used or to unveil a carnivorous smile to make me tremble, scream, beg. That is where he really became great. It was no longer even necessary to touch me for me to be prepared for anything, to accept all humiliations, to confess, if only I had something to confess. When he forced open my mouth with his hand, holding a diamond drill or a scalpel in his other hand, I sobbed like a child, imploring him in groans. When he approached my lower stomach, simply brushing my pubic area or my crotch with his gloved fingers, I reared up with all my strength, enough to break my spine, to faint. So convinced was he that I obstinately persisted in maintaining my silence, my torturer observed me with a kind of admiration mixed with incomprehension. But what could I have in my head to be this recalcitrant? And where did I get the strength to show such determination? Where did I get this almost magical power from? From a potion concocted by some modern Druid, or by Rodrigo Chemicals itself? I would have liked to explain to him, again and again, that I had nothing to reveal, but I didn't have the strength anymore. Suddenly, at the very extreme of despair and suffering, the idea occurred to me to make something up. A guilty person, an informer, a network, something that would give them something to work on. To have a respite, even if only for a day, even if only for an hour, a minute. But in my confusion, in the disorder of my body and my mind, I could not. As the tall skinny man brought a sharp pointed object toward my pupil, I closed my eyes, by reflex.

It is very humid and all three of us are suffering from this damp and oppressive heat as we continue over the dune. In the distance, the Atlantic rolls onto the beach in a thundering roar. The sand acts as a mirror: it sends back to us, from below, the sun. The rays burn us from head to foot and from foot to head. But nothing stops us, We continue our walk in slow strides. Papa is our guide. He is sweating too. He is dying of thirst, but he gives no sign of it. His very light skin is particularly sensitive, even redder than ours, Mama's and mine. He gives us a sign to advance more quickly. I end up passing Mama, who is struggling terribly. I have even offered to carry the basket. She hesitated at first but eventually accepted. Finally, we arrive at the water's edge. Mama spreads the cloth on the sand, letting the ocean breeze help to open it horizontally. I ask for permission to try the water. Okay, but not too far, it is dangerous. We have to be able to see you. I am wary of swims. I promise. But the first wave knocks me over. A second crashes down on me. A third. I am lying on the sand, suffocating. The water has filled up my lungs, I expulse what I can, developing a painful cough. Papa is sitting astride me, and deals me enormous blows as he screams. I am surprised. Papa had never hit me before.

It is not Papa. It is Stéphane. I had been absorbed in a delicious dream, but here there is neither picnic nor ocean. It was the buckets of water they had thrown in my face to get me out of the coma into which I was sinking. Behind him, the man with the face of an undertaker observes me with an indecipherable expression. The corner of his mouth is raised, but he is not smiling. He is beginning to doubt, I think. I imagine. I hope. Why have I still not spoken? I have the impression that in his entire career as a torturer, nobody has held out for so long. Or only guys who really had nothing to confess. So he has doubts, he must. He wonders whom he is dealing with. A real tough guy, tougher than anyone he has seen, or a poor man with nothing to say? Stéphane looks at him questioningly. I cough in torment, I have swallowed water the wrong way. Still leaning against the wall, David sulks, his arms crossed. He seems furious. They took the accused man out of his hands. The result is they haven't gotten anything out of me and I am half-dead. Well done!

Little by little, I come to my senses and catch my breath, I manage to drink. With my haggard eyes, I beg for an explanation, absolution, a bit of pity. Stéphane, with a cigarette in his lips, ventures to break the deafening silence: "He won't say anything, will he? What d'you think?". The torturer-in-chief takes a piece of mint chewing gum from its rectangular package, meticulously detaches the tin paper and methodically devours, using his incisors, the green tab that gives you the *freshness of life*. He chews three or four times before responding to his associate, while continuing to look at me as though intrigued:
"Either this guy is a total idiot, but I'm not sure about that… Or he is a superhuman, as I have seen only once before, back in Algeria, a man we finished with a Tucker telephone, but who had said nothing. Or he has nothing to say. That's what seems most probable to me." Stéphane responds, "All the same, in all three cases, we are wasting our time. I can't take

it anymore, rotting in here. We have better things to do, don't we? I propose that we finish him off and that we get rid of him quickly."

He delivers his idea simply, this gruff Stéphane. Doesn't bother to whisper. Has nothing to hide from me. He does not imagine that I am thinking of protesting. How could I oppose this plan, anyway?

The other chews slowly, seems to hesitate. He lets himself fall into the armchair, set on little wheels, which he makes slide backward with his heel, stretches his legs on the desk, leans his head backwards and crosses his hands behind his neck. The ceiling light gives new signs of weakness and begins flickering again occasionally. Stéphane becomes inpatient. He takes out his gun, an old MR73, which seems to have already been used a lot. He points it dangerously at me, his left eye closed.
"There's no chance I'll miss. Let's do it?"
"Give it here, idiot."
It is David who has intervened, in his fierce voice. He has left the wall and walks assuredly towards Stéphane. The gangly beanpole has become tense, put his feet back on the floor and stands while holding up a threatening hand to his colleagues.
"Calm down, both of you!"
Then he turns toward Stéphane: "He is right. You can't shoot him here. Think about it."
"What? Nobody will hear the sound in this hole! They're not going to ask us any questions!" "That is not the point, Stéphane. What about the blood? And the gunpowder? Scattered everywhere! No, if we want to get rid of him, we'll have to use a little more imagination. We can't just shoot him like that."

29

I observe them and listen to all three of them converse, as though I were a spectator of my own life and of my killing. They do not ask me my opinion, but they no longer bother about showing any discretion towards me. They discuss my fate without the slightest embarrassment. It's almost as though I already no longer existed. They say that at the moment you die, in an accident, you see your life flash before your eyes in the blink of an eye, in the fraction of a second that precedes the impact. And it's true. When they shot my father and the car flipped over, I had the time to see my entire childhood again, Mama's cakes, the cuddles, the occasional bullying at school, the homework, the writing paper, the violin classes, the tango steps, Papa's smile when he lifted me in his arms, the tenderness of his blows when we pretended to fight, when I hit with all my strength without his wavering a single time. He took a bullet right in the forehead. A motorcycle that was driving by us in the wrong direction. The passenger, solidly hanging onto the driver, their black leather jackets stuck to each other, did not miss. Papa's head fell against the horn. The car swerved, the front right wheel climbed onto the embankment. The horizon began spinning like a top. I bounced against all the walls of the cabin. We must have rolled over three or four times, I didn't count. Enough for Mama's face to be bloodied. When the tumult of the car hitting the gravelly ground, the crumpled sheet metal, of bodies banging against the uprights of the door or windows, ceased, when the fury quieted, when there was nothing but silence and the smell of blood mingled with burned plastic, I hoped that she would speak. She said nothing, I called her. She did not answer. Mama, too, was dead. No one has been able to explain to me what miracle allowed me to escape unscathed. With hardly a scratch. The mysteries of the science of accidents. All the same, on this day in November 1960 when my father and mother died together, taking with them their terrible secret, I saw my life flash before my eyes in a few seconds. But today, facing my

30

torturers, who are debating about the most efficient means to put an end to my life, I am taking my time to go through the film of these last thirty-nine years. My childhood in Bueno Aires that ends abruptly on the road, my three years of boarding school, my studies in Paris, paid for by a mysterious benefactor about whom I know nothing, even today, the beginnings of Rodrigo Chemicals, the success of our first anesthetics, the young girls in flower, my first love, Maria Dolores – we were five years old – and the rest up until my latest conquest, Noura, who was perhaps one too many, and whose caprices were not unrelated to my fall. These memories do not jostle each other, they follow one another, in a very well-mannered way, in a tight formation. Thus, I did not see Stéphane put his gun back in its holster and taking the white handkerchief that the tall, bald beanpole of a man held out to him. He reassured him with a gesture that seemed to say: "This will be enough to strangle him; in any case, he cannot struggle against us." When I realize what Stéphane is about to subject me to as the final act of torture, I am overcome with fear again.

Even long after the events I am describe here, as I write these lines today, shudders run through me.

I remember that that day I do not manage to scream, nor to call for help, nor to beg for mercy. I wriggle about actively, in the vain hope of freeing myself from my fetters. Impossible. I see Stéphane again, who gives himself a false air of Robert De Niro playing a bad guy, moving towards me with something sadistic about him. He has rolled up the big handkerchief. He lifts his arms to put it around my neck. It is then than a bang pierces my eardrums. I have the time to read the stupor in Stéphane's eyes, just before they become lifeless. The boss crumples to the ground and is stretched out at my feet. The smoke, the blood, the death. But not mine. Not yet.

31

David has just shot down his two colleagues to prevent them from coldly executing me. He has taken an enormous risk. But even if they were acting totally illegally in keeping me in this pit, even if their deeds and actions could merely have responded to obscure instructions, all three of them were of necessity bound by the unavowable secret of a strange investigation. They obeyed a parallel hierarchy, givers of orders who must not be choirboys. David's act, the murder of his colleagues before my eyes, is more than daring. It is reckless. He who has just spent hours beating me mercilessly, with a sort of relentlessness, or even a kind of pleasure, has suddenly decided to save my life by putting his in danger. Why this change of heart so sudden and unexpected? David will have a hard time hiding the death of these two frightful characters, which will probably be made public. It would be difficult to do otherwise: even if the place of my torture is and will remain a mystery, as well as the nature of this enigmatic investigation, it will not be possible to hide the disappearance of two cops for very long from the public. The police will have to realize very quickly that I have vanished into thin air. That was the plan in any case: I was not supposed to leave that bunker alive. The officials surely have a story to palm off on gullible journalists. Alive, I will be able to speak and demolish the nice story they had made up, and which they had counted on telling the world. And David himself? The police will fear possible confessions and will do everything to silence him. He is now the man to eliminate, maybe even ahead of me. Why has he taken this extraordinary risk to protect me?

The days to come will allow me to find out his astonishing reasons.

David killed Stéphane, then he shot very quickly, firing blind, at the third man. So he didn't hit a vital organ at the first shot. Once on the ground, the injured man, run through with spasms, groaned as though he wanted to say something. David drew close to him, and listened carefully. He seemed to understand since he nodded. He stood up and coldly put a second bullet in the back of the man's head, the latter responding this time only by letting his head drop heavily on the linoleum in a pool of blood. My ears are ringing so much from the third bang that I cannot make out what David is saying to me. He repeats, shouting: "We've got to get out of here, now!"

He sets about undoing the cords in which I am tied up. Just then, the light bulb in the ceiling gives up the ghost, for good this time. We are plunged in the most total darkness. Here I am blind, in addition to having been deafened by the gunshots. But David manages to detach me, helps me to get up and to walk towards the exit that we find by memory. My aching limbs hardly hold me up. It is not that I am in pain; what I feel is beyond suffering. The pain irradiates every part of my body: on the outside, my skin, my nails, my eyes, and on the inside, in my mouth, my stomach, my belly. It feels like all of my bones have been shattered one by one. I have become pain itself. At this moment, I have only one regret: that Stéphane did not kill me right away, before David argued against it. When he pointed his gun at my forehead, relief was intermingled with my natural fear. It was going to be over, Furtively, I recalled that phrase from Jacques Mesrine: "What is the good of crying for the sun? Your tears keep you from seeing the stars." I was going to leave behind the fiery star to find myself in the midst of the firmament, but Stéphane did not shoot. He should have. Here I am alive and crippled with wounds, limping in a dark hallway; I am being supported and pushed forward by the man who has just saved me for a reason that escapes me. Why did I think of Mesrine

33

at this moment? Six years ago, when that solitary bandit was executed by the police in the middle of the street, I had been captivated by the images of that windscreen riddled with bullets, which was shown without stop on television, as well as by the photos of the bloodied head of the criminal, hanging over the steering wheel of the brown BMW. The open door revealing his lifeless body in a leather jacket had reminded me in a striking way of the image of my father in a similar situation. The day of his murder, I had left the car from the back seat, I had opened the door and discovered Papa in the same posture, his face marked by identical wounds as those that they photographed nineteen years later on the face of public enemy number one, shot down by the French police. Behind my father's mortal remains, I saw my mother slumped in the passenger's seat, motionless and silent too, though untouched by the hail of bullets. It was the car accident that did her in. Our blue Peugeot 403, which my father had been able to acquire by saving up and making sacrifices, which had taken us to Sunday picnics, was crumpled up and smoking. Fumes of burned plastic and white-hot sheet metal filled the air. I was fifteen years old. In front of me, Papa's pretty car held nothing but two corpses.

Roused by David who is pushing me, I continue to move forward in little steps in this murky and malodorous tunnel. The damp is streaming from the walls. We are walking up the stairs, still in darkness. Going up dozens and dozens of flights of stairs, I have the impression that we are leaving the depths of oblivion. Otto Lidenbrock, Jules Verne's character, having undertaken his famous voyage to the center of the Earth, could certainly have been found roaming around there. Finally, we see a glimmer of light. A halo that disagreeably hits my retina, already used to darkness. Outside, I recognize nothing. We are in the middle of nowhere. I can see, in the distance, two enormous concrete chimneys. We are in a kind

34

of parking lot, a rectangular space covered in asphalt, encircled by barbed wire and surrounded by triangular panels encouraging wariness in the passerby or the curious person. *Entry forbidden, danger of death.* Not far from us, construction vehicles, trucks, excavators, making an enormous din and showing that construction work is in progress. It is a nuclear power station, without any doubt. David passes in front of me and heads towards a building bearing the logo *EDF,* and adorned with the same warnings as the fence. He removes the padlock from what seems to be a garage door. When it opens, I recognize the Renault 18 that took me here. David has the key. He gives me a sign to hurry up and to get in. After backing up just once, he roars off into the foggy morning, without adding a word. I do not recognize the landscape. I do not know where we are. The air is mild and dry, without being truly hot. The corn stalks and dried-out sunflowers, whose stalks are bending under the assault of the burning rays of the sun, make me surmise, after all, that we are in the south of France. How much time have I spent, finally, in this hole? What day is it? I ask him.

"It is the 5th. September 5th. This is the Golfech nuclear power station. In October and November '81, there were violent confrontations between those opposed to and for its construction, and also with the authorities, of course. There were quite a few incidents, some of them pretty serious. The prefect ended up convincing Paris to set up a police observation post in this bunker and if necessary to house riot police officers capable of responding quickly in the event of a ruckus. But after several years of calm, their presence was judged to be unnecessary and too costly. They emptied the site, but the police maintained use of the space. For operations that are, let's call them…non-standard. Now that you know the place, your skin is worth even less than before. Or more, depending on how you look at things. Well, you and me, we are nothing but deer who must escape from all the hunters of France joined together in a single pack. If we survive and the existence of this place becomes known, it will be a disaster. People will seek to find out what is done there, and, believe me, it is not pretty. More than a few rotten affairs have been finished here. It would be time for them to turn on the first reactor to get rid of a few bodies."

In saying these last words, he cannot repress a sardonic smile at the corner of his mouth. But he quickly recovers himself and, still clutching the steering wheel, without looking away from the road, he continuous, sententiously:

"We have hardly two hours before our car is sought by all the cops in France and... the gendarmes! We are not hard to identify, believe me. The hunt will begin quickly and we are less well-armed than deer, you see... At least they can run. We are easy prey. We have only one way to escape the worst. Flee. Flee quickly, as quickly as possible, and hide."

I wonder if David realizes that, in my state, that's not the question. I don't know if I will be able to overcome this trial, and survive simply, even assuming that we will manage to find shelter and food, in some hiding place. I am nothing but a shell, a mass of bloody skin that is held together in one piece I don't know how. I shake with irregular trembling, long electric shudders run through me. My hands and my feet, sometimes my arms and my legs move suddenly, in a disorderly manner, without my being able to control them.

Without paying attention to the living dead person that I am, slumped on his right in place of the fully dead man, David continues on the highway, his eyes riveted on the shoulders of the road, very focused. Murderous plane trees rush by my window. In the milky light and shade of this dawn at the end of the summer, it seems to me like we are brushing dangerously close to them. That is doubtless just an illusion. I see the trees dancing before throwing themselves on me, in a kind of hallucination, probably connected with my general state. Once or twice, I swing my head to avoid getting hit in the face by a tree trunk. David, silent, takes no notice of my chaotic movements. He drives faster and faster, passes heavy trucks, crosses over the white lines. I am shaken, rocked. Eventually, sleep steals over me. I have not slept for almost two days. Despite the terrible shooting pains piercing me all over, fatigue overcomes me and I abandon myself to it.

How long did I sleep? Probably not very long, since the sun is still not very high in the sky. We are still in the same region. We are now on the smallest, sinuous local roads, occasionally crossing some deserted village in the middle of fields. Here and there, an old woman in black, sitting in front of her steps on an old wicker chair, seems to be waiting… but for what? We finally reach the edge of a still green and leafy forest. David drives onto a dirt path the access to which has been blocked by branches, and which could not be seen from the road. We roll along more slowly, surrounded on both sides by the entanglement of a thicket, by brambles, by trees seeking to reach the light of which their ancestors deprive them. Finally, the car stops in front of a small cob building.

I surmise that this will be our dwelling place for some time. The place seems abandoned, but if we can sleep here, in relative calm and quietude, for me that will largely suffice for the moment. I get out of the vehicle with difficulty and I stagger toward the building whose rickety, moldy wooden door David pushes open. It was not closed; the key is in the lock, on the inside. We enter a dim room whose single window, a dormer window, illuminates what could be a kitchen, equipped with a big ceramic sink, with a tap to which is attached a stainless steel hose, as well as an electric stove and an old refrigerator, which seems to be working, if one can judge by the racket made by its motor. A hallway leads to two separated rooms, each with a desk and a mattress lying directly on the brown tiled floor. Between the rooms, a little bathroom with a sink, a toilet, and a shower with a flower-themed curtain missing half of its rings. Nothing here resembles the luxury in which I lived hardly a few days ago, but this hideout delights me. It gives me a hope that I had lost and that my surprise liberation had not yet returned to me. Having seen myself as a dead man, I had ruled out the idea that I could survive. A very sharp pain piercing my leg brings me back to this desolate reality: I am far from being able to make it through. David has taken several packages of medicine from the cabinet in the bathroom. He gives them to me with a glass of water. Ironically enough, they are anti-inflammatory and pain medications from Rodrigo Chemicals. I administer them to myself. David asks me to lie down and to undress. I do so. Supplied with 98 proof alcohol, cotton swabs and bandages, he undertakes to dress my wounds with a dexterity I could not have suspected in someone who had first appeared to me to be a coarse brute. Despite everything, several times, when he touches a particularly ravaged area, I let out a cry of pain that leaves him indifferent. Then he gives me a cover. "Try to sleep. I'm going out. I'm going to hide the car. We should be able to stay here for a few days."

When my eyelids open, the day has passed and it is almost sunset. I must have slept ten hours straight. Not a single dream, not a single nightmare has troubled my sleep. I am dying of thirst. I would like to rush into the bathroom and put my mouth under the tap. Alas, I am far from being capable of that. As soon as I begin to move, I am run through with horrible electric shocks that must be something like the Tucker telephone the fond memory of which my torturer evoked yesterday. Impossible to move. I call David in my hoarse voice. He eventually hears me. Opening the door of the room where I am lying down, he lets in an odor of cassoulet that helps me realize that I am not only thirsty. I am also terribly hungry. It's reassuring: I am alive, my vital

functions are working again. David has changed clothes. He is wearing dark brown pants and a khaki shirt. With his deerstalker cap set on his head, he is almost unrecognizable. He explains to me, proudly, that this outfit will make it possible for him to go shopping in town at peak hours, hidden in the mass of people. He uses a moped, a 103 Peugeot with a top case. He smiles at me in a friendly way. For the first time, I feel a kind of empathy emanate from him. What a strange situation! He helps me to get up, to drink, to go to the toilet, to wash myself. I have lost all modesty. David's gestures are those of a nurse or a nursing assistant. Rigorous, discreet. We are sitting face to face at the kitchen table, a plank of wood set on top of two trestles. David serves us. I am burning with the desire to ask him questions, but I hold myself back, certain that he won't hesitate to explain himself and to interrogate me. I am wrong; he swallows the pieces of Toulouse sausage in silence, the duck confit that keeps rendering its fat, the pork belly. He smiles vaguely from time to time. After having emptied his soup plate and having mopped it up with the soft part of the bread, he leans against the back of his chair and looks at me straight in the eyes.
"I learned to eat everything. That's how I was brought up. First and above all, survive. The other considerations come after. Too many people have died stupidly from not having followed these rules."
I don't understand anything he tells me. You like cassoulet or you don't, but in the situation we're in, we cannot put on airs. It may have been canned food, yet it will no doubt remain the best meal of my existence, despite the agony that the still raw wounds in my gums and my tongue inflicted on me with every bite of warm food.
"David, I think that we shouldn't complicate things… These cassoulets are as good as any other, but honestly, it's filling…"

He looks at me, as disdainful as he is doubtful. Maybe I have not understood what he wanted to say. He asks me: "The sausage and the pork belly, there is nothing that seems bizarre to you in that?"
"No...It's... it's the recipe, or what..."
"And you don't find it strange that I am eating it?"
"Not really... Why?"
He strikes an enraged fist against the table. The cutlery and the dishes jump. He seems suddenly to be in a foul temper. I would not like for him to feel like beating me. He screams:
"I am Jewish! You haven't understood? I have no choice but to eat pork, although I am Jewish, *capito*?"
Raised with no religion, I must say that it is a consideration that had been totally foreign to me.
My parents had almost never brought up these subjects with me. It was only growing up that I discovered, in the secular country that the Argentina of my childhood was, that the Catholic Church existed, first, and then other altars, other beliefs. David, yes, of course, David is a Jewish name. So what? Non-Jews also sometimes have that name. Just two days ago, this guy was beating me up. Then he killed two of his colleagues in cold blood to put me out of danger. Finally, he took care of me like a sick child. So, Jewish or not, the question had not crossed my mind. Now that he says so, yes...David, indeed... So what?
"So nothing. Except that it's thanks to that that we are here. This hideout was used by my grandparents during the war, starting at the end of '43. They escaped deportation by hiding here, you see. They were never found here. So, it is kind of thanks to this place that I am alive. I lived here with my grandparents for several months until the Liberation in August '44. My parents, they..."
With these words, his voice becomes soft again. His gaze becomes faraway... He remains silent for a few minutes, then decrees suddenly:

"Let's go to sleep. You need a good rest. We won't be able to stay here forever. Times have changed since the war. They will get their claws on us much more easily nowadays. Let's get our strength back while we can."

He goes around the table to help me up, then he supports me all the way to my mattress, where I collapse. Outside, the night is black. There reigns a silence of death, disturbed from time to time only by the rustling of leaves stirred by a breeze. David gives me a sleeping pill to swallow, another product from Rodrigo Chemicals. I abandon myself again to sleep, for a long night.

In the early morning, as the rosy dawn just begins to filter through the blinds, I manage to stand up all by myself. What joy!

Yesterday, I still thought that I would never manage to do that again. I call David. Silence, no response. Where could he be? Our makeshift shelter is devoid of any human presence. While I stop in the bathroom, I perceive the purring of the moped. David is back.

"Fresh bread and croissants on the menu!" he announces proudly, as he warms up some coffee.

Then he puts two newspapers on the table. My face on the front page of the two papers. "Rodrigo Ganos on the Loose Again", is the headline in *Le Figaro*. *Libération* writes: "Does Rodrigo Have a Heart?" The papers publish the same photo of me, the one with the mustache that gives me the look of a serial killer. They have the same information: arrested for insider trading in the context of an investigation of Rodrigo Chemicals, I managed to seize the gun of one of my guards and kill two policemen, taking flight with the third as hostage and human shield. We stole a service car as we left the station. For security reasons, the police have not indicated where these events took place. But they remind people that I can be anywhere in the country right now and that, having been unmasked as the crook described over past few months, I am also a dangerous and violent man. Any information that can help to track me down, any indication is welcome, but utmost caution is encouraged: it is suggested that people remain extremely discreet, avoid approaching me and speaking to me upon coming across me. However, there is no picture of David, his name is not even mentioned by the journalists. We take turns reading the articles as we devour breakfast. The sun comes in through the narrow opening above the gas stove and blinds me. As I turn by reflex, I notice an old radio, its stainless steel glittering brightly, a Panasonic. It is perched on a workbench near the sink. The dial is set to France Inter. *Sweet Dreams* is just ending when I turn it on, then a jingle announces the news. I occupy the main place in this somewhat empty news report. They talk about the discovery of the wreck of the *Titanic* five days earlier, people are worried about the fate of J.R. Ewing, whose adventures continue next Saturday in the upcoming episode of *Dallas*. Rodrigo Chemicals, my escape, my presumed murders, my stock market scam, are the spiciest parts of the program. All of a sudden, David angrily cuts off the journalist, brutally pressing down on and shutting off the poor radio that did nothing to him. He asks me in his serious voice: "Alright, it is time for you to tell me your truth, Rodrigo! How did you know about the AIDOS study before anyone else?"

I can't believe it! He persists in not believing me! I was convinced that he had decided to free me, to pull me from the claws of torturers ready to strike me down with a shot from a revolver, because he had realized that I was not lying, that in reality I had nothing to hide. But no! He remains persuaded that I still have an unavowable secret. He rescued me only to be the first to obtain the information for himself. He is not my ally, he feels no interest in me, he just wants to pursue his investigation alone and get all the rewards for it. I even ask myself if they have not staged and acted out that scene. Seeing that I was not saying anything, even under the worst torture, they had then carried out this artifice. David could have shots blanks at them. The blood? Sacks of red liquid, like in the movies! But I have a hard time believing in this scenario, which I eliminate as quickly as I imagine it. The two cops seemed quite cold, and for good. I take hold of myself, I chase these horrible – and terrifying—thoughts from my head. I must maintain my trust in David. Otherwise, where would I find hope?

"David, I repeated it to you a hundred times down there... How can you imagine for a second that I will deliver to you a truth here that I could have hidden, even while undergoing the worst physical cruelty?"

Embarrassed, he lowers his eyes. I reassure myself little by little. No, clearly, David does not seem like a double agent playing a triple game. There is a sincerity about him that I felt...from the first smacks. He raises his head and continues calmly:

"O.K., let's accept that. So why did you sell the Rodrigo Chemicals shares a few days before the revelation of the information about AIDOS? If you knew nothing in particular as you claim with a perseverance that is, I have to say... impressive, then why?"

Finally! Finally, someone asks me this question! No one has, until now, neither the journalists, nor the cops who held me for two days in this sordid basement. Finally, eye to eye, I will be able to tell him what really happened. Maybe he will not believe me, maybe my words will be in vain, but at least once, just once, I will have been able to explain myself, to give my version of the facts. If I were a believer, I would thank God. But it is David whom I owe my thanks. I begin repeating to him, again, that I had no inside information; I confirm to him that I simply needed money. It's the one and only reason I sold my shares. Of course, this justification is difficult to believe for common mortals. My luck seems considerable. How could I find myself short of cash? It's because I spent like crazy! Not really, though. I am not an enthusiast of fancy cuisine, nor of fine wines, nor of

43

paintings. I gave myself only the minimum of what a man with my financial scope owes himself: a beautiful apartment in the 16th arrondissement in Paris, but without ostentation, a German sedan, an Italian convertible sportscar, a high-end watch, and a few suits whose price remains reasonable. Nothing that can put my affluence in peril. No, to tell the truth, my one Achilles' heel is… yes, I have to recognize it, is Noura, my pretty fiancée, my angel, my madness, my demoness. From the first glance, since the moment her burning eyes lighted in me a fire that I have not been able to put out since, I have realized that I would be unable to resist this siren. What Noura wants, God wants. I obey the smallest of her desires, I submit body and soul to her wishes. She need not demand it, she need merely think in order for me to grovel. It was enough, last spring, that she went into ecstasies in front of a sumptuous Riva, in varnished wood, with a splendid deck chair with green cushions on which she dreamed of lying down, for me to immediately acquire this boat.

I rushed to cede to this caprice that she had hardly meowed. But I had to pay a deposit to the boat-owner. At that moment, however, I found myself a little bit short of cash, having made, hardly a few days earlier, investments that I could not separate myself from easily. In order to make the order and to assure this first transfer, as well as those to follow, I decided to bring in some fresh money by selling some shares of Rodrigo Chemicals. A little more than the amount required, to be sure that I would be able to meet any possible new needs of the same kind in the near future. The quantity of shares sold on the market represented, in reality, a trivial amount, but the stock market price was at its height and I pocketed, on this occasion, quite a sum. Alas, it was this capital gain that would lead to my misfortune. Two weeks after the sale, the share price of Rodrigo Chemicals plummeted. In reaction to our press release underlining the disappointments of the AIDOS study, the share price was

halved in a single session and lost another third of what remained the following day. The OCPB, Operations Commission of the Paris Bourse, examined the operations I had initiated on the shares in the weeks that had preceded these announcements. When the authorities realized that I had sold, even only a small proportion of my equity participation in Rodrigo Chemicals, just before the drama, they saw red. Clear the decks -what a commotion. Multiple accusations and an indictment for insider trading. After a first questioning by the OCPB and a convocation by an investigating judge, I realized that, if I hoped to defend myself and escape from the claws of a justice system that had already made of me a guilty person, I must, first of all, get away and hide. Flee as quickly as possible. And without that idiot functionary in the airport, I could be in Buenos Aires right now, sipping a maté on a beach. Instead of that, here I am in this hovel with a guy who, before saving my life, spent hours redrawing my portrait. My broken nose reminds me with every breath of the savagery with which my liberator first attacked me.
David looks doubtful as he listens to my story. He does not categorically put my word in doubt, but he remains skeptical.
"Let's assume that what you say is true, friend…"
The expression "friend" surprises me. He waits a moment, raises his eyes to the sky as though he were reflecting. Then he continues:
"All that would be nothing but the result of chance…You sold a small proportion of your equity participation in Rodrigo Chemicals to meet an immediate need for money, without being aware of the news in advance. In some way, you… got lucky?"
"A clinical study that fails at the last minute, just when it was about to be completed, the share price collapses, a large part of my fortune disappears into thin air, and my reputation with it, then an investigation for insider trading, leading to my arrest and that, forgive the expression 'friend', as you say,

makes me undergo almost fatal torture… you can call that lucky, sure. In any case, I didn't have the information, no."

"That's what I mean, you understood me. Lucky in the sense that you were not doing insider trading. You made money without really trying on purpose to do it… At least that's what you keep claiming."

I observe David, who looks at me in turn. We look one another up and down for a while, seeking to understand one another as well as to dominate one another. His face is more marked, more wrinkled, more sunken than I had noticed until now. David is older than I imagined. His chestnut hair is abundant and has not gone white, but the marks on his skin, the furrows in his brow, the protuberances of his veins on his hands indicate that, in reality, he is perhaps closer to fifty than I thought. I attempt to decipher this strange character. At once hard and cold, he is capable of killing two colleagues without batting an eye and of showing at the same time a very human ardor, rage. But, endowed with a certain empathy when he took care of me, he can show himself to be almost affectionate when he wishes. What does he want? Without any transition from my legal and financial adventures, he starts to open up. He looks away, his gaze fleeing toward the light entering with difficulty through the dormer window.

"I had just turned six when they came to arrest them. But they had managed to change their identity. We were not longer called Rosenberg. We were re-named Rostand. To keep the beginning of the name, at least the initials, just in case. And also my father was a Cyrano de Bergerac fanatic, and would recite his famous tirade, it seems, as my grandfather told me later. As for me, I was no longer David, I had become Damien. Rachel, my mother, was named Raymonde since 1940, indeed I knew her only under this name. I did not even know that I was Jewish. I was Damien Rostand, son of Jérôme Rostand, of whom I was unaware that he had once been Joseph Rosenberg. Our false papers

worked everywhere. On Sundays, we ostensibly went to Mass. We didn't have the accent of people from here, but that was not very shocking, the neighbors posed few questions, I think. My parents kept from forming close contacts. We had left Paris and crossed into the Free Zone in the first days of '41. We were living in Montauban, in a little three-room apartment on the second floor. In the street, people looked at us a little askance, but I didn't notice. My parents worked in the fields, in silence. Two months before D-Day, to the day, on April 6, 1944, at around eight in the evening, we heard someone knocking heavily at the door. 'Police! Open up!' Mama understood at once. She lifted two floorboards that had been cut out in advance. She grabbed me, put her lips on my forehead with all her strength and made me enter beneath the plank. There were three of them. They had the same hat, the same black leather raincoat, the same revolver pointed at my parents. They were looking for me. 'Where is the kid?' they shouted. Obtaining no reply, they grabbed my mother, held the gun against her temple and screamed at my father: 'You give us the brat or you want us to settle things for him with your wife?" I saw everything from below. She made a sign of yes with her head. I think it was a signal between them…which meant: 'I'm ready. Don't speak. Let's save the little one at least, whatever it costs…'"
David's voice trails off a little. His hands have begun to tremble. He lights a Gitane and offers me the pack. I very willingly accept his offer, even if my aching lips are still in no state to receive the welcome cigarette. My throat tight, I wait in silence for him to continue. A drop has formed at the corner of his eyelid. He does not let it escape. Two or three blinks of his eyelash hold back this tear.
"They did not shoot her in the apartment. The guy contented himself with hitting her with the butt of his gun, breaking her nose and making her fall on top of the boards covering me, plunging me into total darkness. After that, I saw nothing. Protected from the Gestapo's lights by my mother's body, I

47

heard the cops search the home inside out, lift the beds and the mattresses, empty the cabinets, the wardrobes, the suitcases. In desperation, the chief decreed that it was time to clear off. They ordered my still-unconscious mother to get up. In the ray of light, I saw my parents one last time, being beaten by these three men. And then silence returned. Silence and darkness. I remained in my hideout the whole night, without moving. Despite my terror, my sorrow and…and…my anger, above all, I think that I did sleep a bit under the planks. In the early morning, I heard someone enter. Two people. It was my grandparents. I showed myself. We did not speak. They took me here, to this shack that looked more or less the way it looks today. Except for the stove, let's say. We survived here until the end of the war."

I take in the shock of the story. I imagine the poor kid in his hole. David and I thus have something in common. Our parents were taken from us when we were children, even if not at the same age. What brings us together is not so much that they disappeared from our lives early, but rather the way they died. The violence, the brutality with which they were taken away from us. At least he knows why, he knows the historical and ideological origin of the murderous madness that took his family somewhere in the east. He knows why and how those who were supposed to watch over him went to die atrociously, far from their home. I still don't know why my father was shot before my eyes. I have not sought after the reason.

David adds: "In this hut, we lived in near autarky. They procured some rare food, I don't know how. And we went out as little as possible. That's when they told me everything. My real name, that of my family, my history. They told me that they had Eastern European origins, which their accent was enough to reveal. The only thing they could never have imagined was being chased by the French police. The France of the Enlightenment, the France that had been described to them as the country of universal tolerance, the France that had created Victor Hugo and Rimbaud, whose poems they had learned in school, this is the France that had taken away their daughter, Rachel, whom they would never see again. That's really what shocked them the most, I think."

His voice becomes choked at the end of his story. He has let himself go. He smiles at me sadly, almost tenderly. I begin to appreciate this man who has used me, not too long ago, as punching bag, for hours. I could even say that I begin to love him. Until now, I had simply been thankful to him for saving my life. But, after these confessions, I feel a new feeling toward him grow in me, a kind of affection. Yet I do not understand the relation between him, his story, and my current sad fate. I ask him. He responds: "If we survive, you will understand the relation." He puts out his cigarette and leaves the kitchen. Behind the wall, I hear the shower running. I ask myself how long we are going to stay here and what we will do when we have to leave. A cloud passes, the room darkens. I think of Noura. I miss her peals of laughter, her skin, her ample breasts, her craziness, her long, dark, wavy hair, her opaline teeth, her caprices, her beaten-dog-like sulking, her impish eyes, her warm hands. When will I see them again? Has she already forgotten me? Has she already found refuge in the arms of another? Will I again enjoy her sweet lips one day? As my body's pain fades little by little, the absence of my beautiful fiancée now weighs more and more on my bruised heart. She wanted a child. Maybe she is even pregnant, with my child even. Maybe I will never know this little child growing inside her. Will she raise him without any knowledge of his father, while I will remain condemned to the eternal roaming of a fugitive? These thoughts overwhelm me, destroy me.

David reappears. His hair still wet, he finishes buttoning up his jean shirt.

"Don't keep looking like you're going to a burial. We are still alive, you and me. As for those I made cold yesterday, I don't think we'll be invited to the funeral!"

He accompanies his witticism with a blunt smack in the back, which elicits in me a cry of pain.

"If you are telling the truth and you didn't benefit from any information before selling your Rodrigo Chemicals shares, then there are many things you still don't know about. It is more than time that I give you the lowdown. Go take a shower and put on the clothes I prepared for you. They should be more or less your size. Above all don't shave, obviously. And don't forget the cap and the sunglasses. We are leaving. We will not come back."

I remember an event, in Buenos Aires, from a long time ago. I was six or seven years old, perhaps. As I was always first in my class, I did not have many friends my age. But I had one. His name was Bernardo, he was a head taller than me, and had black eyes and a crew cut. We were almost inseparable during recess. He protected me from the sarcastic comments and attacks from the other boys. In the courtyard, we isolated ourselves from the group; we invented worlds for ourselves. We were soldiers, adventurers, sailors, hunters… He was the total opposite of me. An undisciplined dunce, but also funny and imaginative. I loved him like the big brother I never had. There was a cafeteria in the elementary school. Before lunch, they put us into line by twos at the double door that opened onto a covered courtyard. When the teacher gave us the sign, we had to go to the bathroom sinks and wash our hands, before going into the canteen in groups of eight, which was the number of seats at each table.

On this day, for some unknown reason that remained a mystery, the group before us had only seven kids. It had to be completed. The teacher wanted to separate me from Bernardo. I protested vigorously. Nothing to be done. I begged him. He raised his voice, frowning, and ordered me to obey, pulling me by the collar and pushing me towards the bathroom sinks. This man, who was named Miguel, probably a translation of "Michel," as he had a heavy French accent, had never maltreated me before. When he spoke to me, he was always much gentler than he was with the other boys. By nature not a very severe person, he was even tenderer with me than with my classmates. So I was surprised by this sudden reversal and this crisis of authority. My heart skipped a beat. In this ephemeral instant, I nearly lost my senses and gave free rein to an anger that seemed to me entirely justified. As I walked forward, with a heavy heart, I was overcome by an irrepressible impulse. I stared right into Miguel's eyes and gave him the middle finger. He glared at me in turn. I did not allow myself to be intimidated. I repeated my gesture. Then I turned on my heel. He screamed: "Rodrigo! Come here immediately!" I was screwed. The lightning bolts of the entire school hierarchy were about to come down on me. I would be kicked out of school, sent away. My mother would cry. I was already angry at myself for my imbecilic revolt. I expected the worst, as I approached the teacher with my head down. But instead of taking me to the principal's office, instead of beating my fingers or my behind with a stick as I deserved, instead of inflicting public humiliation on me and forcing me to offer my apologies, on my knees, in front of all of the students in the school, the teacher ruffled by curly hair and put me back in line next to my friend Bernardo. He sent us side by side to the next group and he never separated us again.

Later, the same Miguel would patiently teach me French, making me basically bilingual, which allowed me to pursue university studies in France. I think almost every day of him and of this event above all. I re-write the story without end, and I ask myself, still, how valuable this exceptional clemency, on this occasion, was for me.

Often, my father, rather than my mother, came to pick me up at the end of a private French lesson. He loved this foreign language that he knew how to read. He had learned it in school, too.

What was this mysterious school in Ohio where they studied the vocabulary and grammar of an old, almost forgotten

European country? Papa said no more about it. But over time, I realized that Miguel and my father maintained relations that went far beyond the usual relationship of a teacher and a student's parent. Little by little, as I grew up and the world revealed its mysteries to me drop by drop, I discovered that there was, in fact, a profound camaraderie between the two men. A secret, or more than that, formed an indissoluble bond between them. In November 1960, when the police, who had found me on the side of the road, driven from my senses in front of the two bloody cadavers of my parents, tried to find somebody to pick me up from the station, it was Miguel whom they found. I had put him on the right track for that; he was the only adult with whom I had ever entered into a sort of confidence. I had no other family. Miguel came to get me. I would live with him before succeeding in being sent to a boarding school in France. In leaving Miguel and Buenos Aires, I left behind everything I knew in this world. I was born a second time in Brest, when I landed there. I wrapped myself up in my work, relentlessly, I picked up the best degrees in this country, I founded Rodrigo Chemicals, and I put the past behind me. I did not attempt to find out either why or by whom my parents had been murdered. I closed my eyes on my story and on theirs. But today, I have the intuition that my history has caught up with me. They are not hunting me down just because I am the ignoble capitalist the crowd would be glad to see sentenced. David and my two other torturers were convinced that I had something to hide. A secret of utmost importance. It was this conviction that initially brought them together in their dubious undertaking. They did not let up. The more I think about it, the more I believe that there must be a link between their curious certainty and the unexplained murder of my parents.

I am lost in my thoughts and my memories when David enters my room grumbling: "What the hell are you doing, Rodrigo?"

I am sitting on my mattress, my gaze wandering toward the trees. I still haven't taken the time to get dressed.
"You're still not ready? Are you doing that on purpose, or what? You think we're here to daydream? We have to get out of here, right away, as I've explained to you. Let's go, put on these dungarees and these boots that I dug up for you, get a move on!"
His last exclamation pulls me out of my dreams. I get up with difficulty and I get dressed as quickly as my mutilated limbs allow, which is still too slow for David, who is stamping his feet with impatience. I pull a cap over my head and I follow him as best as I can, limping. We leave without pausing to put things in order in the cabin, without even bothering to hide the clothes we were wearing when we arrived. We leave our fingerprints everywhere. It will really not be difficult to reach the conclusion that we stayed here. David doesn't care.
He has also found another car. Where and how? He won't tell me for the moment. In any case, we are leaving the trees in a white Renault 5 covered in rust. The sun is already high in the azure sky. It will doubtless be hotter than in the past several days. As the day before yesterday, David is very focused on the road, at the wheel of the Renault whose wheezing motor lets out a sharp cry before each gear change. We are going as fast as our modest car allows. David negotiates bends at full speed without worrying that this might attract the attention of the local police. But that's what ends up happening. On the edge of a village, a police car that saw us roaring by goes after us, its sirens wailing, flashing their headlights. David slows down, pulls onto the shoulder. He seems very calm, lights a Gitane, then, when the gendarme knocks on the window, he placidly holds up his police card, explaining:
"I am on assignment, maybe you weren't notified. I am transporting a witness in a big case and I cannot allow myself to hang around. He faces threats and is likely to be in danger anywhere, anytime. I must go as quickly as possible."

"Major Roucaud," responds the military man. "Let me introduce to you Deputy Mollard."
He gestures with his chin at a tall beanpole of a man who has left the vehicle just afterwards, whose physiognomy is much less inviting than that of his elder and hierarchical superior, Major Roucaud, who happily accepts the cigarette David offers him. A malicious rictus grin forms on the lips of the gendarme, who narrows his eyes. I wonder if David is not overdoing it with optimism and confidence. He seems convinced that the local guys have not yet heard about our business and thus have not received our description. It is possible, but the major's ironic expression worries me exceedingly.
"A witness? Are you sure?"
He inclines his head to the left, as though to try to seize the details of the features that my three-day beard hides quite poorly, as well as my cap jammed down over my forehead, in conformity with David's instructions.
"He seems a little worse for the wear already, your witness…"
My protector jumps at his opportunity.
"You have figured it out. I managed to remove him from the hands of his abductors…Guys you don't want to meet too often, if you see what I mean…In a day or two, you'll have them too in your sights, I have no doubt about it. But my priority is to get out of here and to get this man to safety."

The major nods slowly, still doubtful, while the deputy also tries look carefully at me through the windshield. Roucaud concludes finally, in a cloud of blue smoke:
"Alright! We're not going to slow you down any longer. Get going…but be a little careful all the same."
When David has already restarted the car and put it into gear, the gendarme reconsiders suddenly, and, leaning into the inside of our car, he asks:
"Where are you going, actually? You want to be escorted?"

With the aplomb that his old experience as a fugitive gave him, David avoids the question and refuses the offer.

"Sorry, pal, but I can't tell you anything. It's top secret. You will be in the loop soon, but for the moment, I have to hit the road and be as discreet as possible. So no escort...but thanks anyway."

The major hesitates another instant. He looks inquiringly at his deputy: the deputy stares wide-eyed and raises his eyebrows in a sign of ignorance and impotence. With a movement of his head, Roucaud gives us a sign to leave. We clear off. A few hundred yards later, going at a slightly more modest pace and incessantly taking a look in the rearview mirror, David lights a cigarette and turns on the radio. The Eurythmics' *Sex Crime* just finishes when the journalist gets back on air and announces, in the midst of other news, that significant progress has just been made in the investigation into the terror attack on rue des Rosiers that took place three years ago, on August 9, 1982. It is possible that those responsible are not connected to Palestine, as was first believed, but to opaque small groups on the extreme right. I am about to comment on the news and express my surprise but, before I can pronounce a single word, David stops me with a gesture. He wants to listen to the report all the way to the end with the greatest attention, and not miss a single detail. It was stupid of me not to have thought of it: this manifestly anti-Semitic attack directly concerns him.

Two years after the attack on a synagogue on rue Copernic in October 1980, a commando alighted on rue des Rosiers, that sad day of August 9, 1982. Going up rue Blancs-Manteaux, men armed to the teeth with machine guns and grenades fired at everything that moved. How many of them were there? Two, five? The eyewitness accounts contradict each other, memories are blurred. The terrorists took aim at the sidewalk outside Jo Goldenberg. They sprayed the storefront with grenades and bullets. Then they left, walking calmly, continuing to fire into the crowd, leaving behind them six corpses and twenty-two injured people. *Action directe*, a very active anarcho-communist organization claimed responsibility for the attack, but almost immediately retracted its claim. Then who? The Abu-Nidal Organization? The evidence is weak. The investigation hardly advances. It has stagnated for thirty-six months. But now there is a new lead, the journalist indicates. Last spring, three Neo-Nazis were arrested planning to commit new attacks. They could be linked to the killings on rue des Rosiers. It is also possible, explains the commentator, that there is a relation with another affair that has made a lot of noise for a few months, the "Rodrigo Ganos scandal."

The journalist's words distinctly reach my ears, but they do not rise immediately to my brain.

I hear my name at first as though it were someone else, or maybe an error, or a dream. It is so surreal, so removed from everything I could have imagined, that at first I do not absorb it. All the more so as David does not bat an eyelid. He remains focused on the road as he has been since we left. He just barely shoots a furtive glance at me to catch my reaction. Little by little, I realize the enormity of what has just been suggested, of the hypothesis advanced by the journalist. My adventure is being associated with the arrest – with the confessions? – of an obscure group of mindless idiots, swastika adorers accused of being associated with or at the origin of the rue des Rosiers massacre, a blind attack, cruel beyond words, obviously aimed at the Jewish community, without being the object of any clear claim of responsibility. As I slowly realize that this unimaginable suspicion rests on me, my heart begins beating out of control, my blood goes to my heels, I feel myself fainting. The plane tree leaves flying past dance the farandole. I feel overcome with heat. I need to open the window, breathe the late summer air, the aroma of dried sunflowers. I need several minutes to recover my spirits. And little by little, I understand better. If David had shown such violence, had let his blows loose on my bruised body during the entire beginning of my "interrogation," it was surely because he was convinced, then that, as I have just learned thanks to the radio news program, I was involved in the anti-Semitic massacre of 1982. I was not only, in his eyes, the pharmaceutical magnate who had unfairly enriched himself on the backs of the shareholders of Rodrigo Chemicals and of his employees, of the entire company, and even of patients, this greedy, cold-blooded being that the media had drawn, the pathological megalomaniac that they had described so many times. I was also, and above all, the accomplice – or the instigator! – of a bloody attack on his people, the Jewish people whose past scars and suffering David held in his heart and in his body. He saw in me the wretched face of those who had taken his parents from him when he was only a defenseless little kid hidden under the fragile boards of a rickety floor, which would have left him in the hands of the Milice if they had happened to give out. When his two colleagues set upon me in turn, when they subjected me to the unspeakable, whereas I had nothing to confess to alleviate my torment, David began to doubt my guilt. I begin to grasp the explanation of his reversal. But I am missing crucial piece of information in this improbable puzzle: how did we get here? Who could have put this idea in the head of the police, or at least in a certain part of the police? How could they come to find credible the hypothesis that I am linked, one way or another, to these sinister political movements, to these small groups animated by an abject ideology from another time? I close the window. As we cross a stream on an old stone bridge leading to a little village called Larrazet, whose octagonal bell tower I am admiring from afar, I ask David:

"You don't seem surprised?" He waits a moment. Lights yet another Gitane, then responds finally: "Surprised? Surprised by what?"

"By what we just heard! You weren't paying attention to what the journalist said? The rue des Rosiers attack could be linked with the Rodrigo Ganos scandal? That doesn't shock you?"

"Why would that shock me?"

David has decided to play with my nerves, which have already been through a lot. He has still not completely exonerated me. He is trying to test me, maybe even to lay a trap for me. I try to keep calm:

"Because that shocks me! That they call me a thief, a tyrant, an arrogant megalomaniac, so be it. It's not pleasant, but I can…let's say…put up with it. But being accused of anti-Semitism? Me? And worse than that, in fact! Of having been behind an attack on the Jewish community in France? Or at least of having been an accomplice, by cooperating with extreme rightwing neo-Nazi muck! Me? But what is this story?"

David believes me, I think. I feel he is swayed by my sincerity. He slows down, pulls into a narrow alley next to a bar with a cigarette counter, whose storefront faces the highway. He parks.

"This story, Rodrigo, is actually History, with a capital H. But I have the feeling that you don't know a word of it. It's no doubt time for you to learn the truth. I will explain everything to you, but come on, follow me, let's get a drink in this bar. You'll need it. No one will bother us here, it's a safe place."

It's the first time that David uses my first name.

He has parked the car under an awning, hidden from view, and he has thrown a tarp over it. We go in through the back door in the smoky bar, where four young men with hair to their shoulders noisily clash in a game of foosball, taking a drag between each point, on a Camel they place, during the game, in one of the ashtrays placed at the four corners of the table. Two other guys sip pastis, waiting for their turn at the counter. They will take on the winner. They glance distractedly and indifferently at the players, who do not look away for an instant from the ball. An old fellow sitting alone at a table knocks back a glass of red wine. He seems utterly lost. A sound system is playing "Big in Japan" by Alphaville. The voices, the synthesizer, and the music box merge together in the din of the bar and the shouts at every goal, hard shots, *spray shots*. The bar owner, an old mustached man with checkered white and gray hair like the squares of his shirt, leaves his spot when he recognizes David across the room. He gives us a sign to go into the back room, which seems used more for dining, but is empty at this hour. We have hardly sat down when he brings us a bottle of Madiran, bread, and pâté. He taps David's shoulder, and says:

"*Adieu*, little guy!"
In this region, "*adieu*" means "*bonjour*." It's curious, but it's like that. Without a Southern French accent, David would doubtless seem stupid if he answered with the same vocabulary. He doesn't risk it, and responds:
"Hey, pal. Can we be left alone here an hour or two? We have to chat."
The guy nods in assent.
"Eat something quickly and don't take your time too much…No one is looking for you for the moment, but that won't take long."
David acquiesces as he spreads pâté on his bread. The bar owner leaves us without another word. I am amazed:
"You are pretty well connected in the region, aren't you…"

59

He shrugs his shoulders.
"Why do you think we chose Golfech for your…interrogation? A secret place, certainly. But there are others. We could have gone elsewhere, but here I had my network. It was my idea…even if, at the time, I didn't know how things would turn out. Cousins, former members of the Resistance, their children, I have a lot of connections in this area. The rare Jewish people who still live in the area—I know everyone and everyone knows me. We help each other. You too, you know what solidarity is, huh?"

He then gives me a meaningful and knowing look. I am not sure that I understand his allusion. He serves us wine, copiously. Before emptying our glasses in one gulp, we toast like two old comrades. In fact, we are at least working together now. Even if, for my part, I am totally unaware of all the twists and turns of that strange investigation that has ultimately led us here. David fills our glasses again. Half the bottle is gone already. He swallows noisily, then asks me dryly:
"What was your father's name?"
I am surprised, but I answer him immediately:
"Juan. Why?"
"Juan, huh? Juan what?"

The second question strikes me as even more bizarre. If I am my father's son, it must be assumed that we have the same patronym. I don't bother telling him something that he certainly knows already. He drinks again, affects a certain serenity, but poorly hides his impatience. He grinds his teeth. He is aching to confront me with his revelations, to test my reactions. It is he who breaks the silence:
"Juan Ganos, yeah? That's it, right?"
"Obviously…What else would he be named?"
He shrugs his shoulders, and tilts backward, leaning against the bars of his chair's backrest. He lights a Gitane with his

60

gas lighter. He offers me one, holding out the pack to me. I decline. He slowly breathes out the blue smoke through his nostrils, and adds, pensively:

"Juan Ganos, what else would he be named…"

He says:

"Wait, we are indeed speaking of Juan Ganos, who was murdered by machine gun fire on November 7, 1960?"

How does he know that? Of course, that information is not too difficult to dig up when you're in the police, that's not the point. What interests me is David's motivation. Why was he interested in what happened to my father? I ask him. Another disillusioned sigh. He retorts:

"You don't have a slight notion, by any chance…?"

I shake my head no. I am lying and he knows it. Or at least he supposes so. I do indeed have a "slight notion," so minuscule that I managed to bury it in the depths of my unconscious. My father's accent in Spanish, which was not as American as he led me to believe, his total panic in May 1960 when I demanded to know the truth about his history, his unsolved murder for which no one claimed responsibility, certainly raised my suspicions, over the years. The trial of Adolf Eichmann did not escape my attention. I was in boarding school in France and people took care not to leave around the newspapers that dealt with that subject. We had neither television nor radio. I would not necessarily have been interested in this topic. But my teachers' obstinacy in hiding the details from me had, on the contrary, the effect of drawing my attention. I ended up digging deeper. Adolf Eichmann had been abducted in Buenos Aires on May 11, 1960, where I lived at the time. On May 11, four days before the day my father could not restrain himself against me, in a unique outburst of rage, when I wanted to know more about him. The coincidence of the date and place left me perplexed. I drew no hasty conclusion. I drew no conclusion at all. I held back from pushing my investigations any further. I forgot that my father pronounced certain words in a German rather than American way. I removed from my memory the word *Scheiße* that escaped him when he burned himself on a pan, or when our old jalopy that he had patched up as best as he could, did not want to start up again after one of our Sunday picnics. I never sought to know why the armed motorcyclists who, one day in November, crossed the path of our 403, had killed him in cold blood. In my heart of hearts, I had understood, but I never wanted to look this reality in the face. So yes, I had a "slight notion." David having told me about his past, I can quite well imagine the reason he looked into the fate of Juan Ganos, and, by consequence, into mine. I would have preferred never to know. But I hardly have the choice. The hidden history of my parents has already caught up with me. I can continue to flee the police and the gendarmes, but I cannot escape the horrible truth. Yet I continue my denial:

"No, David, excuse me, but I don't at all see why you're interested in my father. I don't understand why you researched him in such detail."

"You don't understand, huh? Well I will bring you up to speed then. Drink something because what I'm going to tell you won't be pleasant to hear, believe me."

He fills my glass. I hasten to empty it, aware that what he will tell me is terrible.

"I am not interested in the fate of Juan Ganos, who never existed, imagine that…"

I continue to feign total surprise. I put my two hands flat on the table that separates us and listen wide-eyed.

"…but I am interested in the fate of Johann Gantzer, one of the biggest criminals of the Second World War. Directly responsible for the torture and the death of thousands of Jewish people in the death camps between 1937 and 1944. Thousands, undoubtedly including my father and mother, gassed at Auschwitz, only a few days before the camp's liberation in January '45."

He stops, watching my reaction. I do not manage to control the nervous, mechanic spasm of my lower lip. With a trembling hand, I grab the pack of cigarettes that he has left next to his plate. Magnanimously, he gives me a light. I continue my absurd tactic of feigning ignorance, though my mind has been overrun with so many suspicions, for so long: "Johann Gantzer…I've never heard of him. A real son of a bitch, no doubt… But what does that have to do with my father?"

At this instant, of course, he knows that I have understood. He has no need to say anything more. He could get up and leave; the conclusion is self-evident. But, I feel, he really pities me. He wants to hammer the truth into me himself, perhaps to prevent me from having to discover it myself. He puts a reassuring hand on mine before adding:
"Juan Ganos is nothing by the Hispanicized pseudonym of Johann Gantzer. Ganos never existed. Your father…was Johann Gantzer. He was assassinated by the Mossad in November 1960."

Even if I have been waiting feverishly for long minutes, for long years, forever, for this, the information, thus divulged abruptly by David, stuns me. As if it were not enough it itself, it is accompanied by the rumbling of thunder outside. The little lightbulbs that illuminate the restaurant's dining room day and night, the windows being too small to distribute enough light, flicker with the bang. The sky has darkened, the thunderstorm is approaching, large drops of rain carried by the whirling wind come crashing against the window panes. I can hardly breathe. I had understood for a long time, at least since I turned fifteen, that Juan Ganos had an unavowable past. The marvelously gentle and loving man that I knew, and who had cherished me so much, remained largely shrouded in a shadow. I was unaware until this instant that the shadow was this black. My chest is as tight as my throat. I cannot speak a word. I hold out my glass to David, who fills it, giving me a sad smile. Two days ago, he was my torturer. It is worse than that today: he is the voice of horror and of scandal. I drink. He continues:

"Adolf Eichmann, whom they had just abducted, had given the name of your father to the infiltrated agents who interrogated him. The guys could not, or did not, act right away. They had to exfiltrate Eichmann first. A commando returned a few months later. Its mission, this time, was to arrest your father and bring him back to Israel. But the operation went bad. Your mother suspected something, no one knows how. She had gotten wind of the plan. She went to the bar where your father worked at night, where he was supposed to be abducted upon leaving. She managed to get him out through a hidden door. The Mossad guys, on guard duty, were noticed by the bar owner, who asked them what they were waiting for. The operation was in a bad way. Right away, they were given the order to eliminate Gantzer, or Ganos, as simple as that. The assassins gunned him down the next day... You were in the car, I believe."

David, embarrassed, lowers his eyes as he finishes his sentence, as though he himself were guilty, as though he were responsible for the death of my parents before my eyes, as though it were he who had pulled the trigger. I ask myself how he knows all these details. I gather my strength and I try to speak. I manage to articulate in a whisper:

"You...you tell it as though you were there... How do you know all that?"

He shrugs his shoulders.

"I looked into it..."

"But these events are from over twenty-five years ago and took place in Argentina, over six thousand miles from here."

A long flash of lightening, then two short flashes fill the room. They are followed by the rumbling of thunder, which makes David flinch. It's the first time I see this cop on the run tremble. Ashamed of his fearful reaction, he shakes his head vigorously and laughs, as though to erase his momentary weakness, before continuing:

"I was raised by my grandparents. I went to public school, we spoke no more of Judaism. I never set foot in a synagogue. My thing was soccer. In '54, I was sixteen, I was able to go to the World Cup final in Bern, in Switzerland. My grandfather had saved some money and drove me all the way there. It was an extraordinary journey! The best day of my life. In our enthusiasm, the star of David that I wore around my neck on a gold chain came out of my shirt when I raised my arms to applaud a goal. I also accidentally elbowed my neighbor in the face, who pushed me back violently, screaming: 'Hey! Watch out, kike! Get out of here! No one wants you here.' The war had been over for nine years, I thought that we were done with the problem of 'kikes.' But no! On that day, I realized I would forever remain the subservient Jew. With or without a kippa, I would not be able to escape my condition… I decided to become a hunter of Nazis, old and new. I began to spend my free time on that. And then I studied law and I entered the police, which made my task significantly easier."

He has taken a serious tone again. His fixed gaze is hard, devoid of the emotion he expressed a moment earlier. He gets up, goes towards the window, watches the rain that has started to fall forcefully and that is making an incredible noise. Then he returns, stops in front of me, his hands on the back of his chair.

"Your father was, for a long time, a key figure in my investigations. His name, in different forms, his identities, appeared everywhere. Even though he was dead, I worked on him more than anyone else. That's why I know so many things about him. At the same time, I followed your career, hoping for you to stumble, to put me on a new scent. When the scandal of your insider trading happened, I told myself that, this time, I had you for good. We were going to unravel the mystery. I needed to see you resist the treatment that we inflicted on you at Golfech in order to imagine the possibility of your innocence…"

I really have a hard time understanding what insider trading, of which the authorities and public opinion accuse me unremittingly, could possibly have to do with my father's past, however inglorious it was. It is all the more difficult for me to make a connection between the two subjects, as David is one of the only people who knows that I am the son of the ignoble Johann Gantzer. Even myself, I had no idea until today.

"It's true, but the two other cops knew, too. They belong, like me, to a special division, a group created at the end of the war, whose sole mission is to hunt down former Nazis. In reality, at the same time we had to hush up affairs that were too embarrassing for politicians in power, erase the traces of disagreeable memories for the reputation of this or that person. To put it briefly, one for them, one for us. They gave us a collaborator to denounce in exchange for saving someone's honor. That was the deal. I accepted it. I wanted to put my hands on the real bastards, on the executioners of my parents and so many others. We had all the best information on your father, on those still alive who were his friends and his potential allies in Europe. I repeat to you, Johann Gantzer is a key figure."

He does not hesitate, David, he does not hesitate to pour salt in my wounds. He looks me straight in the eyes. He empties what remains of the wine in the bottle, and he continues, speaking a little louder to overcome the pattering of the rain, interrupted by the rumbling of the departing storm.

"In the fifties and sixties, the biggest criminals of the war mostly succeeded in leaving Europe. Nobody really hunted them down. People more or less closed their eyes. The old generation did not want to hear anything more about all that, especially in Germany of course, but also in France. What mattered was reconciliation and peace. It's my generation that started to truly become interested in the subject. We set out rummaging around to track down those who had gone into hiding. We pulled them out of their holes, one after another. So those we hadn't yet flushed out tried to flee when they could. And for that, they needed a network, and financing. That's where you come in!"

He lets fly these latter words with uncontrolled enthusiasm. He bangs his fist on the table, making the glasses and utensils jump, and he points his index finger at me, interrupting himself to check and see if I have understood his point. Indeed, I believe that I begin to glimpse the logic leading to my abduction, which is what my arrest and the treatment I had to undergo over two days must be called.

"What you are telling me, David, is that in the name of what my father did during the war, and of which I am entirely ignorant, you got it into your head that I financed the escape of Nazi criminals? Is that it?"
David is not proud to admit that this was indeed his simplistic reasoning.
"Yes, that's not totally false, it's sort of what we believed…"
"But what does that have to do with the AIDOS study?"
"When the scandal broke in the press, we went straight to the stock market authorities. At the Financial Markets Regulator, we met the man in charge of the Rodrigo Chemicals case. The guy affirmed to us that there was no doubt about it: if you had sold shares fifteen days before the news came out that rocked your company and provoked its share price collapse, it's because you had found out about it. Someone had certainly given you the info. You had to be guilty of insider trading. At least, it was highly, highly probable, according to him. You indeed knew the scientific director

who conducted the study. You even knew him very well in reality… He is more than an employee, he's a friend, isn't he?"

Decidedly, David is well informed. Indeed, I have more than professional relations with the man in charge of clinical trials at Rodrigo Chemicals, the man who had discovered that a cardiovascular signal invalidated the AIDOS study. We had become friends in the boarding school where I had been a student since my arrival in France in the winter of 1960-1961. He was a student at the school, and someone had asked him to welcome me, to take care of me at the beginning, while I adapted to my new surroundings. Who was this "someone"? I never found out exactly who it was. One of my mysterious protectors, no doubt. All the same, Loïc and I become inseparable fellow travelers. At the end of his pharmaceutical studies, it was only natural for me to hire him to conduct the clinical studies of Rodrigo Chemicals. He began with the company, with me, and he was there throughout our development. Even if he has been my employee for fifteen years, Loïc is also my best friend.

"Loïc? Loîc Martin? Yes, he is more than an employee and associate… he is a friend! I don't see why I would deny something so self-evident"

"Exactly, perfect, we're making progress. It is precisely this 'friend' who could have given you the tipoff in advance?"

"You don't know what you're talking about, David. Obviously he was the one to call me to inform me that the study had bombed…But his phone call came after I sold my shares! That was two weeks later… I did not benefit from any tipoff, I don't know how else to repeat it to you. The fact that Loïc is my best friend changes nothing…"

"Yes, I wound up accepting your version of the facts… That's why we are both here, face to face, here and now. It's because I thought that you couldn't continue to conceal the truth in the state you were in that I took all the risks I took to get you out of Golfech. Otherwise, you would already be rotting six feet underground, my friend! You were a billionaire, you didn't need the money. So why take such a risk? We presupposed that, as we imagined you had done before for a long time, you still financed clandestine groups seeking to aid former Nazis or organizing murders or targeted attacks, like the rue des Rosiers attack. And you will also admit that this closeness with Loïc, in charge of the clinical study, only reinforced our suspicion about you."

These accusations are appalling, but I can understand why he is uttering them. When I decided to disappear, to flee the authorities, I totally cut ties with Loïc. I suspected his phone would be tapped right away.
"Why didn't you arrest him too, if you were convinced the information came from him?"

David seems to hesitate. Outside, the rain is stopping, the pattering has ceased. I allow myself to be distracted by a majestic rainbow extending behind the restaurant's windows, like a peacock's feathers as it spreads them. Calm has returned. The noise from the bar filters back through the glass door separating us from it. We distinctly hear cries of joy, of rage, the sounds of spray shots, and the games of foosball. David finally decides to respond:
"We hoped...to lay a trap for him. We had him followed and had his phone tapped. He didn't walk into the trap. He watched his step."
"Why would you have wanted for him not to watch his step?"
"Loïc Martin...the one who welcomed you at the boarding school...you never asked yourself why he had taken such good care of you when you arrived in France? Nor who asked him to do so?"
A ray of sunlight suddenly sweeps through the window. It spreads over the mosaic, forcing me to squint. David is back-lit, but I perceive his slight smile.

"No, I have to admit that…no…I thought it had to be the headmaster who chose him at random." "I see…So then you didn't wonder about much since your adolescence, huh? Neither about your father's history, nor about the reasons for his murder…Nothing, really?"

David hits me where it hurts. I had noticed that my father's accent sometimes sounded more German than American, I had heard his cursing in the language of Goethe, I had noticed his distress four days after the arrest of Adolf Eichmann in Buenos Aires, when he had hit me in front of the door of our little apartment. I knew, without admitting it to myself, that Papa had a dark past to hide, but after his death, I didn't want to dig any deeper. I tried to turn toward the future, to efface my childhood memories, this impoverished and happy childhood that was mine. When Loïc Martin offered me his friendship and his support upon my arrival at the boarding school, I accepted both without worrying about the reasons for his devotion. Today, David forces me to reconsider my own history, in light of everything he has just told me.

"Loïc Martin, the son of a famous collaborator and member of the Milice. One of those who participated in the organization of the Vél-d-Hiv rafle, among other feats of arms. His father is held directly responsible for at least fifteen thousand deportations."

Alright! Him too. David will spare me nothing. My chest tightens a bit more over my heart, like a vice. The bar owner comes back into the room and yells, in his gravelly voice:

"How's it going over here? You want something else? I have confit de canard, want me to warm it up for you?"

David shakes his head no, but asks for more wine, shaking the empty bottle with a smile. The old fellow leaves us to go dig up another Madiran that he brings us jovially. Before going, he gives David a friendly tap on the shoulder. Then he closes the door behind him.

"Loïc Martin's father was sentenced in absentia in 1948. He had left France well before all that. He left…for Argentina. Buenos Aires, to be precise. We think it was he who helped your father to run away too. Just after he did."
David stops, watches my reaction. I am speechless. I wait for what follows. I am now ready to hear anything.
"He was named Martin, Michel Martin, simply. He renamed himself Miguel Martinez when he arrived in Argentina. The father of your friend Loïc died there, in 1967. Once again, it was the Mossad that tried to catch him, but it was another failure. He identified the infiltrated spies who were about to get their hands on him, and he managed to put a bullet in his head, before the agents came to his house."

Miguel! Miguel Martinez! The teacher who liked me! He of whom I had intuited that there were particular ties between him and my father. He who had demonstrated a strange indulgence towards me, he who had also taught me French. Miguel Martinez, whose real name was actually Michel Martin, had been a hardcore collaborator, hiding in Latin America. Not one of these Frenchmen who, through negligence, through ignorance, through weakness, or simply through spinelessness, had closed their eyes on the horrors committed by the occupier. No, a collaborator, a real one, like you see in films, with a black leather raincoat and armband. One of those bastards who must look like those who arrested David's parents. Who knows, indeed, if he wasn't among them? And Miguel was also the father of my friend Loïc. I am starting to have trouble assimilating all this information, which is tumbling about my bewildered mind. I feel like retching. David pours the wine and offers it to me. I decline.

Suddenly, he freezes. A blue light is flashing outside. It's a gendarmerie van. Through the window panes, we recognize Major Roucaud, who stopped us just before for speeding.

Followed by his colleague Mollard, he approaches the bar entrance. David was mistaken when he told me, an hour ago, that this was a safe place where we wouldn't be bothered. We have to flee. Too late. We're trapped.

Two gendarmes are keeping guard in front of the windows of the restaurant. They are very young, they look like boys wearing costumes. They walk hesitantly, their movements are awkward. They keep their hands on the handgun in its holster, as though they were ready to draw. But it's clear that they wouldn't be capable when the moment comes. That has not escaped David, who has turned around to look at them. They don't even dare to take a step towards the building. We see Roucaud and Mollard walk in front of them and enter the establishment through the bar door. David remains very calm, still. A professional, he scans the place to find a way out. We remain frozen stiff. The foosball game fell silent when the major and the deputy came in. The din has ceased too. Roucaud breaks the silence. He asks the bar owner, our protector. David's friend plays innocent:
"Who? Rodrigo what? Oh! The businessman, on the run... The guy who ran away with the cash register, right? No luck, buddy, I didn't see him. But I wouldn't have recognized him, anyway. I saw his face the other day, in the newspaper, but yeah I kind of forgot..."
A moment passes. One of the two gendarmes must be showing him a photo of my mug, with or without mustache.
"Oh! That's his face? Nope, that doesn't ring a bell, sorry."
"And you know Inspector David Rosenberg, don't you?" asks Roucaud.
"David? Oh yeah, definitely! When he used to live around here, I saw him often. I even knew him when he was little, poor kid. It was not fun in those days. But when he grew up, he left. I haven't seen him for years now..."

There are footsteps on the other side of the restaurant door. Roucaud and Mollard seem to be walking around the bar. Will they come in here? The sound departs again. The gendarmes must have returned to the bar counter. Deputy Mollard continues:
"We saw them both on the road just before. In a white R5. But we hadn't received the information that they were on the run. We only found out later. They are wanted men, do you know that?"

"Who is wanted? The police? The gendarmes are chasing after the police now? Well fancy that!" And the boss lets out a loud laugh, accompanied by a chorus of his amused customers.

Annoyed, Mollard raises his voice: "Don't joke around too much with me, sir, if you don't want me to lock you up right away for public insult, got it?"

"Calm down, Mollard..." interrupts Roucaud. "The gentleman is not aware of the matter. He is surprised that we are looking for a policeman! That is quite understandable... It is true that may seem surprising. Let me explain: David Rosenberg is said to have, how can I put it, went off the deep end, imagine that. He is said to have shot his colleagues at point blank and then taken flight with Rodrigo Ganos. In a white Renault 5, as the deputy explained... And it so happens that a witness saw them hanging around here. That is the occasion for our visit."

We perceive only silence. Then footsteps. A firm, regular step, military. The gendarmes draw near again.

In a single leap, like a cat with velvet paws, David rushes noisily, fast as lightning, to the bathroom. The door closes behind him, he has disappeared. I remain by myself,

paralyzed. I hear the bolt creaking; someone is coming into the restaurant. I do not turn around. Roucaud's voice calls me. My heart is racing. My mouth and my throat go dry. Here I am once again caught like a rat.
"Sir? Sir?"
My cap still pulled down over my head, my three-day beard screening me, I stupidly hope that the cop won't recognize me. I do not react. But he repeats:
"Sir?" I cannot avoid turning towards him.
I answer him: "Ah? You are speaking to me?"

Roucaud winces at the sight of my face. I am not sure if he recognizes me, but my strange appearance confirms to him that I am the guy he saw on the road. Rodrigo Ganos, the most wanted man in France.
"Is it you, Monsieur Ganos?"

Mollard has come in behind him and peers searchingly around the room to try to find where David has hidden himself. The restaurant is not very large, the deputy has quickly realized that there is no possible hiding place. He rushes to the bathroom, violently slams open three doors, and comes back out looking pale.
"He has run off, Major. Rosenberg went out the bathroom stall window: the R5 is parked back there. He must have escaped on foot."
Roucaud digests the information. He turns toward me. Turns back toward Mollard. Me again. Him. He shrugs his shoulders, raises an eyebrow.
"At least we have Ganos, all is not lost."
In a disillusioned breath, he commands me:
"Monsieur Rodrigo Ganos, you are under arrest. I will ask you to be so kind as to follow us." Discretely, he has lowered his hand towards his revolver, just in case, while the tall beanpole approaches, brandishing the handcuffs that he's about to put on me. My time on the run was as short as it was

intense. At least I understand now what I am accused of. And why.

I have been held for several hours, and nothing. No interrogation, not a single question besides: "Are you hungry, thirsty? Do you want to go to the bathroom?" They hardly asked me, on my arrival, to state my identity. They took away my shoes and my belt, and they stuck me in a grayish cell smelling of urine and locked the door behind me. They gave me a blanket I am not using, since it is hot as hell in this hole. I've had to ask for something to drink several times. It's always the same guy who answers. A youthful-looking gendarme who is incapable of providing me with the information I ask him for. He blushes each time I speak to him. When will I be interrogated? Have Mollard and Roucaud been able to come yet? What exactly am I accused of? He doesn't know, the good young man. He would like to help me, I can see it, I can tell. He does not dare to look me in the eye. He is impressed by the caliber of prisoner he has been put in charge of. I am not just anybody, some petty thug passing through, some vulgar receiver of stolen cars, some armed robber of tobacconist shops, some dealer of knockoffs, some second-rate pimp. No, I am Rodrigo Ganos, the billionaire who packed his bags with his fortune tucked under his arm, the fugitive caught by the border police, the man who has possibly killed two of his jailers in cold blood, or made David do it, they aren't very sure, they can't decide, but whichever is the right version, I am a big fish. I was already on the front page of the newspapers before my first arrest. I have since become a veritable myth, public enemy number one. Mesrine, his sun, and his stars can forget about it. I am the boss. The big shot. The Godfather, that's me. They knew I was gifted at embezzlement, rackets, and perfidious strategies. Now they have learned that I was also capable of physical violence, that I was brutal, that I was not afraid to spill blood. According to what my young guard has told me, and the noises in the hallway that I manage to discern since I have been in my cage, I will henceforth be depicted this way on the outside. A major criminal, a dangerous man. It is possible that I kidnapped David Rosenberg, and that I got rid of him before being arrested. Did I murder him? Nothing is ruled out.

If this is the version that is ultimately accepted, it could have quite disagreeable consequences for David. If they eventually decide to put the blame on me, they won't hesitate to put out his lights to silence him, and thus I would seem like his murderer. Kill two birds with one stone.
I am waiting in my cell. I am alone. I vaguely hear the drunken drivers complaining of the unacceptable treatment inflicted on them: things aren't going to go like that, they've got connections, the gendarmes will regret their initiative… An old prostitute wonders aloud: since she has been working and is well known by the gendarmes, what is she suddenly being reproached for? Solicitation in public… Twenty-four hours in police custody for so little… She finds it excessive. A young minor is also accused of shoplifting. A trifle. They are keeping him a few hours, to give him a scare, but nothing will come of it. The door of my jail cell finally opens. they lead me into the office of Major Roucaud. From a distance, his feet on this table, he gives me a sign to approach, to sit. On his right, Deputy Mollard is waiting, in front of a typewriter, for the instructions of his superior. Roucaud has seen others—that's what his entire attitude seems to express. He let me marinate for three hours without a word of explanation. He has not bothered to open his mouth since I have entered, he has not sat up, he has addressed me only by movements of his hand. Even if he is sitting in front of Rodrigo Ganos in the flesh, whom he arrested himself, moreover, he is not easily taken in. These are the subliminal messages he is sending me. For my part, I am disoriented. My soul has been even more wounded than my body since David threw the truth of my father's past in my face. My heart is more bashed up than my bones. How can I accept the idea that the man I loved most in the world, the hero of my

childhood, he who incarnated tenderness itself, was, before being my father, a bloody executioner much crueler than my torturers from the Golfech basement? I do not resolve myself to do so. I would like to die, to disappear, never to have existed. I take a seat in front of the major and I let out my grief, this grief that has inhabited me, without my being fully aware of it, without my knowing truly, for twenty-five years. I let out my tears, which come pouring out my eyelids. They stream over the still-open wounds on my cheeks. I cry like a baby. That's what they always say. To cry like a baby. Well, in my case, I had to wait forty years to let myself go. Roucaud clucks his tongue. My crisis of weakness is irritating him. He finally sits up, puts his feet on the ground, and leans over his desk. He strikes the table, with his two hands. Without yelling, but in a strong voice, he asks me to state my identity, my date and place of birth, is surprised that I was born in Buenos Aires. His surprise reassures me a little. If he does not already know my biography in detail, that means he is not obsessed with the Ganos case. He is not full of assumptions about me, has not devoured the press, which has spoken of nothing but me for weeks.

Roucaud lives kind of in another world, another time. He has a television, he tells me, but he never turns it on. He only became interested in the affair after having received the order to arrest me. Until then, he had simply heard my name going around. He had read neither any article nor any report about me, had not imagined he would run into me in that region. On that point, his hierarchy cannot hold it against him; even me, I would never have imagined it. He remembers having seen me in the passenger seat, traveling under a false identity, in a Renault 5. He found us. Well, not exactly "us." He could only get his hands on me. Rosenberg disappeared. Or am I the one who made him disappear? That's the hypothesis the authorities are going with for the moment. Roucaud doesn't waste any time. He tells me that I am now suspected not only of embezzlement, but also of the murder of three police officers on duty. That's to say, I am going to do major time. A lot of time. Life, without parole, simply. And that is without counting the possible links that might be established between my activities and the rue des Rosiers attack. Mollard conscientiously types out what he hears, transcribes our conversations as accurately as possible, without asking me any question and without asking himself any question either.

It is my turn to speak. I deny everything. What else can I do, in any case? First of all, I did not commit any financial crime, never had any inside information. Secondly, I have killed nobody. Neither David, nor his colleagues. How was I able to escape them? I do not dare to denounce David. He is toast, whatever happens. He is a fugitive whom they will not hesitate to kill when the moment comes, to silence him. It is not so much to protect him that I don't want to tell the whole truth. It is above all because the lower levels of Golfech are themselves secret places. The story of my first arrest must be rewritten. Nobody will believe my version of the facts. I risk falling into dubious explanations that will discredit me. I have to find something else. I plead ignorance. I fainted during my interrogation at the Bourget airport. Maybe I was drugged, I have no idea. In any case, I woke up in David's car. I don't know what happened in the meantime. Inspector Rosenberg left me in the bar where I was arrested. He left well before the arrival of the gendarmes.

My story isn't believable at all. Roucaud lights another cigarette. Mollard coughs. The major gets up and walks up around, smoking, preoccupied, like Lieutenant Columbo. Since the series is very popular right now, I ask myself if the repeated tics of the actor have influenced the attitude of our gendarme. This idea amuses me. It's the first time in days, in weeks maybe, that a pleasant, even funny image, crosses my mind. An involuntary and unconscious smile forms on my lips. Roucaud is startled.

"What is happening to you, Ganos? Two minutes ago, you were crying like a little boy, and now, you are amused? You're not putting me on, by any chance, are you?"
His reaction brings me immediately back to my sad reality. My mouth closes at the severe expression of the major. As for the somber Mollard, who expresses nothing, just looking at him is enough to dishearten me.
"No, no, absolutely not, Major. I hadn't smiled for a long time. It was a reflex, nothing more. Believe me, the situation I find myself in has nothing amusing about it."
He takes a drag on his cigarette, and breathes the smoke very close to me. I am dreaming of a Gitane like those David offered me for two days, which were far superior to the light tobacco cigarette Stéphane had offered me at Golfech. But Roucaud doesn't care about my taste in tobacco, or about bothering me with the spirals of smoke he gives off.
He continues his reflection: "Let's summarize, Monsieur Ganos. You were born in Buenos Aires in May 1945."
"That is correct. Orphaned at fifteen. My parents were murdered for reasons that I never understood clearly. I managed to come to France at the end of 1960."
"I see…"
In an abrupt movement, he half puts out the glowing cigarette end, then he sits back down. Mollard finishes typing what I just said. Roucaud scratches his cheek.
"But…how, in fact? How were you able to come to France? And why France, first of all? Did you have family here?"
I am ill at ease. I will be obligated to put Roucaud on the track of my father's friendships. He will pull at that thread, and realize what David has known for a long time. Out of a sense of discretion, I hope he will never know the truth. But it is there to be discovered. That's his job. He waits.
I finally respond:
"No, I did not have family here. But I had learned French with a friend of my father. A teacher. He is the one who helped me to leave. I got into a cargo ship. I was fed and

treated well throughout the whole journey to Brest. Then, I was given an identity card in my real name, in due form, and a certificate of French nationality. I was sent to a boarding school. A classmate welcomed me, Loïc Martin. He then became my best friend and my closest partner."

"Loïc Martin, yes... I saw that name. But one detail escapes me. You keep saying 'I was fed,' 'I was given papers...' But who were all these people you didn't know?"

I desperately try to buy some time.

"We are not here to speak about my childhood... That was over twenty-five years ago, it's not exactly the point, is it?"

"My dear Monsieur Ganos, if you please, I will continue to distinguish what is part of the point from what is not. Everyone has his role to play. I ask the questions. You answer them, okay? Who were these 'people' you referred to?"

"I never saw any of these people. When I arrived in France, a woman was waiting for me on the waterfront. She was wearing a dark gray dress. She gave me a sign when I disembarked the boat. I approached her and I followed her. She took me to the boarding school. I never knew anything else and... I never asked anything."

The telephone rings. The major picks up. "Roucaud here! Yes. Yes, he is here, in front of me... No, I don't know. No trace, no... Yes, okay. Understood."

He hangs up and explains to me:

"Your arrest is already making a lot of noise. The authorities are looking into what you could have done with this poor David Rosenberg. We will get to that right away. But first of all, I would like to know a little more about you. So you were orphaned at fifteen. Mysterious protectors allowed you to go to a French boarding school in which you had a brilliant career as a student. You continued to benefit from financing of an unknown origin, and which accompanied you also during your university studies."

Faced with the brute simplicity of his words, I become aware of the willful ignorance in which I lived throughout all these years, without ever trying to understand who these benefactors were, nor why they wished me so well. Here I am up against the wall.

Roucaud sniggers. Mollard imitates him mechanically, probably out of an obsequious reflex. "You never asked yourself any question, Monsieur Ganos? You had been aided and financed until 1968, when you finished your studies of..."

He rummages in a pile of papers confusedly spread out on his desk. He moves a few papers to pull out others, but he brings them to close to the still smoking ashtray. They catch fire while he is looking for a form. I draw his attention, he blows on the paper, then taps on it. Irritated, he stubs out his cigarette harder than his first attempt, before continuing: "...studies of chemistry in 1968? Is that right?"

"Yes! Exactly... The end of my studies was a bit disturbed by the month of May... I didn't participate much in the events. I was never interested in politics. In any case, it didn't seem to have anything to do with me. I had no reason to revolt. The idea of chasing away the "old fools" did not particularly preoccupy me. Anyway, I got my degree one way or another, and I took advantage of the ambient void to start my business as quickly as possible. With the help of my friend Loïc Martin."

"Oh yes, that's right! Yes, Loïc Martin, yes..." Roucaud mumbles, in his gravely smoker's voice, clearing his throat.

He rubs his chin, knitting his brows. Colombo is really not far off. Behind his exaggerations, his theatrical gestures, his noisy exhalations, his posturing, his irritation, his drags on his cigarette, his shouting, there is something endearing about Roucaud. A strange mixture of harshness, of cunning, and of weakness. But thus was he caught who thought to catch me. His little blue-green eyes seeking to pierce my secrets also let me see his. There is unhappiness in this man, a fragility that he attempts to hide with his seeming confidence. I feel close to him. Me, whom people have seen as a superhuman, as the devil incarnate, me, whose tough-guy image preceded, at Rodrigo Chemicals itself, his image as a criminal forged by the media in the meantime, I feel puny and weak, on the contrary. They call me brutal, but I see myself as tender. They think I am authoritarian, but I am timid. They say I am swaggering, daring. I was ambitious, certainly, but at heart I am a chicken.

"And this Loïc, well?"
"Well what?"
"How did you meet him?"
"At the boarding school, as I have told you. He took me under his wing from the very first days." "Oh yeah, that's right, at the boarding school! But then you fell out of touch?"
"Not at all. He studied pharmacy. When I founded Rodrigo, I naturally turned to him to back me up. At first, I thought I would start a chemicals company that would develop solutions for everyday household use: disinfectants, sunscreens, nothing revolutionary. It was unfashionable, at that time when everyone extolled the virtues of returning to nature, when young people left for Katmandu or the Larzac. And then little by little, we recruited other chemists and biologists, and we developed and began to sell active molecules, anti-inflammatories, antipyretics, sleeping pills, and anxiolytics. Finally, Rodrigo Chemicals became a pharmaceutical company in the strict sense."
"Rodrigo, yes… Rodrigo Chemicals. Your friend Loïc wasn't jealous that the company that he had helped build bears only your name and that his appears nowhere?"

The question surprises me. I must admit that I had never asked myself that.

"Loïc is an intelligent, rigorous, methodical guy. He was one of the first to create medical studies with a control group and thorough statistical analysis, with my help for the math. He contributed a lot to the success of Rodrigo Chemicals, that is undeniable. But he didn't have the spirit of an entrepreneur or a leader. He never showed any desire to have that position. It was always obvious that I was the only executive."

Roucaud nods his head dubiously. He circles the name Loïc Martin with red ballpoint pen.

"And you never wondered about this point either? You never suspected that your friend and collaborator might feel some secret rivalry in his innermost being?"

It is another blow from Roucaud. After the revelations about my father, must I now learn that my friend, my ally since always, my brother at heart, was jealous of me, hated me, without my suspecting it? The major fixes his gaze on me with a slight sneer. Behind him, Mollard unfolds his large body and takes a few steps to stretch his legs. I remain speechless.

"You never wondered, Monsieur Ganos, what could be the cause of your problems?"

"Uh…I…I mean, yeah, of course. I was accused of a crime I didn't commit. The press seized on the case, even before the courts. It was impossible to defend myself against slander. So I tried to flee, that's all."

"That's all? That's all, what?" Either you lied, or you didn't lie! If you told the truth, why flee?"

"I couldn't prove it…"

In pronouncing these words, I see better what Roucaud's point is. My only recourse was Loïc Martin's testimony. Before a judge, Loïc was the only one who could assign a date to the information he had given me, thus proving that it was posterior to the sale of my shares. Why didn't I use his testimony as incontestable proof of my innocence? I wonder if, as with my father, I did not turn a blind eye on purpose.

Roucaud insists: "Only one man had the power to testify for you and to prove your innocence. But you did not try to lean on him, on his word. You preferred to flee justice and to attempt a desperate journey to Argentina rather than defending yourself here, in France. Of course, that only adds weight to the idea that you are guilty. Nothing is more logical. But as for me, you don't quite look the part... Mollard, please do not write that down."

The deputy is surprised: "Huh? Why?"
In a single bound, Roucaud throws himself at him. I am afraid he's going to give him a smack, but he contents himself with screaming, in a fury:
"Fuck! Mollard! When are you going to stop disputing my orders? You want me to request your transfer to the Mirail projects? I have friends in high places, you know! I can use them! Understood?"
Mollard goes pale, and stops typing. Roucaud catches his breath, turns back toward me, sits halfway on his desk, and continues:
"I shouldn't say that, you know. You shouldn't presume the guilt or innocence of someone based on their face or the look they have about them. But, try as you might to be a gendarme, to have a sense of duty and a respect for rigor, you're still a man. Oh! Yes, you're going to tell me, sexual perverts who look like butter wouldn't melt in their mouth, crooks with the face of an angel, guys who beat their wives to death and bury them in the garden and whom you would pity like tearful widowers, yes, I have known them, definitely. And the other way around, little hoodlums I would have thought guilty a thousand times over and whose conduct has proved to be irreproachable after investigating, yes, I have seen them too, it's true. But honestly, between us, they are only a few exceptions that prove the rule. The truth – Mollard, above all, do not write this down! – the truth is that, more often than not, our candidates for the clink look the

part, yes. The armed robbers look like armed robbers, the dealers look like dealers, the white collar crooks look simply like crooks. And with you, I don't know, but I just feel that you are not capable of an iota of what you are accused of…"

He gave me this speech in a cordial, almost warm, tone, like a retired cop telling his memories to a journalist or to an old comrade from his regiment, with a beer in the shade of a plane tree. He has drawn nearer to me with a smirk that I don't manage to interpret. Is he trying to make me trust him in order to trap me more easily? I remain on my guard. In a shrill voice, I respond only: "Thank you, Major."

"Oh, no, don't thank me! I am only telling you things as I see them. But my belief won't allow you to leave here! You can't imagine the pressure I am under! If I let you marinate for three hours down there, it was not for the pleasure of it, believe me."

"Really? Actually, it was a long time. I thought that…"

"You were wrong! It was a matter between the police and the gendarmes. I spent all that time on the phone with Paris negotiating. I had quite a hard time winning my case."

The deputy interrupts him: "Major, be careful! If I may allow myself to say so, maybe you should not reveal…"

Roucaud fulminates: "He won't shut it, will he?"

Mollard frowns. I ask: "What case did you win?"

"To keep you for twenty-four hours. They wanted me to hand you over to the court right away, or to give you back to the police."

These last words give me the chills. These cops he is speaking of, maybe he doesn't even know them. They are the ones who carted me off from Bourget to Golfech and who took care of my case. Oh, not they were not the ones Roucaud has dealt with, to be sure! All the more so as two of them are dead and the third is on the run. Guys like me. I

86

don't feel like reliving, at their hands, the episode from four days ago. I do not want him to deliver me to them again. I shiver at the thought of it, despite the humidity and the heat of this cramped atmosphere. The two gendarmes dab at their foreheads regularly. As for me, the fear is literally making me drip with sweat.

"Would it be possible to open the window? Could I please have something to drink?"

Roucaud gives a sign to his deputy to open the big windows that are not protected by bars. A welcome breeze wafts in. We are on the ground floor. For an instant, I imagine leaping in a single bound into the courtyard, which is plunged in shadow at this late hour. I see myself fleeing as fast as I can go. But I am handcuffed and incapable of attempting anything like that. Mollard sits back down, chuckling into his beard.

Roucaud shouts at him: "What is it that's amusing you so much, Deputy?"

The other man begins laughing openly.

"Excuse me, Major. It's the expression, '"have something to drink'…like what? A pastis? Does our candidate think he's the postman or something? 'Oh, you'll have something to drink…'"

Mollard doubles up with laughter. Roucaud reacts:

"Alight! Listen, if that amuses you, that's fine, but for the time being, go get some cold water and bring us three glasses. I am dying of thirst too. And you know what? Time is short. We have no more than twenty-four hours ahead of us and we will have to sleep a bit too."

While Mollard is gone, Roucaud confides:

"This guy is an ass. He is a mean bastard. He was imposed on me, I didn't have a choice. It's hard to lug him around the whole damn day, let me tell you. But I also have to admit, he's an excellent detective. Once he catches the scent of a clue, he doesn't give up."

Why is he confessing these things to me? What he is trying to tell me? That I should be more afraid of Mollard than of him? That, if I am lying, I will certainly be caught by the deputy? I wonder. The tall beanpole returns, armed with glasses and with a jug. He serves us. I swallow it all in a single gulp. He pours me another glass. I begin again. I am nauseous.

The major then continues the interrogation by the book. Mollard has to type out the whole story, from the beginning and the rise of Rodrigo Chemicals, up to my arrest in the restaurant, including my supposed insider trading crime, my hideout in Paris for a few weeks, my abortive flight to Argentina, and my improbable story about waking up in Rosenberg's car after a massive blackout several days long. Roucaud does not bother contradicting me, he insists on having my deposition in full, maybe in order to highlight its weaknesses more easily afterwards. I have my suspicions about this man's intentions. But I am, whatever the case may be, at his mercy. It has taken two more solid hours to transcribe everything, at the pace of the typewriter that jammed several times and needed its ribbon and carbon paper replaced.

Night has now completely fallen. They have closed the windows and turned on a neon light that gives off a pale and sad light in this room which is no less so. The only decoration is a glacial photo portrait of the current president, François Mitterrand. His frozen image, his false half-smile, his vague gaze remind me all of a sudden of the rumors circulating about him. Did Mitterrand have an ambiguous attitude during the Occupation? The press refers more and more freely to the embarrassing friendships of the head of state. They speak in particular of someone named René

Bousquet, a multifaceted personality who is said to have escaped the purge after the Liberation, but whose career was perhaps no better than my father's. An article in *L'Express,* in 1978 sparked things off, leading the former prefect in the Marne region, who had become a businessman, to step down from all of his administrative tasks. Certain journalists go as far as to claim that Bousquet was at the origin of the Vélodrome d'Hiver roundup in July 1942, of which Loïc Martin's father is said to have been one of the organizers. Could there be a link between that investigation, which is beginning, and my indictment?

The two gendarmes yawn together in silence while my thoughts wander. It is after ten at night.

Roucaud slumps into his armchair. "Let's drop it for today, Deputy! I am exhausted."
"But, Major…"
"I am telling you we're going to drop it, that's all! I need to think. I'm going to eat a casserole I left in the fridge and go to bed. We'll meet here at six tomorrow morning and we will take stock of things with our candidate."

Then, addressing me: "I don't know what you have done, nor what has brought you here. But I think you are a cog in a machine you don't understand. In Paris, they are convinced that you have killed Rosenberg. At least, they pretend to believe that. That is not my opinion. I am convinced that the cop is your accomplice, on the contrary…"

He looks hard at me for an instant, watches for my reaction, staring mischievously at me. I don't move a muscle.

"…and you're going to help me find him! In the meantime, rest up. We have our work cut out for us tomorrow."

With a nod, he gives Mollard the sign to leave. One minute later, the young-looking gendarme who took me here comes to bring me to my cell.

They served me a lukewarm meal after everybody else, after Roucaud decided to cut off my interrogation. There was vermicelli noodle soup, chicken with a carrot purée, and plain yogurt. I could not finish it. I called and they came to take away my plate. The last time that I had been subjected to this kind of regimen, it was during a two-day stay at the hospital for a minor surgery when I was around twenty years old.

I manage to fall asleep, a bit before midnight, when the episodic protests of other detainees have finally ceased. My sleep is troubled. The Golfech torturers reappear as monsters, their features blending with my fathers', who raises his right arm in front of the portrait of the Führer, while my mother, who strangely has the face of Romy Schneider, tries to save my fiancée Noura from the clutches of a member of the Milice. The scene unfolds in our ramshackle apartment in Buenos Aires; I am still a child, but I accuse my father of having lied. He is about to punch me in the face when I wake up with a start, covered in sweat. It takes me several seconds to catch my breath. I hear the locks sliding. I stare at my cell door, which opens onto the silhouettes of two men I recognize immediately. One is holding the other at gunpoint. I blink, I pinch myself to see if I am still in my nightmare, or if what I see is real. David holds his MR73 against the temple of the young non-commissioned officer, whose heart is in his boots. The gendarme has just opened the door. He is still holding the key ring in his trembling hand.

"Give me the keys and get inside," says my liberator in a calm but firm voice.
The young man obeys. David gives me a sign to join him, without another word. He locks the poor kid in and we get out of there. On the ground floor, two other gendarmes whose mouths are duct-taped shut, handcuffed to the radiator and disarmed by the cop, watch us flee, without moving. We

leave under a starry sky. David tosses me the keys to a red Peugeot 205 towards which he walks. The car is carefully parked on the left side of the one-way street. It seems to be waiting for us in complete tranquility.
"You drive!"

Still in the fog of sleep, haggard, lost, disoriented, I get behind the wheel. David sits in the passenger's seat. He opens the window, does not put on his seatbelt, and turns his head in every direction to try to see any possible pursuers in the darkness that the streetlamps only partially dissipate.
"Start the car, hurry up."

While we are leaving the parking space, a glance in the rearview mirror allows me to see that the gendarmerie seems completely calm. The entrance hall is bright, the front door is ajar. One imagines our brave on-call soldiers ready to receive the night's complaints as they patiently await the return of their colleagues who have gone on patrol. David is right, let's not dally. I put the car into second gear. We traverse the silent little town. I stop at the stop sign. David guides me, take a right, take a left, go straight, he's told me to lower the window on my side too. Fresh and damp air rushes into the car. It both wakes me up and soothes me. When I stop at the stop sign, I can hear the rustling of the wind in the leaves, which are starting to dry at this summer's end. An owl hoots in the distance. The night is warm. The town is sleeping soundly. Not a soul on the sidewalks. Fleeing seems easy. What has David done since escaping being arrested? How did he procure this new vehicle for himself? He says nothing. But he has lost the calm assurance that he had before. He is anxious. He delivers his instructions in a staccato voice. He is no longer the confident cop, who a few days ago, killed his two colleagues in cold blood or who, yesterday still, described to me the shameful service records of my adored father. He almost seems afraid. I still hardly know him, but

enough to know that he is no chicken. I have rarely read such determination in somebody's gaze. But, between yesterday and tonight, he has changed. What is bothering him so much? I break the silence:
"Thank you, David. I mean...for freeing me. Even if that major, Roucaud, seems honest to me, at least, I was not necessarily going to manage things like that. I find him to be sincere and I am convinced that he tried to untangle the true from the false. But I'm not safe from the risk of going to do a stint in prison."

David lights a Gitane and orders me to buckle him up. He even furtively aims his gun at me, before resting it on his knees. I keep quiet. I try to go over the last few hours... Suddenly, a detail comes back to me that could very well explain Rosenberg's sudden worry. A detail that I had noticed during my interrogation by Roucaud. When Roucaud was rummaging around in his things to look for notes he had taken on me, and when he had inadvertently let some of his papers catch fire, I clearly noticed David's photo on one of the papers that flied away. So far, there was nothing surprising about that since he is one of the key personalities in the major's investigation. What troubled me more, without my truly realizing it in the moment, what that on the same page appeared the names of various public personalities, including René Bousquet, born in Montauban, not far from here, according that what I had read before the beginning of my scandal and my first arrest. I had the time to see the other family names that sounded vaguely familiar to me: Leguay, Darquier, Baylet... Red and blue arrows connecting all these individuals, certain of whom were surrounded by several lines. I realize now that it was not directly Mitterrand's portrait that made me think of Bousquet. That name had already been running through my head since I had seen it associated with Rosenberg among Roucaud's papers. When my eyes fell on the photo of the president, I thought of his embarrassing friendships because I had just seen *René Bousquet* on Roucaud's list. Other public personalities—politicians, artists, business leaders—were aligned in alphabetical order on this list connected to the photo of David. I only fleetingly glanced at the document; I did not catch all its details. I wonder if these could be the personalities my savior has committed to rehabilitating "by hand." He had to clear certain names. In exchange for which he had carte blanche for the most sordid executioners. David explained it well to me: "one for one." Might Roucaud, who seems to be quite nosy, be about to figure out this strange procedure and reveal the truth to the public, jeopardizing David's work? My curiosity piqued, I would ask the cop, but I can tell he's not in the mood to chat, and even less to confide in me. I hold my tongue for the moment. We are leaving Beaumont towards the north. Tomorrow evening, we will head towards Bordeaux. There, a smuggler will hide me in the hold of a cargo ship, David announces to me in a formal tone that does not invite debate or contradiction. I will leave France clandestinely. He needs me, so he wants to know I am safe. In a few days, I will dock in Casablanca. My heart skips a beat: Casa is the native city of Noura! Her family still lives there: her father, an grouchy old mustachioed man of whom she has spoken to me so often with tremors in her voice, two of her sisters, her mother who drinks whiskey on the sly as an aperitif without ever separating herself from her colorful hijab. Will I finally see my pretty fiancée again? David quickly dampens my hopes. I will be unloaded at the port by his friends there. Before arriving, I will be locked in a container whose serial number they will tell me. They will let me out when the time comes, no more than a few hours after landing. But all the same I should bring enough water, and an empty bottle to urinate. They will take me to a riad within a medina quarter, a place kept so secret that David himself does not know it precisely. No one will be able to find me as long as I do not show myself. No one will know where I am, aside from a few of David's allies. How much time will I have to remain in hiding?

"As long as it takes!" David responds. "You have no questions to ask. You don't have a choice, you obey, that's all!"

He has cut off every other attempt at objection. We are driving in silence for a half-hour to the edge of the little village of Saint-Nicolas-de-la-Grave, the birthplace of Antoine de La Mothe-Cadillac, founder of the city of Detroit in the 18th century, who will inspire the creators of the car brand that bears his name. I wonder why David, so somber this moonless night, suddenly bothers to tell me this anecdote. He has me stop in front of a telephone booth. He needs to make a call to finalize the details of my trip. The call doesn't take long, and he returns quickly.

We leave the village towards the west, and a few miles further on, we drive into undergrowth growing alongside the Garonne River. Once the car is stopped in a hidden spot that seems hard to find, David decides that we will stay here until dawn, enveloped by the long branches of white willows that merge with black poplars covered in lianas, and protected by centennial oaks.

"Let's try to sleep. Tomorrow, we will have to wait here the whole day, keeping on the lookout, before leaving for Bordeaux once night has fallen."

It is almost three in the morning. David reclines his seatback almost horizontally, and curls up in the fetal position, his eyes closed, his gun tightly held in his right hand. I imitate him, but it is impossible for me to fall asleep. My fatigue and stress stir up the after-effects of the painful torments from my stay in the Golfech basement. Fear gets the best of me. I am trembling. The forest has retained its dampness from the afternoon storm. The scent of decaying plants wafts into the car whose windows we have left open. It chases away the odor of stale tobacco, caresses my nostrils, reminding me of the summer rains in Buenos Aires, which we welcomed like redemptive gifts from the heavens. When Papa was home, he took me running in the deluge. We came home soaked. Mama scolded us, undressed us, rubbed us down despite our protests, hung our clothes at the window to dry. Often, my parents would then share a beer to celebrate the event. Sometimes I had the right to a glass of milk. These memories finally calm me. I manage to doze off.

A few hours later, daybreak pulls me from my slumber. David is up, I see him seated rather close to the river. I go sit down next to him. He is mechanically throwing stones into the Garonne, not very far, out of fear of being seen. He remains in the shelter of the trees. From here, he thinks, no one will be able to see us. If a barge were to pass, there would be time to draw back. He offers me a plastic bottle of water.
"It's all I have to offer you for breakfast."
But I do not refuse. I swallow a quarter of the bottle in large gulps.
"What else do you know about… about… Johann Gantzer? I almost don't manage to call him 'Papa' anymore."
"Johann Gantzer was born in Bonn on December 16, 1905, one hundred and thirty-five years after the birth of Beethoven in the same city. For his father, a math teacher named Ludwig, passionate about classical music and himself an instrumentalist, it was a sign of destiny. From early on, he imagined for his son a career as a musician. He initiated Johann, named after Strauss, to the violin from a very young age. The Great War arrived. Ludwig died at Verdun in spring 1916. It seems that Johann absorbed Germany's surrender as a terrible humiliation, a blow to the memory of his father. He

nonetheless pursues a brilliant career as a student in physical sciences, distinguishing himself numerous times, and frequents the greatest minds: he is noticed by Werner Heisenberg, who mentions him several times in his letters to his family, and even in some of his works. he describes Johann as a hardworking young man, hot-headed, gifted with a prodigious intelligence, but he regrets his excessive exaltation. Johann spends long stays in the United States, at the University of Columbus, in Ohio. He returns nearly bilingual, but also convinced that the Great War, and above all the German defeat, can be attributed to the treachery of the Jewish conspiracy, an ideal circulating actively there too. He commits very early to Hitler, and is among the very first to join the SA."

A small wave splashes David's feet, obliging him to step back quickly. I jump in turn, and am run through with a long chill whose exact origin I cannot determine: the waft of fresh air that has just caressed me or the cop's chilling story. I don't want to know any more, but at the same time I am burning to know the whole truth. I persist:
"And then?"
"And then? And then what?"

David can well imagine what I want to find out, without my being sure, however, of truly desiring it. What was the exact role of my father during the war and the Occupation? Was he involved in the deportation of Jews? The cop gets up. His hands in his jean pockets, he is strolling between the trees, scratches at the dirt with the toe of his Adidas Stan Smiths and does not turn his eyes away from his feet. He hesitates to lay out everything.

"Your father was part of the Paris Kommandantur. He worked under the orders of General von Choltitz until August '44. He then deserted and he probably managed to flee the capital at the beginning of the month of August, no one really knows how. As a German officer, he was able to cross still-occupied France, all the way to Bordeaux. From there, he probably embarked a fishing boat and reached Spain. Then it seems he reached Portugal. It seems he left from Porto in September for Argentina, on a cargo ship…"

Once again, what David tells me has an effect as though he stabbed or clubbed me, knocking the breath out of me. Trying, with difficulty, to catch my breath, I manage to articulate:
"What you are telling me, David, is that I am about to leave France, tomorrow, clandestinely, by the same route my as father forty-one years ago? I have become a pariah like him in this country that has become mine over time. As though I had committed the same crimes he did."

David takes his hand out of his pocket to pass it through his thick brown hair. He crouches down right next to me. He has something else to tell me and his embarrassment is noticeable.
"Rodrigo, listen…"

It's the second time he pronounces my first name since we've met. His tone is more solemn than ever.
"Rodrigo, this departure from Bordeaux, you have… how can I put it… done it once already, in August '44."
I am not sure what he is getting at. I remain silent, taken aback. He nods as a sign of approval, as though to confirm that he knows what he's talking about. He has not suddenly gone mad. He is completely lucid, and I am the one who doesn't understand, once again.

"Yes, when your father left the port in his little trawler in the middle of the night, he had, bundled up in a blanket, a newborn a few days old, or maybe a few weeks. And that baby, Rodrigo, was you…"

He uttered these last words in such a faint whisper that I wonder if I have heard right. That baby was… me? I am lost. The sun is already rising above the horizon and is beginning to warm the atmosphere; birds are chirping cheerfully, are busy looking for worms hidden beneath the leaves, while insects begin to buzz around us. I have to swat away a cloud of flies that is threatening to nestle under my eyelids. Existence continues to take its course here just as elsewhere at the end of this summer, indifferent to my fate, to my story, and indeed to History. These poplars, these wasps, and these spiders don't care a fig about our somber torments. They ceaselessly repeat the absurd cycle of life that, from ameba, gave birth to multicellular organisms, to algae, to mollusks, to fish, and finally to mammals. From reproduction to reproduction it happened that one day in 1943 a man and a woman met and made love. In July 1944, a new being was born of the union of the gametes of Johann Gantzer with those of an unknown woman. That infant was me. My name is Rodrigo Ganos, and until a few seconds ago, I thought I was born on May 15, 1945 in Buenos Aires. When I was very little, I was considered to be advanced for my age… I understand better now why: I was almost a year older than my official age. Since two days ago, I know that my papa was not the tender barman Juan Ganos I knew, but the ignoble Johann Gantzer, physicist by profession and bloody tormentor on occasion, a barbarous, sadistic criminal. I now have to accept that I was not born in the city where I grew up, nor even in the right year. These terrible revelations torture me to the core, but soon they give way to a new, even more troubling doubt. Mute worry pierces my gut as it takes shape. If I was born in France, that means… My God! No, I cannot believe that. Yet I hear myself asking him:

"And my mother, Soledad? She was born in Argentina and, as far as I know, always lived there. She didn't speak French... Johann couldn't have met her in Paris, where she never went?"

I have hardly finished my phrase when I suddenly see my naivety. Obviously! David only has to deal me the final blow: "Your mother, your mother is not...who you think. Your father met Soledad soon after having arrived in Buenos Aires. We don't know exactly when, but we think that she is the person who helped him procure a new passport. Johann called himself John, an American communist who had fled the United States. Thanks to his near-bilingualism, the deception worked, and he thus obtained, with his wife's help, a new identity. Soledad adopted you and raised you as her son.

What pain to have these revelations told to me by this cop whom I didn't know a week ago, even if he seems to feel a certain compassion for me!

"And... How should I say... my... my real mother? Who was she?"

David shakes his head back and forth. He is sorry.
"We looked for her. We looked a lot. But we never found anything We assumed that she had abandoned this shameful child..."

Realizing the monstrosity of his expression, he excuses himself:
"Sorry, it's not what I wanted to say..."
"Continue!"
"...yes, sorry. We assume that she attempted to abandon the child, to get rid of this proof of her affair with a German officer, when she learned that Allied troops were headed

towards Paris. Maybe she avoided having her head shaved that way. In any case, we have no trace of her. To be honest, we know absolutely nothing about who she was. There was not a single rumor about any affair your father might have had."

It's strange, but I am almost relieved by this last avowal. It's been forty-eight hours that David has been bombarding me with stupefying revelations. My entire life had so far seemed to be an open book to him. Paradoxically, I am happy that he is missing a piece of the puzzle. My story thus doesn't completely belong to him. The identity of my real mother, of which I also know nothing, will have escaped them. A part of my private life still remains intact.

We remain seated a moment next to one another, in silence. David has started again to throw pebbles or little pellets of balled-up dirt into the Garonne. I take off the hiking boots that I haven't removed in two days. I massage the soles of my feet. I feel bad. David too. I suggest that we take advantage of the nearness of the water to wash up.

"You're right. I even have what we need."

David goes to the car and returns with Marseille soap. Each of us washes quickly while the other keeps guard. After the brief rinse, I lie down. I wind up falling asleep again. When I wake up, David has disappeared. I spring up. The car is gone. I am seized with panic. I rush to the river, retrace my path, start running toward the road on the edge of the woods, run back as soon as I hear the sound of a motor. I stop finally, crouch down, huddle against a tree. Soledad's loving face appears to me. Her wrinkles at the corner of her eyelids, the softness of her hands, her warm voice that put me to sleep when she sung me a nursery rhyme. I was her *Rodri*, her *cariño,* her *ángel*. She was my little dear mama. She is no longer. I must mourn her a second time. I have to begin a new quest, to discover the identity of the woman who really brought me into the world. After years of investigation on me, as well as on my father, the specialized police did not manage to find my biological mother. Their many investigations did not even lead to a vague clue! The task looks to be even harder for me, as I have no means at my disposal and will be obliged to leave France as of this evening, without knowing if I will be ever be able to return.

The red Peugeot 205 reappears on the path. David gets out, with a satisfied smile at having accomplished his mission. He proudly displays a large bag with many sandwiches, sodas, candies.

"We have to eat! Especially you. You may not be able to eat again right away. Take your strength!"
"But.. where have you found all that?"
He smiles:
"Well it doesn't grow on trees! I went to the village grocery store, what do you think?"
"But...how did you manage not to be spotted? Are you sure you weren't followed?"

He laughs at that.
"Look at that, our businessman on the run is worried about my professional skills! Listen, as far as surveillance goes, I am very competent. It's even, I could say, my specialty. Anyway, my face hasn't been in all the papers for months, like yours. Nobody knows me. Only the police services and the gendarmes know what I look like, and... I had no trouble mixing in with people from the area calmly doing their shopping."

He gives me an enormous sausage sandwich. I do not refuse it. We chew in silence. Then his eyes begin to sparkle again.

He grabs me by the arm, helps me up, and takes me toward the trunk of the car. He opens it.

"It was market day today. I also bought new clothes!"

He unfolds two red shirts, two pairs of jeans, and two caps with the Ferrari logo.

"Starting now and until this evening, we will be *Scuderia* aficionados out for a good time, as indeed the color of our race car shows, he says cheerfully, and giving a kick to the car's lower body frame. Alright, let's go, get changed!"

David seems to have found the confidence he had lost overnight. I am still itching to know what had troubled him so much. Once I am dressed, I ask him right away:
"You were very nervous when we left Beaumont. What was worrying you so much?"

He hesitates. His fate and mine might be linked forever, but he is not sure how much he can trust me, nor of the counter-intuitive friendship the he can offer his former victim. His recent questions when we were first hiding out prove that he has still not decided definitively about my indirect but still possible participation in the rue des Rosiers attack. Must he, under these conditions, confide in me the subject of his torments? After a sigh of indecision, he admits:

"This gendarme... Roucaud... he worries me. He is going to stick his nose everywhere. He is just a hair shy of understanding the way our special unit worked. He knows that I have investigated René Bousquet for a long time. And it was by following that track that I discovered the existence of your father as well as that of Michel Martin."

As I seem skeptical, he explains:

"Martin worked for the Milice under the more or less unofficial orders of Bousquet, then secretary-general of the police. He reported directly to Jean Leguay, René Bousquet's delegate. Gantzer, for his part, was among their German counterparts, just like Adolf Eichmann. They organized the Vél'd'Hiv raffle all together."

These words cruelly scorch my ears. How can I bear to hear my father's name associated with "Vél-d-Hiv, "Milice", "Adolf Eichmann"? But I don't have a choice if I want to understand the reasons for David's worry. In order to have a clear view, I must not interrupt.

"I don't understand, David. Even if your methods are…muscular (I touch my still swollen jaw as I speak), and even if it is true that you regularly work out an arrangement with the law, your unit is still not a secret society. A gendarme can very well know of its existence and your areas of investigation…"

He raises his eyes to the sky, annoyed by my naivety.

"Do you think that we had even tacit authorization to treat you as we did? Do you think that our hierarchy would have approved if it had known about it? We had carte blanche as long as we did not get caught. Let's say that the General Inspection of the National Police didn't butt into our business too much, but, at the slightest underhand trick, they would abandon us. We knew that and we worked fully aware of those conditions. And, I repeat, it was a principle of quid pro quo. Bousquet is one of the protected guys. He was already tried. *Non bis in idem*! You can't try somebody twice for the same reasons. That's why we need new elements if we want to get him. But nobody wants him to fall, especially not up there, at the summit" (David points his finger at the ceiling).

"I play a double game, you understand? I feign trying to rehabilitate him, but, in reality, my inquiry is advancing, I am putting myself in position. That is why I need you. I could not let my two moronic colleagues bump you off. You are indispensable. But now this stubborn Roucaud must not rummage around in that, he would screw everything up."

Little by little, the pieces of the puzzle are beginning to connect. The overall image is gradually becoming clear. I catch a glimpse of the plan simmering in David's head. I will serve him as scout as well as bait. Through me, through the identity of my historical protectors, he will try to trace the web of financing and to catch those who help Neo-Nazi groups or give them money. Through my name, too, he will try to trap Bousquet, or others. To make them believe that there is in me, because of my heritage, an ally.

As for me, I have no more future. I will flee, like a criminal, this country that welcomed me, that offered me glory and prosperity, that will have given me everything before taking it all away. My best friend Loïc is beyond reach; my fiancée has disappeared, or rather it is I who have absconded. With neither parents nor children, I am alone in the world. I do not know if Noura carries within her the child that she wanted from me. I imagine her stomach becoming round, her breasts becoming heavier, I see her walking down the hallways in the Samaritaine shopping center, her hands resting on the small of her back, looking for a cradle, a play mat, a music box to ceaselessly add cheer to the cradle with Brahms... He will be brown-haired like his mother, with curly hair and large black eyes. Unless it is a girl. What will we name her? What will she name her? I will not be there to see her born. To see her at all. When will I be able to return? When will I be able to see Noura again? I stand up, move away from David and walk along the river to drown my sorrow in the current.

When I have retraced my steps, David is seated in the car, absorbed in paperwork, taking notes.

"These documents are a goldmine…"
I do not respond. He continues:
"Get changed, we are not going to delay leaving here."
I do so.
"And then? Once you have leave me in Bordeaux, what will you do, David?"
"Don't worry about me. I have a million places to stay. And I will not reveal a single one of them to you. As you have experienced during your stay in Golfech, the best way not to speak is to know nothing. If you are arrested, whether they pull out your toenails and fingernails one by one, or pour salt in your wounds so they cannot heal, or drown you in a basin, you will not say where I am, simply because you will not know. You will not say when I plan to come get you in Casablanca because you will not have the slightest idea. You will not give away the identity of our smuggler because you don't know it. You understand?"

I understand very well, yes. I even feel it in my skin. But if David is capable of keeping a secret to make sure that I don't speak, even if driven to the last extremity, I wonder why he told me so easily about his investigation about René Bousquet. I ask myself. I do not understand any better the importance of my supposed insider trading in this immense affair. Loïc is undeniably the missing link. Everything began with him, and it was through him, ultimately, that the first scandal broke out.

We bury our old clothing and we finally leave the underbrush. The traces of our passing and our stay will be discovered before long—in a few days at most. Who cares. By then, we will be far away, God willing. *Inch Allah*, as Noura would say.

It was indeed God's wish, as proved by the muezzin's singing, which reaches me in the container in which I am locked up: so here I am in the Port of Casablanca. Fortunately, I had stocked up on extra water before stowing away. David's advice was very wise, as the heat is stifling. The total darkness no doubt increases my sense of suffocation, but it has the advantage of making my hearing keener. Creaking, clinking, rolling, shouts, the murmuring of one engine, the sputtering of another, the lapping of waves, I can hear even the slightest noise. My brain attempts to interpret each sound it perceives, to organize them into some kind of logic. All this noise reminds me of the Port of Buenos Aires, when we would stroll along the docks with Papa. Juan would take me to see the huge cargo ships casting off in the estuary of the Rio de la Plata. Was he coming to do something other than to take a simple walk with his son? Was he bringing false papers or food to someone who had run away from Europe and whose too-murky past had led them toward our shores?

I feel the container rising. It must be on a forklift, or hanging from a crane. I am jolted around until the movement ceases. Long minutes pass in this way, in complete night and silence, broken from time to time by a faraway echo. Finally, I hear the locks sliding. The top opens up; a ray of pale light, that of a warehouse, floods in. An affable little face with curly black hair appears above the sheet metal wall, like a puppet. The figure leans sideways and tries to make out my face in the darkness still enveloping me. In a high voice, with a singsong intonation in which the vowels *i, e,* and *u* merge into a mysterious resonance, he asks me the code question:
"Where you from, Monsieur?"

His Moroccan accent makes my heart leap. It reminds me of Noura's, and of her father's when she called him on the

phone and I heard the old man through the handset. I respond to the boy following David's instructions:
"From the nuclear power plant."
"Okay. Grab hold, I will help you to get out."
He extends his hand. I hold on and manage to extirpate myself from my steel prison.
"Welcome, brother. Don't worry, we'll take care of you. Here, we protect Jews like you, no worries."
"Thanks... What's your name?"
"I'm Jawad. And you?"
I notice that he has a little, short mustache, probably to try to make his youthful features look older.
"Rodrigo. My name is Rodrigo. Thanks for you hospitality and the protection you are offering me. But, I am not Jewish, you know..."

Why did I need to give this clarification? Why did I believe myself obligated to do that? I ask myself and I almost immediately feel ashamed. Could my father have transmitted to me, with his genes, his visceral anti-Semitism? Might I be the victim of a sinister atavism, so deeply anchored in me that it pushes me to deny the Judaism that this young man offers me? At least it isn't fear that motivates my denial. Not much more glorious, whatever the case may be. Jawad breaks out in laughter.

"Whatever you want, brother. Jewish or not, we'll take care of you. Alright, get in there."
He points to a gray Berliet pickup whose bed its covered with a rounded dark khaki-green tarp. It contains tools, cans, all kinds of gadgets, and even two chickens in a cage. In an enthusiastic voice, my protector gives me his instructions:
"Zigzag between the crates and hide in the back. There's a big empty wood crate attached to the driver's cabin. Lie down in there, you will be fine. I made holes for you to breathe, at the bottom, and an opening for your eyes, you'll

be able to see the countryside. There is even a pillow for your head, you will be fine, brother. We have to drive for an hour and then we'll be there. Take water with you."

I get in as he asked me and I wait. After two or three minutes of commotion, the motor starts and we head out. A half-hour passes. Through my mini-window, I actually do see sidewalks, the trunks of palm trees and the feet of passersby, the white djellabas, the doors of Peugeot 104s, or sometimes of Mercedes that pass us. We stop at traffic lights, at stop signs, at crossings. Or at least that's what I imagine. But suddenly the murmuring of the diesel engine stops. The driver door creaks as it opens, and slams shut. I recognize Jawad's voice, but he is speaking Arabic now. A man replies in the same language, in an authoritative tone. I manage to make out the hips of the two speakers, the jeans and white shirt of my driver and the black belt on the beige pants of the man who seems to be a police officer. Surreptitiously, Jawad moves away from the truck while continuing to argue. The cop follows him. I can see their silhouettes in full. They argue on and on, accompanying their words with grand gestures. They look around furtively several times before Jawad decides to slip him a bill. In a fraction of a second, the other grabs the money. He hides it in his shirt pocket as fast as a chameleon's tongue catching a cricket. Neither seen nor recognized, the two men return to the truck with a debonair gate. The cop draws near. I hear his fingers sliding along the tarp until they reach the hole through which I observe the exterior. I have the reflex to withdraw just in time to avoid his index finger being stuck in my eye. That was close! He speaks to the driver. I have the impression that he is telling him off. But, as Jawad responds to him in the same tone, I conclude that that is just how they speak to each other. I hear the tarp being opened, and someone climbing onto the pickup bed. He walks around the clutter, and finally reaches the trunk I am hidden in. Through the opening made to allow me to breathe, I see the policeman's boots. I am trembling. A second person climbs into the vehicle. It must be Jawad. Here they are ranting on and on again. The tension mounts. The officer outright screams. I am jolted, and I ask myself if they have come to blows. Then, suddenly, I hear a much more peaceful *shukran,* an almost friendly *hamdullah,* and the two men get out of the truck. We drive on again. I don't know how Jawad got us out of this mess; maybe he slipped him another bill. In any case we drive another twenty minutes before stopping again. This time, my protector comes to open up and helps me out of the trunk and out of the truck. The landscape I see around me is not at all like what I expected. We are in the middle of what must be a shantytown, far from palm trees and from any kind of medina, or especially any riad. There is indeed the ocean on the horizon, but the beach is covered in garbage and bordered by run-down houses, made of cement bricks, some of them painted over with a layer of color – quite few – all are covered by corrugated sheet metal roofs. There are a few windows here and there. There are large plastic canisters placed regularly next to houses: they seem to be used as water reservoirs. Boys run around barefoot, and chase each other with little branches serving them as a sword or a whip; women dressed in black or in colorful costumes, protected by a dark hijab or chador, attend to their chores in the dusty roads. Behind the shantytown are tall factory chimneys expelling smoke that is sometimes white, sometimes dark gray. In the distance, you can see long buildings for workers and machinery.

"We're here, brother. Here, this is the Aïn Sebaâ quarter. Here, there is no police, no army. There is nothing, No one will come looking for you. Follow me. There are also no stores and no telephones. We are all alone here, in the middle of nowhere. Nobody thinks about us. We don't exist. As long as you stay in Aïn Sebaâ, brother, you won't exist either!"

He concludes with a friendly pat on my back. We walk away from the pickup and navigate around the shacks to reach a rectangular dwelling whose walls are painted pink, and covered by a metal roof. This dwelling is bigger than the others. It has a little courtyard, delimited by the walls of the neighboring shacks. A few chickens are shuffling about and pecking at the sandy ground. We enter. An old woman wearing a veil welcomes us with a wide, toothless smile. She gives Jawad, who is a head taller than her, a long hug. The young man lets himself be hugged, and then he points to me with his hand and says something in Arabic that I don't understand, even if I hear my name in the middle of his phrase. The woman opens her arms as though to bless me, then says her name, tapping herself in the chest:
"Fatima."
As I don't react, she repeats herself. I finally nod in a sign of greeting and I announce:
"Rodrigo."

I have nothing to give her and I cannot express anything in her language. Jawad declares:
"Fatima is my mama. I am her eighth child, the youngest. My brothers and sisters have all left. They are in the country, somewhere else. Now we have room for you. You will sleep there, you will be fine, brother, we will take care of you. You will be fine, don't worry."

I am a little ashamed. A few weeks ago, I was one of the richest men in France. Here I am being sheltered by the poorest in Morocco. Fatima says something. Her son translates:

"You are like a son for her. Even if you are Jewish, it's no problem, it's all the same. In my house, we like the Jews. Peace on you. She will look after you, Mama."

"Thanks, Jawad. Thanks a lot. And thank your mama too. But I assure you still that I am not Jewish… If I were, I would tell you, but…"

He laughs suddenly this time, which obliges me to interrupt myself.
"It's all the same, no worries… it's the same thing for us. So, let's go!"

Jawad pulls me by the arm to show me where I will sleep. We pass the portable stove and we go down a little hallway made of breeze-blocks and submerged in darkness. We end up in a space closed off by a piece ochre clothe. Jawad moves it aside and reveals a cramped room, one of whose walls is missing two cement bricks, which lets some daylight in. But the hole is also closed off with a piece of blue curtain. A mattress on the dirt floor will be my bed.

I did not know it yet, but I would spend long days and long nights in this narrow rectangular room.

When we return, Fatima is pouring us mint tea. I accept the burning-hot drink that quenches my thirst despite the ambient heat. I already love these two beings as though we have known each other forever, even though I have hardly met them. They give me sympathetic looks. I feel good with them, within these dilapidated walls. Reassured for the first time, finally. I have an impression of safety with them. Foolishly, I suddenly feel obliged to explain:
"You know, Jawad, I have a lot of money in France. When I can, I will help you, your mother and you, that's a promise. I will get you out of here."

Immediately, he stiffens up, He jovial face darkens. Fatima, who could not have understood anything that I've just said, frowns in the same way, doubtless in a mimetic reaction, because she has guessed that I have upset her son, who replies dryly:

"We don't ask you for anything, Rodrigo. I didn̩'t do that for the money. We don't ask you to get us out of here. Here is our home, Yours too, now. We don't go begging."

He briskly puts his glass down on the silver-plated tray and, walking quickly, leaves the shack. I remain a bit stunned before the old lady, who smiles tenderly at me and makes a comforting face. "It's not a big deal, Jawad is impulsive, he will come back with he's calmed down. Drink your tea," she seems to tell me. I do so. With a gesture, she invites me to sit down on a brown leather ottoman. She does the same thing, facing me. The relief of her wrinkled face is reinforced by a ray of sunlight entering through a crack. She narrows her eyes to protect herself from the light, maybe also to flee my gaze. A certain embarrassment takes hold between us. We can communicate only by signs. To touch would be indecent. Wanting to break the ice, I say the one Arabic word that I know, in order to thank her for the tea: *shukran*. This moment is the first of many long afternoons that I will spend with Fatima in the months to come. Soon it will be autumn and winter, mild, sometimes damp, but never cold. In the meantime, here we are, face to face, mute. From time to time, I have the impression I have found Mama. We would sometimes remain seated without saying a word in our rundown apartment in Buenos Aires, enjoying simply the presence of the other, her odor, her breathing. I still call her Mama. Yet I know now that Soledad, the best tango dancer in Buenos Aires, with a straight back and chin held high, her black hair in a bun tied up above her neck – except for when she kissed me in the evening – this woman of ample bust was not my mother. My chest tightens. I keep my dignity and express nothing. After a few moments, Jawad returns and isolates himself without a word.

The first dinner takes place in silence. We share a couscous, serving ourselves directly with our fingers in the plate. I am not familiar with this custom, I say nothing, I imitate my hosts. In the days to come, Jawad begins speaking to me again and even to joke with me. I think he has finally forgiven my blunder, and I have made him understand I won't be caught doing the same thing again. He gives me a tour of the neighborhood, shows me where the latrines are, the sources of drinking water, teaches me how to wash. He recommends that I drink nowhere except at his home or from the tap that he showed me. I scrupulously follow his advice, but that does not suffice. On the fourth day, I have terrible stomach pains. I empty my intestines as best I can through the entire night; toward dawn, I am running a fever. I am delirious for over a day, almost two, until I recover my faculties enough to ask Jawad to procure antipyretics for me. I even name the brands of antalgics and paracetamol sold by Rodrigo Chemicals – a reflex that proves to me that I still hope, in my heart of hearts, to take back the reins and full ownership of my business one day. But he doesn't want to hear anything of that, this guy. Stubborn as a mule. In my moments of lucidity, I beg him. "No, no, and no." Jawad refuses the medicine. He has something better. He would rather send for a local healer. A gray-haired guy dressed in a long blue-gray djellaba arrives in the den where I am bent over with pain, my forehead covered in a piece of cloth soaked in cold water that Fatima replaces for me regularly. He takes out a Koran from his pocket, reads several verses in Arabic without my understanding a single word, except for *Allah,* of course. He implores the heavens countless times, raising his eyes and his arms towards the Divine, then he puts his hands on top of my head while uttering new prayers. Then he leaves, not without putting a little bill into his pocket. I can't tell from the episode whether his service is remunerated or whether the money is destined for good works. As surprising as it may seem, the healer heals me. Not

115

only does my fever fall a few minutes after his departure, my intestinal pain also disappears in the afternoon. Jawad makes fun of me:
"You see, brother, here, you don't need medicine. Here, you don't need anything! Now you can eat and drink all you want, you are protected, you won't be sick anymore."

Behind him, as though she had understood everything he told me, Fatima begins laughing. As for me, when he says the word "drink", I think of a beer, or a good whisky. Since Golfech until now, except for in Beaumont, I have not absorbed a drop of alcohol. I would have enjoyed a little comfort.
"No problem. You want beer? Whisky? I'll bring you that. In an hour, I'll be back, I'll give you all that."
"But…"
"What?"
I still hesitate to speak of money. These people have given me shelter and fed me for several days already, and I have given them nothing in exchange. But the earlier incident makes me cautious. Still, I wonder how my new friend will find and buy these drinks, which must be so expensive, if they are even sold anywhere. I bring up this point:
"But… it's allowed here?"

He shrugs his shoulders, smiling so wide that I notice, for the first time, that he is missing a lower molar.
"Of course it's allowed! You're not a Muslim, you can drink… Jews are allowed to have alcohol."
"But Jawad, since I tell you that I am not…"

I do not finish my sentence. Who cares, at the end of the day, whether he believes me to be Jewish or not. I am annoyed with myself for having tried again to defend myself. Timidly, I bring up the other problem:
"Jawad, I also wonder… It is it expensive?"

116

"Expensive, what? Alcohol? No, it's not expensive. Here, nothing is expensive; in Aïn Sebaâ, you can trade anything. I will manage, *inch Allah*, and I will bring you back your drinks.
"Thanks, Jawad, but I'd like to pitch in one way or another…"
"You're my brother, you know? I don't want money. But soon, yes, I'll ask you for something, you'll see. You'll be able to help us."

Days pass. Jawad brings me back a large quantity of alcoholic beverages of all kinds. He even shares a beer with me if Fatima has gone to bed early and left us alone. It's not that he is trying to hide from her, he explains, but it's a matter of respect. He cannot see himself drinking in front of his mother, that's all. There is really neither justification nor explanation. Just a matter of respect, he insists. I do not attempt to understand more. It's his right, I have nothing to say about it. There is no refrigerator here. We leave the cans in the shade in a basin of seawater, which we renew regularly. We drink them lukewarm. It's not very good, but it's better than nothing. I have gotten used to it. In exchange for all that, contrary to what he indicated, Jawad never asked me for anything. Neither money, nor a favor, nor a secret. He brings me what I desire, I don't know how. In any case, I give him nothing for it.

During the day, I don't have much to do. Jawad leaves early and returns only for the evening meal. I don't know what his activities are in the meantime. Fatima and I wait for him. She asks him a few questions in Arabic, he responds onomatopoetically. To me, he explains nothing. In the morning, I walk around the shantytown a bit, participate in two or three collective chores. Because I want to; nobody makes me contribute. Old men, still steeped in the colonial times, call me *Sidi* and bow when I walk by. Others give me, on the contrary, surly, provocative looks. There are a few bearded men, too, who are always wearing their white djellabas. I am a little afraid of them, even if they never speak to me, have never threatened me. Every day, I refresh the potable water for the house, and I take a shower in the gloomy community sanitary facilities. I hear almost no one speak French in the alleys. Rare are the people who try to speak a word to me. I keep my eyes down and in general I walk with a steady gate, avoiding all contact with the local population. From time to time, I content myself with kicking back a ball to kids playing soccer. The afternoons are interminable. Jawad was able to dig up a few books in French for me, luckily. I have devoured several adventures of the Rougon-Macquarts, I savored the marvelous *Silbermann*, by Jacques Lacretelle, a touching story of friendship and – perhaps more than that – between a Jewish child and a Protestant in the interwar period, both minorities, both persecuted. Above all, I was able to dive back into *The Count of Monte-Cristo*. I identified myself more and more with this brilliant hero. I am waiting for the opportune moment when, like Edmond Dantès, I will return to where I am from, and when I will have the heads of the slanderers and conspirators. From one idle moment to the next, from long moments spent in silence with Fatima to short walks outside, sometimes all the way to the ocean, where I even ventured to swim in the muddy water, autumn passed. Then winter. I have lost my sense of time a bit, I must constantly ask Jawad to remind me what date it is, what day. When spring arrives, a vague odor of jasmine, which traverses our area, is mixed with the acidic effluvia of the factories. The articles about René Bousquet increase in number this year, 1986. His murky past is referred to more and more openly, his friendship with François Mitterrand is exposed. The President of the Republic is accused of obstruction of justice. His Vichy past is laid out before the eyes of the public which, for the vast majority, discovers it for the first time. Everything is being laid out in the open. I wonder what role David has played in these revelations. What role he still plays. Here and there, people are indignant. To crown it all, the Socialist party has taken a beating in the last election. A new word has appeared in the vocabulary of French people: cohabitation. The prime minister is the head of the main party in opposition to the president. But he leaves no doubt that, in two years, they will confront each other in the presidential election. They are assiduously getting in each other's way in the meantime. Who knows if Chirac and Pasqua aren't maneuvering to exhume a hardly glorious story about the president whom the people affectionately nickname Tonton? In all this political topsy-turvy, David has perhaps managed to join up with a more or less clandestine network. Unless Roucaud, furious at having let himself lose the big fish I was, one of his best catches probably, has tried to put a spoke in his wheel. Perhaps even despite his talent, his pugnacity, and his infallible knowledge of the territory, the super cop Rosenberg has gotten himself locked up. And if that is the case, nobody will come looking for me here. Yet with the new season, desires of elsewhere are reborn. While I have been sunk in a sort of hibernation, for long months, no longer measuring the passing of time, nor elaborating any project for the future, contenting myself with living in the present moment, without hope and without desire, now springtime solicits me to move, to go see what is happening outside, that is to say, beyond Aïn Sebaâ, beyond the coast and beyond the ocean. Jawad gives me an occasion. He gives me the task of going to Casablanca. There, at the bar of a hotel whose name he tells me and of which he describes certain details to me, a man will be waiting for me. I will only have to sit down with him, he will tell me spontaneously what I need to know. I mustn't worry and I mustn't ask any questions! I will not be disappointed.

Since my arrival, I have cut my hair little, and I have stopped shaving. Sometimes, I maladroitly trim my beard with an old pair of scissors. My chin and my cheeks are nonetheless covered in already graying hair. This is aging me; until now, I had never had a single white hair, and now my beard is giving away my age that is advancing inexorably. Already I'm past forty, time is accelerating, soon, old age. It is urgent to act if I want to take back control over my life. I must go into town. Jawad orders me to. I point out my grimy and frayed clothes and, in general, my Neanderthal-like appearance. He shrugs his shoulders.

"People will know where you are coming from, from this neighborhood. It's very good like that, my brother. And that will help you hitch-hike, the truck drivers will take pity on you, they'll stop."

He is not wrong. I am hardly positioned, with my thumb up, on the side of the road, when a van transporting fruits and vegetables stops. The driver, a mustachioed man in his fifties, spontaneously gives me a sign to get in, before I have even uttered a single word. I sit down next to him, in death's place, as they say in France, an expression that is more realistic here than anywhere else. It is already hot at the beginning of June, but the man does not seem to be troubled by that. I ask him, with gestures, if I can open the window. He responds to me in French:
"Of course. And you can speak to me in French too, I am not illiterate."
"Ah, no, not at all, that's not at all what I thought, but I had noticed that few people speak French here… And I don't speak Arabic. Anyway, I have started to get along as I can, since I have been here, but…"
"You've been here a long time?"

I realize that I have already said too much. At the first difficulty, I let myself go and confide in someone. If I reveal to this man, about whom I know nothing, that I have been living in hiding in Aïn Sebaâ for a year, the questions will not be long is coming and I will be obliged to lie. I change the subject:
"So, you know French?"
"Yes, like all those of my age who went to school. You know, not long ago, it was our language here. Now, young people, don't understand it anymore, but we, even among ourselves, we still use it."

I think of Fatima, Jawad's mother. She must be pretty much the same age as my driver, or maybe she is a little older. Yet she does not seem to understand a single word of French, and even less to be capable of expressing herself. She doubtless belongs to the excluded among the excluded. The colonist's language has not reached her. It can also happen that I speak Spanish in the area. For some, the language of Don Quixote is more familiar. I seized the occasion, which I hadn't had for a long time, to reconnect with the sonority of my childhood.

We reach the hotel indicated by Jawad via the *boulevard de la Corniche*. We have driven along the ocean from one end to another. We have stopped often, letting pass children, farmers, fishers carrying their crates full of fish. The roads we have driven down at full speed are also full of pedestrians. Motor vehicles are intermingled with carts drawn by a donkey, wheelbarrows, women and their offspring. More than once, our tires have screeched upon a sudden slam on the brakes. More than once, I saw terror in the eyes of a boy in danger of going under our wheels and I trembled terribly. From time to time, we also had to stop to pay a baksheesh to a threatening cop. One way or another, we have reached our goal: the Hôtel Suisse. My driver drops me off in front of this slender building, constructed simply and dazzlingly white, facing the ocean. A large entryway leading to a vast hall, crowned with an inscription in gold letters, aims to conceal the paltry reality of the place. An aging, seedy, establishment with old-fashioned decorations, frequented by broke tourists. I thank my guide, I ask him to excuse me: I have no money, I have no means to compensate him. He understands, wishes me good luck, takes me in his arms as though he were taking his leave from an old fellow traveler. I walk confidently into the hotel. The doormen look me over, scrutinize my sinister look, but they ultimately let me in without intervening. I go to the place Jawad indicated: a long patio, lit only by the daylight entering through a glass roof, where there are low tables surrounded by wicker armchairs and luxuriant plants. At the end, a man in black glasses, his hat pulled down over his head, his neck wrapped up in a Berber scarf, is seated in front of two half-pints of beer. He has had a few sips from his glass. The other one is for me, according to what Jawad had announced to me. I approach with a slow but decisive gate, when suddenly my heart leaps into my throat. All of a sudden, the face of a woman I feared I would never see again is turned towards me: Noura's face. Her gaze paused on me for a fraction of a second before turning away. It is her, I did not hesitate for a single instant. I do not know if she recognized me, but for my part, I feel something like an electric shock, a shiver that ran through me. Her fiery gray-green eyes pierced me through and through. She is here, in front of me, unreal, like a ghost appearing from out of nowhere. She turns back toward her interlocutor, begins to laugh, revealing her teeth, white as the edifice of the hotel. The man speaking to her is clearly her age, less than thirty in any case. He puts his hand on hers. This kid could be her new fiancé. I freeze, unable to take another step, my breathing is blocked. It's been a year, a long year that I have been dreaming of seeing once more the woman who upended the course of my life. Months, nights spent imagining her body united with mine, her warm voice murmuring in my ear, her skin against mine. So much hope nourished by the unconditional passion I feel for this woman, so much expectation shattered, faced with this cruel reality. Noura is here, alive, more beautiful than ever, in front of me, and so despairingly far away. She has found refuge in the arms of another, has abandoned me to my sad fate. Perhaps she has even forgotten me entirely. I want to jump up, pull her away from this man, embrace her and run away with her. Yet I know that is impossible. But how could I draw her attention? I cannot let pass this chance, which will perhaps never come again. I must inform her that I am alive and that I am here, in her hometown of Casablanca. I approach the couple.

"Excuse me for bothering you, Madame, Monsieur. I don't want to interrupt your conversation, but I have a little question to ask you…"

With my beggar's look, the man, a tall, curly-haired guy, jerks backward. He holds his hand on his thigh, as though he were going to draw a gun. I am afraid, but I do not back up. It is the chance of my life, the chance to start things again with Noura. This time, she must have recognized the timbre of my voice, because a flame has been ignited in her gaze. She looks me over intensely. We are very close to one another, so close that I could plant my lips on hers. I could kiss her with the same ardor as back then, embrace her as when she had given herself to me just after our first encounter. I gather my strength to hold myself back from yielding to this insane impulse. I finish my sentence:

"…maybe a stupid question… but…"
I am short of ideas. I find nothing plausible to say. I improvise: "It seems to me I have seen you in the movies recently. Aren't you in the French movie *Les Spécialistes* with Lanvin and Giraudeau? The role of…"

The guy stands up and eyes me scornfully.
"No, Monsieur! We are not in anything at all... Leave us please!"

I give in and back away without further ago:
"Excuse me, I didn't want to bother you, but I thought that.. It seemed to me... I really thought that.. But sorry, my mistake, I will leave you. Have a good day."

He nods in agreement. She smiles no more, and does not cease looking at me. I am sure that she has recognized me. We were so close to one another that she couldn't possibly doubt it. I walk away from them to sit down in front of the man who is waiting for me without showing a sign of impatience. My second surprise, when I am at the table of the man Jawad has sent me to meet: I immediately identify the face hidden under a hat, tortoiseshell glasses, and a red beard. From up close, the assumption becomes a certainty; it is David. David Rosenberg. The cop has come all the way here. He has given Jawad notice of his arrival, I don't know how nor through which intermediary, but the conduit was the right one. He is here, in the flesh, and I am in front of him. He is smoking a Gitane, offers me one, holding out the package toward me. I refuse with a gesture.

"I ordered you a beer, he says, indicated the glass in front of me. You are late, it must have gotten a little warm. I took the liberty of starting mine."

Late? Late with respect to what, to whom? I only received the instruction to come here however I could. I left right away. I did not take a single detour. No meeting time was specified. I suppose that David is trying to test me, to gauge my psychological state, to find out if, after a year of almost total isolation, during which I was in the company only of

inhabitants of the shantytown who communicated with me only by smiles and onomatopoetic sounds, I am still alert, solid, and capable of keeping my calm. In reality, these long months were at once difficult and pleasant. I suffered a form of solitude and idleness, but I received a sincere affection that I had not felt since the loss of my parents. Here, how wonderful were those wild boys I kicked the ball back to when it came to my feet and who baptized me Platini, the only French personality whose fame had reached them. How warm were those friends of Jawad who welcomed me, who procured for me all sorts of merchandise and contraband, who drank with me. How tender were their mothers who pampered me like a son, even if their sisters were distant, not daring to approach me or not being allowed to. And finally, in the midst of this new and very big family, I was happy, but alone. Throughout all this time, I knew nothing of what had become of my business, I could not enquire about my employees, my old friends who, it is true, were ultimately mere social acquaintances, for the most part. Still, their company was agreeable to me. I have not had any information about my case, about the development of the investigation, about what was probably waiting for me upon my return. David is perhaps here to enlighten me. I ask him:
"Late? We had a meeting at a specific time?" He smiles sardonically.
"I am kidding. I thought you would arrive earlier, that's all."
"When you hitchhike, you don't impose your rhythm on your driver. We took the time that was needed…"
"You are here, that's what matters."
He suddenly turns towards Noura and her companion.
"A hell of a coincidence, huh?"

So he knows her. Since he knows she exists, he will not have neglected to gather together everything it is possible to find out about her. Of course, since he knows everything about me. But was he able to provoke this unexpected meeting? Was he informed that she would be here at this exact time?

"We don't have much time. Let's get to the point. Things are progressing in France. I have a lead."

David gives me a frank, penetrating look, as he utters these last words. I feel that he is not alluding to the pursuit of former Nazis, nor to the state of his inquiry into Bousquet, nor even to the origin of the rue des Rosiers attack. Nor even to my financial and legal troubles. No, what he is thinking of is an inquiry that is much more anecdotal from the perspective of History. The lead he refers to, I am sure of it, is that of my true mother. Incontestably, there is in David, behind the brute who smashed his fists with all his strength against my face a year ago, behind the cop in disguise talking to me today, a tender-hearted man, marked like me by the premature disappearance of his parents. Out of the corner of his eyes, he observes the movements of our neighbors. Noura is there, behind me. I feel her presence, her scent that I have not forgotten; I hear the rhythm of her breathing. I would like, for my part, to land my fist in the face of that tall guy that seemed to me like an unpassable barrier between her and me. Murderous thoughts pass through my mind. I make an effort to chase these dangerous ideas away.

"I went through our archives up and down, I examined everything your father had left at the hôtel Meurice, which served as a German military command center during the Occupation. Each of the objects he touched was catalogued, entered into a repertory, seen and reviewed countless times. I examined each of his relics with the energy of despair, scrutinized, observed, turned over and back everything that could have gone through his hands, even temporarily. Rereading his agenda, I noticed that meetings with someone named Marcel reappeared regularly. I moved mountains to understand who this man was. A member of the Milice, of the Gestapo, a spy? Nothing that resembles that name, neither veritable identity not pseudonym. I searched in other papers abandoned by German officers. There too, there were traces of this famous Marcel… By cross-referencing, I finally understood."

David knows how to produce an effect. He allows silence to hover, catches his breath, raises his glass, invites me to toast, drinks one or two sips of beer. A certain commotion behind me makes me think that Noura and the man are preparing to leave. I don't know any more if I should continue my conversation with David in order to find out who Marcel is or if I should stand up brusquely, swipe aside the colossus accompanying my princess, take back from him the woman who lives in my heart. In the time it takes to ask myself this question, the lovebirds have already moved away. When I turn around, I see them leave the patio. Noura gives me another furtive look before leaving the hall. I notice something that should have been obvious when I went up to them just now. There were not only two of them, there were three. Nourra is pushing a stroller.

I take a drink and ask:
"Don't make me wait any longer. Who was this Marcel?"

"In reality, it's very simple. It was Marcel Bricourt, the concierge of the hôtel Meurice in Paris, who became a jack-of-all-trades for the Germans during the Occupation. Arrested at the Liberation, well defended by eloquent lawyers, he spent only a few months in prison and was sentenced only for national indignity for his real but not zealous collaboration. He contented himself with doing minor favors for some compensation. No denunciation of Jews or members of the resistance, and even no veritably malevolent act seems attributable to him. He was forty years old at the Liberation. He is eighty today. He is still alive…"

David takes a sip. The sun entering through the glass roof has invaded the patio and gives a multicolor sheen to the green plants surrounding us. He smiles again, takes pleasure in making me wait on his every word.

"Since you ask me, I will respond in advance. Yes, I found this Marcel Bricourt. He lives in Paris, in a modest apartment in the 15th arrondissement. Rue Vasco-de-Gama, to be precise, in a little three-room on that narrow and discrete street. He lives with his wife, who has gone off her rocker a bit, I think, which is not the case with him. I went to their home to speak with him."

David's tone is solemn, even if he is whispering. He knows how to make the most of his effects, but I am sure that he has essential information for me up his sleeve. It is getting later, and it is less hot on the patio. I finish my beer. David too. With a signal, he asks a waiter to serve us two more.

"Your father was a charming man, Marcel told me. Cultivated, well brought-up, he spoke French as best as he could, knew English, and even a little Spanish. You see, you can have deaths and thousands of deportees on your conscience, and behave like an honest man in everyday life, even in the outfit of an officer of the Occupation…"

Just as a year ago, David likes to go out of his way to remind me of the supposed ignominy of the father whom I so loved, and whom I still love. I am filled with anger, but I tamp it down. I am aching to know more. The waiter brings us two beers. David leaves him such a big tip that he doesn't stop bowing and saying thanks, slapping himself in the chest with flat of his hand. The bowing and scraping prevent him from continuing his story. After drinking his pint, David continues:

"Nonetheless, according to this Marcel, your father was present, sort of by chance, at the arrest of a family on rue du Sentier. His little tender heart was overwhelmed, imagine that!"

He chuckles, shrugs his shoulders, and suddenly seems to be speaking to himself dreamily:
"Maybe, ultimately, if the occupation officers had seen the reality of deportation with their own eyes, they would have been less cruel... It's easier to order forced labor, torture, and deprivation from far away, when you cannot see how things happen... Confronted with the horror, maybe they would have been less zealous... In any case, on that day, Johann Gantzer went soft. Nazi through and through that he was, he was touched by this family, gathered in a truck whose destination he didn't really know. Taken with a sudden mad idea, he ordered soldiers and the Milice not to put the young girl aboard. She must have been around twenty, in winter '43. The negotiations took place afterwards, at least according to the echoes that reached Bricourt. Your father used his authority, at his own risk, and finally ensured that she be put in his hands. He drove her in a car close to the hôtel Meurice and called Marcel Bricourt, supposing that the man with a million tricks up his sleeve would perhaps have an idea to help hide the girl. He was right, the concierge had a plan. Bricourt entrusted her to one of his old aunts, a nun in the couvent de l'Annonciation, on rue du Faubourg-Saint-Honoré, a few minutes away by car from the Meurice. It was there, it seems, that Officer Gantzer subsequently paid regular visits to Sarah Goldstein, a young abandoned, hidden, orphaned Jewish girl. I don't know how they managed to avoid being noticed by the nuns, but Marcel did not seem to have the slightest doubt: the girl gave birth there to the child

she expected from Gantzer, with the help of another of Bricourt's cousins, who was a doctor, and of a nun who had become a midwife. There. That's how you were born, Rodrigo. I think that at the time, they were careful not to give you a first name. You could have been named David! Moreover, since we know that your mother was Jewish, you are one of us. You belong to the community."

Upon hearing these words, I suddenly realize the ridiculousness of my denials to Jawad. I am indeed Jewish. I am the child of a Nazi torturer and a Jewish woman he saved from deportation! It is difficult for me to fathom. For the first time since I have met David, I see on his face an expression of sincere benevolence towards me. I am one of his own. If so far we had had in common having suffered the early loss of our respective fathers and mothers, under tragic circumstances, that was not enough for him to feel a veritable and deep affection for someone he saw above all as the son of a high-ranking Nazi. Now, he is beginning to see me as a brother. But I need to dig deeper:
"David, you are saying that this Sarah Goldstein gave birth to me in this convent?"
"Exactly. In July 1944. Bricourt has forgotten the exact day. Possibly around the 10th…"
"Okay… let's assume that's right. But afterwards?"

The cop looks away for a fraction of a second, long enough for me to realize that it is unpleasant for him to tell me what happened next.

"There was… a denunciation. Who, what, how? Bricourt claims not to know. In any case, the French police arrived by surprise in the convent. The nuns had the time to hide the child. But the collaborators succeeded in putting their hands on the mother and sent her away. She was never seen again… Drancy, Auschwitz, Dachau… nobody knows. I have found no trace. But I keep looking. Keep in mind, I have also gone into hiding in France. My means are very limited right now."

He is right to remind me that. I had nearly forgotten.
"And then?"
"Then, everything happened very quickly. The Allies landed in June. They moved towards the capital. Well informed, your father understood that it was only a question of days until the liberation of Paris. He decided to desert and to flee to Bordeaux, taking the kid with him. The nuns took care of the baby since the deportation of your mother. He... well, 'you' survived. Through resourcefulness, Officer Gantzer managed to procure food to nourish you on the way and succeeded in his incredible gamble: leaving France, arriving in Argentina while the war was still not yet over, with his child safe and sound in his arms. Loïc Martin's father, your teacher in Buenos Aires, a hardcore collaborator, no doubt played a decisive role in helping him to give you contraband milk, enough to last you all the way to South America. As for the rest, no one really knows how he managed to cross occupied France. Maybe he got himself a phony mission. Or a real one, even. In any case, he played his cards right because he arrived safe and sound in Buenos Aires, with his illegitimate son in his arms. After the Liberation, your father no doubt helped Michel Martin to get to the Argentinian capital in turn. The two men reappeared a few years later, with new identities. Your birth date changed, the name of your mother too. The whole story was forgotten, or so they wanted to believe. Moreover, it is true: if countless forces are employed to find your father, from Nuremberg to Jerusalem, people knew nothing of your existence and that of Sarah Goldstein, temporarily saved from the clutches of the French Gestapo by your father."

This story comforts me. Not only was my beloved father not "only" a monster, since he took immense risks to save my mother from the first truck that would have taken her to an almost certain death, but he also put himself in other kinds of danger to save my life. Even if it is true that he protected himself at the same time, that nevertheless makes him rise in my esteem. I would have a million more questions to ask, but David doesn't give me time.

"That's it. About your mother, that is everything I know for the moment. I continue my investigations. With his name, it will but easier, obviously. But another thing brings me here."

I've thought as much. I take a sip, waiting.
"It is not by chance that we met here in this place at the same time as your fiancée, Noura. I have information on her and I was sure that she would be here this afternoon. She was able to see that you are still alive and that you are in Casablanca. It's important, you will have a chance to get in contact with her."

Our glasses are empty. The waiter – black pants and vest with a white shirt, short hair, slicked and plastered to his head – approaches again and asks if we would like anything else. David sends him away with an irritated tone. Is this nuisance a bit strange? To come back so regularly without our calling him, might he not, by chance, be trying to spy on us, to glean morsels of our conversation? David seems more and more nervous.

"Today I am possibly more wanted than you, Rodrigo. I have to finish my job and disappear forever. I trust no one and now that you are going to surface again, you should adopt a similar attitude. You don't have a single friend or ally, apart from me; remember that well. In me reposes your welfare, and reciprocally. We are everything to one another, bound together by the secrets we share. And now, I need you. You will need to speak to Noura and obtain her intervention."

No mission could have given me greater joy. To see Noura again, to touch her, to kiss her, even. And run away with her to the end of the earth? That would be for later, maybe. First, I have to find her.

"We will separate in a few minutes. You will wait until I have left. Then you will leave in turn, and you will go to Boulevard Mohamed-V. Number 12."

He hands me five bills of ten dirhams.
"Take a taxi. That should be enough."
I stick the bills in my pocket without answering.

"You will enter the building, a large white edifice from the thirties. Next to the entrance, you will see a little neighborhood grocery store. If you see that, you are sure to be at the right address. There is a door code at the main door. The code is 2706A. In the hall, there is only a stairway. You go up two flights and you ring at the door to the right of the elevator. A woman will open the door. She is French and is named Marthe. You tell her this: 'You are the accumulating present.' It's a text by René Char, the poet and member of the resistance, you know it?"
"No, I…"
David chuckles, shrugs his shoulders, suddenly turns cruel:
"One thing's for sure, you weren't rocked to sleep by resistance writers' poems as a child…"

What pleasure could he find in bringing up such a sensitive subject? His attitude sickens me. Who does he think he is, this guy? Is he certain he is more of a victim than I am? Of what is he innocent, of which I am guilty? After all, I piss him off! I owe him my life, fine, I owe him my liberation from the gendarmes in Beaumont, I owe him Jawad and Fatima, and I will perhaps owe him for seeing Noura again;

but what he has done was in his own interest. That doesn't give him the right to humiliate me, to make me share the guilt of my father's acts. The martyrdom of his parents back then does not make him, today, heroic, nor confer on him any moral superiority. I rebel, for the first time since he got me out of Golfech a year ago. I am suddenly sick of his insinuations. I stand up, interrupt him, and grab his forearms tightly. He lets himself be pushed around while I liberate my bile:

"Starting now, David, you keep your reflections to yourself, okay? You know a lot of things about my life, and about lots of people's lives. But you are far from knowing everything. You know nothing about my childhood and what I was given to read. I'd bet I have more literary education in my little finger than you, including writers of the resistance. Maybe you are one of the many victims of the Nazi plague, just like your parents. It's sad, but that's the way it is. Don't imagine that that gives you the right to judge me. I am innocent of the crimes that others have committed, even when it comes to my father! And you, you are not the bearer of humanity's innocence, got it?"

I wouldn't say that David is afraid of me, but I perceive slight apprehension faced with my barely contained anger that I let out through gritted teeth. He repeats in a more timid tone:

"It's… It's René Char and it's an excerpt from his poem *Marthe*: "You are the accumulating present." That will be your password. When you will have pronounced it clearly, she will let you in and will tell you how to meet Noura."

Every time he utters that name, my emotion rekindles.
"What is Noura supposed to tell me?"

"Tell you? Nothing. You are the one who is going to say something. You will ask her not to reveal that you are still alive, nor where you are going. And you will insist that she make contact with Loïc Martin and that she get him to speak. I believe he is at the heart of our affair... You have to convince her to help us. Out of everyone in your circle, she is the only one never to have been followed or spied on. She is not yet in the sights of the French cops. She is our trump card."

Our trump card? A woman I love utterly, whom I abandoned without even saying goodbye when I saw I was being pursued, and who is raising, in another man's arms, a child who is perhaps mine! If Noura is our ace in the hole, we might as well say right away that we don't have anything in our game... David is already getting up, he puts his hand on my shoulder and walks away. Before he disappears, I come bounding towards him.
"David, David!"
He turns around, furious. What an imbecile I am to shout his name here! I pinch my lips, realizing my mistake, but still I grab his arm. I don't want him to leave before I have asked him:
"David, tell me. That child of Johann Gantzer, since he was born before my official birth, how are you certain that it is really me? Couldn't it be a half-brother? Dead and buried before my birth and before my father met Soledad? What do you really know after all?"

He pushes me back forcefully and holds me at a distance with his hand on my chest. He makes me understand that I would do well to stay away from him. He then says in a calm tone:
"I don't have the slightest doubt, Rodrigo. You are the son of Johann and Sarah."
"How can you be so sure?"
"Soon, you'll understand. In the meantime, go to Marthe. Time is short."

A taxi, a red Peugeot, stops almost immediately when I leave the Hôtel Suisse under a blazing sun. It takes me at full speed along Boulevard Mohamed-V, just barely avoiding children crossing and policemen giving us dirty looks. The driver tells me that his meter is broken and that he will make me a deal, the trip for thirty dirhams. I accept, not having the choice, nor the least idea of what the official, regulated rate could be.

"You are the accumulating present."

Upon these words, an old lady opens the door, after I have rung the doorbell. She is rather plump, with fulsome breasts on which her chin seems to rest. She stands straight as an arrow, and seems to look me up and down despite her small stature. Curiously, this face that I am seeing for the first time is not foreign to me. I fleetingly perceive something familiar in the mute expression of the woman eyeing me severely, without smiling, as though to assure herself that I am not an usurper who has procured for himself the magic words.

"You have come on behalf of whom?"

Surprised by her question, I hesitate a moment before saying: "David. David Rosenberg."
She nods, visibly satisfied with my answer. She did not recognize, under my abundant hair and behind my long beard, the man who had been in the news just a year ago. She asks me to sit down facing her, on the other side of a round yellowed wood table. She is wearing a black dress decorated with some geometrical motifs. Her gray-white hair is permed, as though it were fixed for eternity in its current position, as though the curls were as old as Methuselah and will last forever. Despite the deep wrinkles dug in her cheeks and forehead, I have the feeling that she is not all that old. There is a liveliness in her gaze, in her gestures, that makes me

think that she looks older than she really is. Each year of her life must have counted double.

"You are looking for Noura?" she says abruptly.

"I haven't been looking for her anymore since I have found out that she is here, in Casablanca. I just saw her at the Hôtel Suisse. What I don't know is her address and how to get in touch with her. David told me that you would be able to help me. That's why I'm here. I love that woman."

"You love Noura, you have just seen her, but you need me to get in touch with her? I am not sure I follow you…"
The old lady observes me mischievously.

"Noura was my fiancée. But we… how should I put it… lost sight of each other more over a year ago. I found her here again by chance. At least, I think so. She did not recognize me. She was with another man, I did not speak to her."

"Are we speaking of the same Noura?"
"Mine is beautiful as can be."

For the first time, the trace of a smile brightens Marthe's face. She gets up slowly to rummage around in the chest of drawers behind her. She pulls out an album of photos that she opens in front of me. She points her index finger, bent by arthritis, at one of the first pictures in color. A baby seems to posing for the camera.

"That's her," declares Marthe, pointing to the child in its bassinet. That's your Noura. I've known her since she was a baby."
Who is this woman? How is it that she knew Noura so long ago? The mysterious Marthe quickly closes the album, as though she wanted to avoid my looking for too long at

certain pictures, or perhaps out of reserve, in order not to reveal to me the details of her private life, her memories carefully organized in this ageless collection. She puts it back in the chest behind her and anticipates my questions:

"I took care of this child from her birth in 1960 until she was fifteen in 1975. I raised her and I loved her as though she were my own daughter, until she returned to her true family. We stayed in touch with each other. And we always will. She knows that she's not my biological daughter, but that in my heart I will always be her mother."

I do not know what to respond. I do not dare ask her to continue. I remain silent, concentrating on the tick-tock of an old clock covered now and again by the voice of the muezzin in the distance. The call to prayer leaves Marthe indifferent. Her chestnut-gray eyes gaze into the void, looking at without seeing the faded wallpaper. In a tremulous voice, she adds:

"I did not have any other child."

After having uttered these words, she stares at me for a long time. Timid tears gather at her eyelids. She holds them back. Nervously, she scratches the waxed cloth with her fingernails, which are covered in ruby-red nail polish. The withered skin along her arm vibrates with the movement of her hand. I wonder what could have happened. Why did this woman whom Noura never spoke to me of raise her until her adolescence, to let her go finally, when her family was known since the beginning?

"It's complicated," Marthe continues, as though she read my thoughts. That child was born under difficult conditions. Noura is an illegitimate daughter… That's in itself unacceptable here, in Moroccan society. But making the scandal even worse: her mother was Jewish! Her father, Aziz M'Barek, had had an adulterous relationship with a woman from the Mellah in Casablanca, the Jewish quarter. How did they meet? It's a mystery. But the young girl found herself pregnant. Despite the fear of opprobrium and dishonor, M'Barek begged her not to secretly get an abortion. He hid her, he took care of all her needs during her pregnancy, he made it possible for her to give birth under good conditions. But then he asked her to abandon the little child in an orphanage, and that's what she did. They picked a Moroccan name for her to hide her origins. When I received her, I knew she was Jewish, for it so happens that I am Jewish too."

I don't believe my ears. So Noura and I have identical stories, with fifteen years' difference. We are the illegitimate children of a Jewish mother, both of us abandoned. I think again of that papa, austere and tender at the same time, his mustache as thick as his eyelashes, whose praises Noura sung in a serious voice, she who feared his anger, but to whom she also seemed so attached. I risk another question:

"Marthe? That's not very Jewish..."

She shrugs her shoulders and raises her eyes to the sky.

"What do you think, that it's my real name? I am French and I miraculously escaped deportation. I took refuge here at the end of the war, in 1945, after a strange journey that isn't your business. I chose Marthe, since that saint was a disciple of Jesus Christ, so she was Jewish too..."

She throws me a mischievous glance. As for me, I am a bit ashamed. I wonder why I asked about her first name, as though that detail were important, as though there were nothing more interesting and more urgent to elucidate. But my curiosity brings me back to the essential point:

"Why did you decide to send Noura back to her family? What happened?"

Marthe sighs, annoyed, as though she felt she were repeating herself. Maybe she has already told David everything and is surprised that he did not inform me. She continues wearily:

"Aziz M'Barek never lost sight of his daughter. He came every week, on Wednesday afternoons. They spoke together. He told her the truth from the very beginning. A strong bond was established between them over the years. Noura lived with us, in the orphanage, but she knew her story and her origins. Yet she never asked to go live with her father, she knew it was impossible… Still, she adored him and had a limitless admiration for him."

"And her mother?"

"She came to see her too, from time to time. But less often. It was more difficult for her than for Monsieur M'Barek to hide in order to visit her daughter. And then one day…"

Marthe gets up with difficulty and walks hesitatingly toward a gas stove to boil some water.
"Do you want mint tea…, Monsieur…? Monsieur what, actually? I don't even know your name!"

"Rodrigo. Rodrigo Ganos. No thank you, I will not take tea."

She starts, recoils.

"Rodrigo Ganos! The crook on the run?"

I never imagined that my forty years of life – forty-one according to David – could be summed up in these four words: crook on the run. That's how public opinion represents me: a mere bandit who has taken flight. Maybe I even have the honor of being considered a criminal, the murderer of two honest policemen on duty. After her brief reaction of stupor, Marthe pours the mint tea with this entirely oriental gesture she has adopted and that consists in moving the teapot up and down as the tea pours into a narrow glass. She sits down again in front of me.

"Rodrigo Ganos... So you were that 'businessman' Noura saw in France?"

"That was me, yes."

Marthe stares at me for a while, hesitates a bit, scrutinizes my features carefully, drinks a sip of tea, and says:

"It's true... Now I recognize you, despite your beard and hair. It is you. David told me your story. But he had not told me that it was you that he would send to me."

I am startled in turn.
"David told you my story?"
She laughs.
"Yes. I met David not very long ago, but we have spoken a lot. We exchanged a great deal of information about what preoccupies both of us. We are conducting the same investigation, each of us. That is how our paths crossed. We got along well right away. I understood that he was also on the run, like you and no doubt because of you, but I don't care. That is not what interests me."

"You are with the police, too?"

She seems taken aback, observes me with a form of disdain, pity. She seems to be wondering if I am really as stupid as my question might suggest.

"No, my poor friend, I am not with the police, as you say, and I have no intention of joining, especially since they prove their incompetence a bit more every day. But my sister died in the rue des Rosiers attack, three years ago now. I want to know who is behind the crime. And take my revenge on him.

I realized that it would not be thanks to the 'police' that I would achieve my aim. The cops are totally lost."

Rue des Rosiers! Again this attack, which seems to be following me. You would think that everything leads me back to it. What dreadful coincidences! At least Marthe does not seem to believe in my involvement, even indirect.

"I know that people once thought that you were involved in that horrible act… For my part, I believe that accusation is ridiculous, even if it might seem logical in a certain way."

"I thank you for not crediting that stupidity, but I don't see what you can find logical about it."

Marthe shrugs her shoulders and wearily shakes her head back and forth.
"You are not very perceptive, clearly… Well, where were we?"
"I was asking you why you ultimately returned Noura to her father, even though you raised her and loved her like your own daughter."

"Ah, yes! Oh! It's not very difficult to understand! One fine day, Aziz M'Barek's wife died in a car accident. Even if religion did not oblige him to, Noura's father respected the socially acceptable period of mourning of six months' time. During this time, Noura's mother converted to Islam. She decided to wear the Islamic veil and married Aziz, whose two older children, a girl and a boy, had moved out. The new couple then decided to 'adopt' Noura officially. They lived happily together, I believe… Noura gave me news of her mother, who continued to have her before-dinner drink secretly… She still managed to make me laugh."

The hidjab and the whisky, the entire portrait Noura painted for me of her mother… A shadow passes over Marthe's face. In a breath, she confides:
"I had to separate myself from the girl…"
The old lady swallows a sip of water, before concluding:
"That's the way it is. I accepted a long time ago that I have to tolerate the trials life imposes on me. Do we have a choice, after all? But I am still able to get in touch with Noura and I can organize a meeting for you. Do you want me to?"

How could I want anything else in the world! It is my only hope and my only expectation. I am overcome with emotion. I nod affirmatively.

"Wait here a moment. Don't move."

Marthe gets up and goes to the room next to the kitchen and that seems to me to be her bedroom. She leaves the door ajar. I hear her dialing a telephone number. The very brief conversation is in Arabic. Marthe returns and tells me:

"Tomorrow at 6pm, she will be waiting for you in the Jardins de l'Hermitage. She will be covered in a full burka, you will not see her face. That way, your meeting will be as discrete as possible. However, have no doubt, it will indeed be Noura behind the veil."

I am not worried: I will recognize her easily by her voice.

"Sit on the first bench on the right as you enter. Do not be late. Your meeting cannot last very long."

"Don't be late" – no doubt an allusion to my meeting with David. As I rise to leave, Marthe asks me:
"Where do you think you're going?"

Surprised, I stop. She seems to me waiting for my answer. I eventually mutter:

"I... I'll try to go home."
"Home?"
Marthe is well informed. She must know that I don't really have a home here in Casablanca, that I am hosted only by Jawad and Fatima.

Suddenly, I think of them. I regret not having been able to pay them back. Deep inside, I still hope I can. I hope to rise from my ashes one day and unleash my revenge on those who wrongly accused me or – worse – who sought to ascribe to me acts I did not commit. But I also plan, in this blessed future, to cover in gold the Just who helped me. First of all Jawad and Fatima.

"My home, yes... Well, where I live right now, in Aïn Sebaâ. Marthe smiles:
"The round trip to Aïn Sebaâ between now and tomorrow is useless and would even risk making you late for the meeting, which would ruin its interest. I have an unoccupied room... You need only stay there for the night."

She points to a closed door, which I had not noticed until now. The proposition is tempting. A real room, with a door, a window that I can maybe crack open and, who knows, a real bed with a box spring mattress. It has been almost a year since I have enjoyed such comfort. For long months, I held back from nourishing this kind of fantasy. I effaced from my memory the thoughts of nights spent in palaces, of my vast bedroom with its ceiling decorated with molding sculpted like lace and its bed so wide that I could spread myself out with my arms extended without even reaching Noura's body, while through the bay window, I admired all of Paris. During this period of privation and clandestine wandering, I did my best to transform myself into a new man, with neither past nor future, to live in the present moment, expecting and especially missing nothing.

The slightest exception to this conduct would have thrown me into insurmountable distress. But now Marthe's proposition reveals in me my taste for comfort, for well-being. I cannot resist her offer:

"Thank you...Marthe. Can I call you Marthe?"
She gives a sign in the affirmative.
"Yes, listen, I think I will accept your generous suggestion. I will allow myself to be tempted... I will sleep here."
She gets up and exclaims happily:
"That's a fine idea, my boy! I will show you the way..."
She passes in front of my and opens the door to the room.
"You have a shower, there in the back, if you want to refresh yourself. Dinner is a 8 o'clock."

I go in. She closes the door behind me immediately, as though I were not allowed to leave until supper, in two hours. I am alone. The walls are covered in wallpaper with a motif in the form of multicolor flowers and crowns of dubious taste, but the whole has the effect, for me, of unheard-of luxury, compared to the gray cinder blocks that kept me company at Fatima's home. The floor is worn and creaky, but it seems solid. I collapse onto the little double bed that welcomes me, next to which a lamp is sitting atop a wooden pedestal table. Indeed, from my recumbent position, I see, behind an ajar door, a bathroom with a shower. I get up. It has been such a long time since I have luxuriated in such pleasing lukewarm water. I lie back down and I nod off. Decidedly, this Marthe whom I did not know two hours ago lets me re-experience the simple pleasures I had no longer imagined, for what seems to me to be an eternity. When she calls me to join her for the meal, I get dressed in haste, putting back on my dirty clothes, and I hurry to the living room. Marthe is awaiting me standing up. She has changed, has put on makeup, has gotten ready as though she were receiving an important person. That individual is me: Rodrigo Ganos, shaggy hair and beard, covered in rags. I feel ridiculous. In front of my hostess, a plate of meatballs is placed next to a cucumber, fennel, and tomato salad. I have eaten almost nothing since last night; I begin to salivate at the sight of these colorful and appetizing dishes. Marthe invites me to sit opposite her. We dine in silence. It is delicious. Aromas of a thousand spices delight my palate. I make a superhuman effort not to devour, empty my plate with vulgar gluttony. Marthe, on the contrary, savors her cooking parsimoniously, in little mouthfuls. She does not cease looking at me, scrutinizes me attentively, as though she were afraid I will run away. I feel a strange sensation of embarrassment. We finish the meal without saying a word. Marthe stands to clear the table. She does not refuse my help; she even asks me to serve her a coffee, once she has sat back down after having gone to get, in the sideboard, a brushed steel cigarette case that looks like it is at least a hundred years old. She opens it and offers me one. I accept. She feels the need to justify herself, explains to me that she only takes one per day, after dinner. But I do not reproach her at all. We smoke in silence, then she takes her leave, and asks me to excuse her: she has the habit of going to sleep every night at ten pm. She will be up at six in the morning. I also return to the room that has been given to me, but I have a hard time falling asleep, having slept deeply just before the meal. A bit after eleven, the muezzin makes the call to prayer for the last time, the nighttime call, the *icha*. For almost a year, in the time I have lived in Casablanca, I have gotten used to this rhythmical ritual. That faraway voice, that long and guttural sound pacifies me, tranquilizes me. I will miss it when I leave the country. Is that departure near or far away? I manage to nod off, then I tip into the land of dreams where

Noura's smile merges with the faces of the Golfech torturers, while the judges who condemn me for insider trading that I did not commit wear the mask of Loïc Martin. At the end of the night, I sink into a deep sleep, which the day filtering through the Venetian blinds does not even trouble. It is after ten in the morning when I open my eyes. I leave the bedroom. The apartment is empty, Marthe is gone. She has left a note: *I made you coffee. I will not be back until you have left for your appointment. 6pm in the Jardins de l'Hermitage. She will be waiting for you on the first bench on the right when you see the little lake. Don't be late.* She signed: *Marthe*. I couldn't say why this first name written by her, this careful and old-fashioned calligraphy procures a strange emotion in me, a sensation of familiarity, of intimacy with the woman who has hosted me. I remain stupefied for a moment. By reflex, I put the paper in my pocket. I am briefly tempted to rummage around in the dresser where the photo album is. Maybe it contains other documents, other secrets that Marthe has chosen not to reveal to me yet. Ultimately, I do not do it. I have a cup of coffee and I also swallow two *cornes de gazelle*. The apartment is already bathed in sunlight, I walk towards the window as I drink my lukewarm coffee. I observe the agitation of the Boulevard Mohamed-V: the fruit merchants meeting the businessmen in white suits, the notables of Casablanca, the bankers, a few beggars, the women who wear the hidjab, some, rarer, who wear the niqab, but also those wearing a flowery dress or a chic suit and walking with assurance, hair blowing in the wind. They rub shoulders with one another, run into each other, kiss, cross paths in the tumult of motors and car horns. Since my exile in Aïn Sebaâ, it has been a long time since I have had the chance to contemplate city life, a spectacle that I had almost forgotten. Paris, my large apartment and its immense terrace opening onto the Eiffel Tower and furnished with deckchairs on which Noura would lie down languorously, my brand-name suits, somber, sober, elegant, that had nothing in common with the rags I am wearing today, all that seems to me so far away. I let myself dream, recalling my society cocktail parties, those that traditionally celebrated, at Rodrigo Chemicals, the creation of new active molecules or the authorization to put the latest medicines on the market. I see again the trips in a convertible to the Côte d'Azur with Noura, or our first awkward turns on the Avoriaz trails, we who had not, neither the one nor the other, had the opportunity to discover snow in our childhoods. I recall the Saturday afternoon shopping trips with my Oriental woman, the nights of insatiable love, the Sunday mornings golfing with Loïc. We never talked shop during the games, that was the rule. We shared the green with adversaries we knew: with pharmacists, notaries. The only authorized subject of conversation was the quality of the this or that person's swing. We would finish the game with a beer, sometimes with a croque-monsieur, in the clubhouse where there always reigned an odor of cigars. When I came home, Noura, would be in bed. She would be watching an episode of *The Love Boat* or devouring the latest Barbara Cartland novel. I would lie down beside her and we would dream of the name of the child we would have one day. Has that baby been born? Could it be the baby in the stroller yesterday at the hotel? Maybe she will tell me later. It is past noon. I am pacing like a caged lion in the hot apartment, awaiting the hour of our appointment. I take a shower to refresh myself and I go out to walk the boulevard. I go into a shisha bar, which is also a restaurant. I'm not really hungry anymore, but I force myself to swallow an eggplant salad. The minutes and the hours tick by laboriously, before it is time to leave for the meeting. I arrive at the Jardins de l'Hermitage at five to six. I walk up the palm tree path, all the way to the lake. I do not see anyone who looks like Noura. But I walk to the place where she is supposed to be waiting for me. Certain benches are occupied by old men smoking and conversing, embellishing their discussions with grand gestures. There is no woman.

Noura is not there. I continue looking for her among the silhouettes, imagining that she might have disguised herself as a man, in a thick white djellaba and with a false beard. But no, all these guys seem like they are really men. I take a seat on the only free bench, a very classic bench you find everywhere, made of a cement base and boards of wood painted bottle green. I wait, becoming more and more feverish. The hour has long passed. No one. My nervousness increases. Marthe had, however, insisted on the need for punctuality. The conversation would have to be quick. I was exactly on time and I am alone. Have I understood the place for the meeting correctly? It is here. Was Noura prevented from coming? Or did David or Marthe, or both of them, lay a trap for me? I scan the lake, the grass surrounding it. I look at the people walking by. Having arrived from behind me, a man sits down beside me. At the moment, I pay no attention to him, but I feel that he is observing me insistently. I pretend to ignore him for a moment, but, despite myself, I end up turning towards him. It is then that I recognize him. My blood freezes in my veins, I cannot breathe. He stares at me with his steely gaze, with his eternal smile in the corner of his mouth. Short hair, heavy chin, back slumped against the backrest, Major Roucaud, the gendarme who let me get away a year ago, is there, facing me, in civilian clothes. He has come to Morocco – *Al-Maghrib,* the Arabic name for this country of the setting sun, at the far west of the Maghreb – to get his hands on me and no doubt to lock me up. Marthe, whom I, stupidly, trusted blindly and without justification, delivered me to him. Happy with himself, the major lights a cigarette and offers me one. I would like to flee, but I don't manage to. I am glued in place. I don't have the strength to bolt, hardly even to extend my hand to the cigarette pack he offers me.

Roucaud sits up, brings the Zippo flame towards my mouth, covering the top of the lighter with his left hand to protect it

from the wind, and lights my cigarette. Since I have been in Aïn Sebaâ, I smoke much less tobacco. From time to time shisha or cannabis, hashish, but more rarely simple cigarettes. The taste of light tobacco surprises and disappoints me. But I still take a few drags and stammer:
"Major Roucaud… what are you doing here?"

He raises his eyelids in a questioning manner, still smiling. He is wearing jeans and an old navy blue t-shirt, spotted with sweat stains. If I had not seen him before in uniform in his office in Beaumont, I would not guess that he belongs to the gendarmerie. Here, seen up close and in civilian clothes, has the look of a vagabond, or a beggar. He stands up and plants himself in front of me, his hands in his pockets, cigarette in his lips, leaning slightly backwards, his chin tucked down:

"What am I doing here? You are asking me that question? Don't you think you are reversing our roles somewhat? Isn't it rather your job to tell me what you have been up to here since you escaped me a year ago?"

Of course, my question had something ridiculous about it. It is not for the fugitive caught by the patrol to ask the gendarme what he's doing there! With almost childlike naivety, I respond:

"I… I have a meeting with Noura."

Roucaud raises his eyes to the sky with a look of exasperation. He murmurs into his beard, as though he no longer addressed me:

"Yes, that. Noura, I know, of course…"

He shrugs his shoulders with exasperation, turns abruptly on his heels, takes a few steps before walking back towards me. From a distance, he shouts:

"Fine, so, what are you doing? You coming?"
I join him.
We walk side by side, leaving the garden for the sidewalks of Casablanca. I can't tell if I am following him, or the other way around. We advance in the same direction while we speak. Actually, it's mostly he who speaks. He is not here to arrest me, he explains first of all. That's a relief, but I am waiting for more complete information before rejoicing completely. He is not on duty, he tells me. Officially, he is on vacation in Morocco. And he tells me: when he entered the gendarmerie in the early morning, the day after my spectacular escape, and found the two poor orderlies tied to the radiator and the third locked in my cell, he realized that I had been aided by a professional, an expert. That intuition was confirmed by gendarmes' account, in which he recognized the description of David Rosenberg, the cop driving the Renault 5 when Roucaud had stopped us on the highway. He admits it really got his goat to be taken in so easily and to have let escape a catch as precious as what I represented. Poor Mollard paid the price of his rage. Despite the little esteem and affection he has for his subordinate, the major reproached himself for having yielded to his impulses and having humiliated the deputy in front of all his colleagues. He was even obliged to excuse himself in private. He hopes that Mollard doesn't hold against him too much and will not become an enemy on the inside. He will have to be careful from now on.

Such a free confession surprises me by its apparent sincerity. I wait for the rest, but he interrupts himself suddenly:

"Ganos, I am talking and talking, but you told me that you had an appointment with your fiancée, the ravishing Noura, right?"

Absorbed by his tale, I had almost forgotten Noura! His question jolts me.

"That's true," I say.

"And you don't wonder what happened? You hadn't already asked yourself how a meeting between you and the beautiful Moroccan you left behind could have been arranged. That doesn't interest you at all?"

I have the impression that Roucaud takes a crafty pleasure in destabilizing me. I don't know what to respond. I reflect. I unravel in my memory the film of events that led me here. Jawad sending me to hitchhike to Casa for a supposed mission that would be given to me by someone at the Hôtel Suisse. David Rosenberg in person waiting for me there. The strange conversation with the no less mysterious Marthe, this improbable meeting in the Jardins de l'Hermitage with Noura, who does not show up, replaced ultimately by Major Roucaud. Nothing in all that has the least coherence. I don't even know how David could have warned Jawad. Since the beginning, I have known nothing about their relations. Persuaded that Roucaud is not there by chance, either, and convinced that he was informed of my meeting with Marthe, I explain myself:

"Marthe revealed to me her connection with Noura. But she told me she knew how to find my fiancée and proposed this rendezvous to me. I believed her... I shouldn't have, no doubt."

Roucaud looks dubious. I stop suddenly, taken aback.

"Marthe? Who's that, Marthe?"

His question is genuine, I think. He does not know the old lady, does not see who I'm talking about. He fears, clearly, being taken in and tricked, but by whom? And if it was not by Marthe that Roucaud was alerted to my presence here, since he does not know who she is, then who was it? By Noura herself? Roucaud does not like having been caught out. He was the one who was supposed to surprise me, not the reverse. His affability suffused in irony has suddenly left him. His nostrils dilate, he grates his teeth. There's no doubt, he is livid. Now I have information, a mine of information, to which he does not have access. I have the advantage once again.

"Yes, Marthe. You don't know Marthe? That's strange, I would have imagined, seeing you arrive instead of Noura, that it was Marthe who had informed you. I guess I was mistaken."

Roucaud is silent. He lights another cigarette and gives me an aggressive look. Offended. No doubt about it, the gendarme is offended. In the complicated game of this story, the entrance of Marthe disconcerts him. He could almost reproach me, the hare of the story, for not having put him on the right track. It's a bit much. As it happens, I do not deny myself a good thing. For the first time since this adventure has begun, since the imaginary insider trading, and even before, since my childhood in Buenos Aires until Aïn Sebaâ, including the sweaty basements of Golfech where the odor of blood and powder are mingled, I have always been the fall guy, the ignorant person, the happy (or not) idiot, who had always been a bit slow on the uptake. But now the unexpected ignorance of Roucaud gives me a semblance of initiative. Thus was he caught who thought he would catch, I tell myself. I choose to let him marinate for a moment. He will have tell me something if he wants to obtain information from me. But if Roucaud is himself manipulated, if he is, like me, nothing but a marionette, then who is pulling the strings? With this question, I remain perplexed. In a now more confident tone, I ask him:

"But then, if it was not Marthe who suggested to you to meet me instead of Noura, who was it? Noura herself? That is the most logical hypothesis. But, you see, I have a hard time believing that. Yes, my fiancée is doubtless hurt that I abandoned her last year, that I haven't given her a sign of life since, and she certainly holds it against me a bit. But I do not think she is capable of laying a trap for me, of giving me up to the cops…"

All of my pride is in this claim. Definitively, for a year, I have not often had the chance to gain the upper hand. I glimpse a good occasion to get back part of my haughtiness of yesteryear. Roucaud takes it without batting an eyelid.

"You are right, Ganos. It was not Noura who gave the game away. And if I am in Casablanca, it's not by chance, of course. My informer is David. The strange David Rosenberg, who got you out of Golfech – after having put you there, that cannot be forgotten, indeed – and who also helped you to escape the Beaumont gendarmerie. It was he who told me that you had taken refuge here. I jumped on a plane. It was also he who gave me the lead about this appointment in the Jardins de l'Hermitage, naming the exact hour and place."

A new surprise – but a surprise that, to tell the truth, is not really one, since if it was not Marthe who informed Roucaud, it could only be David. Thus, the major having begun again to walk slowly, his hands crossed behind his back, shutting his eyelids to protect himself from the still bright light of the sun in front of us, I simulate surprise that I only feel halfway:

"David?"
"David, yes. Your David. I have gotten in touch with him."
I raise an eyebrow. Roucaud decides to tell the truth:

"Yes, okay, I can guess your thoughts and... I admit you are not wrong. In reality, it was he who approached me."

I smile. Another little victory over the gendarme. I who reigned over the largest pharmaceutical empire in Europe, I who was courted by everyone, the bankers, the pharmacists, the politicians, the ministers, and the corner baker, I am reduced, today, to contenting myself with the most meager satisfactions. Getting ahead of the gendarme in his reflections, understanding who called whom. *Sic transit gloria mundi.* I am now nothing but a hunted fugitive. But the pursuer is here, standing sheepishly before me, and he shows no intention of arresting me. We walk and talk like two old comrades. We turn towards the north, then we walk along the ocean, by the Sidi-Mohamed boulevard, before arriving at a wasteland opening onto a beach where there is an immense construction site. There are barriers, fences, that make it impossible to advance. Behind the enclosure, men protected by helmets work, talk, plan. A bit further on, we discover a poster indicating that here, Bouygues will soon begin the construction of the biggest mosque in Casablanca, the Hassan-II Mosque. My mind wanders for an moment, I try to imagine where the gigantic minaret will be raised above this Pharaonic project. Roucaud brings me back to the present moment.

"You know, Rodrigo... How can I explain it to you? I have had great misfortune in my life. I lost a son, my only son. You don't recover from that kind of blow from destiny.

Worn away, each of us, by sorrow, incapable of living with that of the other, my wife and I ended up separating. Today, I am alone and I will tell you, I no longer taste of the pleasures of existence. Cigarettes, a Madiran, a good mushroom omelet, that's about all... I no longer know what joy could be. It is as though my life stopped with my son's. I am living on borrowed time on this earth. I do not have a suicidal temperament, so I wait. I wait for death to deliver me, and I try to occupy myself in the meantime. And, you see, nothing occupies my mind as much as a complicated investigation. Flushing out a guilty person, nosing around, following a lead, that is what retains me still in this world. As for you, I repeat it to you, I have believed you are innocent, since the very beginning. You do not have the look. You escaped from me, certainly. But you would have been quite incapable of that without Rosenberg's help. You are not a professional swindler or runaway."

Roucaud has decided, like David in Larrazet, to call me by my first name, just when he gets to the heart of the matter. He begins walking again with his heavy tread. I follow him, eager to hear what comes next. He continues his monologue:

"Rosenberg is an excellent sleuth too. He is riling people up with Bousquet but ultimately, I think that he doesn't give a damn about that collaborator's fate. You know that he also contributed to obtaining the extradition of Klaus Barbie from Bolivia? The trial of the "butcher of Lyon," as he is called, will begin soon, I think. But all that is ancient history. Hunting Nazis is good, that's the job that David chose and he did it better than anyone. But if he decided to go underground, putting bullets in his colleagues to save your skin, it was not to find yet another doddery old man who was a camp guard at forty, no. He is beyond that stage. What he wants is to find the guys who are committing crimes today, who will commit them tomorrow, more than those who perpetrated them yesterday. In fact, he's obsessed with the rue des Rosiers attack. Officially, the Fatah lead is still given preference, but Rosenberg is convinced that the cliques of a certain "far" far right are responsible for it. You've heard of those Neo-Nazis they've arrested in France?"

Yes, I heard about them on the radio, in the Renault 5 that David was driving. And I won't likely forget it because that was the moment when I heard the journalist say that the French police suspected me of being linked to that horrible event. I acquiesce. Roucaud continues:

"These people nostalgic for the Führer are crazy people capable of anything, of any ignominy for the sake of their 'cause.' They very well can, temporarily, create improbable alliances with Pro-Palestinian groups, or even unnatural bonds with Communists, Maoists, militant environmentalists, Wahabi Salafists, or with the Muslim Brotherhood, depending on the situation, why not? It can be with anyone, as long as it creates chaos and puts peace in danger, or perturbs the tranquility of Jews. These guys define themselves as being defenders of the Aryan race. You find them everywhere in the West, in the ranks of the Ku Klux Klan in America and among English skinheads. We have them in France too. Since the beginning, David has thought that it's necessary to look for them there. He wants to infiltrate that milieu and follow that lead. He was convinced that you were part of that system, of that universe… When he realized that he was wrong, but that the two other cops would still not spare your life, he decided he would rather leave his colleagues cold and dead in order to protect you. You are the indispensable link in his investigation and thus also in… mine!"

As we continue to walk, the ocean darkens and the sun sinks over the horizon, casting an orange glow on the coast. A maritime breeze has stirred, which refreshes us pleasantly. We soon reach the port docks, the very place where my container was unloaded over a year ago. We sit down on a barrel lying sideways, in a corner that Roucaud seems to have chosen carefully, facing the boats, but hidden from view. Alone, along the longest dock that we can see, the silhouette of a woman in black, her face covered by a full burka, seems to advance towards us.

Although hypnotized by this gait that I would recognize out of a million, even disguised by the ample black clothing, I remain concentrated on the Major's explanations. He too, himself, he assures me, has been interested for a long time in the rue des Rosiers attack and has followed several leads. And he is also convinced that the murder was not committed by isolated crazy people. The massacre was meticulously prepared by an organized group, and thus… financed. It was the angle of the financing that led people to suspect me. Roucaud, through the same reasoning, finally concluded that Loïc could be involved. And it was in his investigation of Loïc that he crossed paths with David. Rosenberg was also following that lead. He got in touch with Roucaud and proposed joining forces. The gendarme in the spotlight, the cop in secret. The Major accepted; they met, they spoke, and reached an identical conclusion: it was necessary to make Loïc Martin talk. David can loosen recalcitrant tongues. Roucaud countered that the end did not justify the means. You have to refrain from using the same methods as those you are pursuing. So they agreed that the best way to get him to speak was to use Nourra. He knew her and, if she told him that she was speaking in my name, he would trust her. If Loïc is not entirely innocent in this affair, as they imagine, then he will certainly be very curious to learn what has happened to me. That I am alive, lost in the wilderness, possibly in the process of unraveling the tangled web all the way to him and bringing the secret to light—that is what must worry him.

Loïc will cooperate despite himself, since he will be too impatient to know more. And the best way to convince Noura to collaborate was to have me intervene. For her love of me, maybe she would accept playing along.

I have known, in the past, docks other than Casablanca's. The foggy and shadowy docks where I arrived in France. I was fifteen. It was winter. A wet but not very cold winter, in Brest, in December 1960. I disembarked from the cargo ship that had transported me here, in France, a country whose language I had vaguely learned, but of which I knew nothing—neither its geography nor its climate, nor its customs. Without any family and separated from all that I had known until then, unaware of the reason for which I had found myself so brutally made an orphan, I was alone and lost. If it was not from cold, I trembled from fear, as I advanced towards the unknown on this sopping dock, enveloped in fog mingled with engine smoke. I walked straight ahead, surrounded by dock workers unloading cargo, who did not notice me, until someone named Anne, as she introduced herself, called me by my first name. I walked towards her. I was shivering in the drizzling rain. She covered me in a yellow raincoat far too big for me and led me to her car, a Renault 4 CV in the inimitable color of a lump of butter. The four-cylinder car took us, its engine spluttering, along winding and at times picturesque inland roads. It took us three hours to arrive in Ploërmel. In that Breton town was the boarding school where I would spend the following three years, until my school-leaving exams. The gray stone L-shaped building was austere, but the cold architecture was only an imperfect reflection of the monastic rigor that awaited me within those high walls. Anna stopped in front of the majestic entrance and kissed my forehead. Before I had the time to react, she had readjusted her headscarf and had gotten back into the car whose motor she had not turned off. She left without another word or sign. I never heard from her again, I never knew who she was. I had no choice but to cross the courtyard and walk towards the man in a black cassock waiting for me in the doorway. It was around noon. He took me straight to the refectory, where I took my place next to other boys of my age who did not greet me. It was against the rules to speak during meals. A bell rang and I saw all the students rise and get in line. I imitated them. We went out in silence, then another bell could be heard. It was the signal for recreation time. The boys began running, chasing each other, amusing themselves under the severe watch of two short-haired and eagled-eyed seminarians. It was crucial never to break the strict rules of propriety, under any circumstance, including during recreation, on penalty of pitiless sanctions. I remained alone in a corner, waiting for another signal ordering us to get in line again to join our respective classes. I did not know where to go. The chaplain who had received me on my arrival – a tall and lean man of around fifty, who walked with long, nervous steps and who wore little round glasses – appeared on the steps. "Ganos!" he called, in a stentorian voice. I approached. He led me to the dormitory. Around eighty beds lined up, separated from one another by around twenty inches. Father Cuvelier – that was his name – indicated the mattress that was for me. As I did not move, he whom the boarders secretly called, as I would soon learn, "hairy ass" (or "Cul velu," which the name *Cuvelier* sounded like), urged me to hurry. At La Mannais, he explained to me, neither laziness nor procrastination, nor day-dreaming, was tolerated. Those who stood around gaping were brought to order and would remember it. If you were not studying or praying, you had to be active, while remaining disciplined. There was no place here for disorder, havoc, decadent mores. The priest knew that I had not yet received a religious education, and thus had received no education at all. I therefore had much to learn before having the honor of being considered a respectable member of the institution. Only with iron discipline and real efforts could I make up for my delay. In the meantime, I should hurry up and make my bed! I must then swiftly go to his office so that my measure could be taken and so that I could be given a uniform. I did not know how it was done. I managed to line up the sheets, imitating as best as I could what I saw on the neighboring beds. This first failed attempt would soon earn me an exemplary punishment. I still did not know, at that moment, that Father Cuvelier was in reality a cruel and sadistic tyrant, who saw to it that terror reigned throughout the boarding school. He would martyrize me, like the others, throughout the three years that I spent at La Mennais. But he also had to keep me. Someone was financing my studies and much else. This mysterious donor contributed also to building repairs, improved the everyday fare of the ecclesiastics, maintained the athletic fields. I was thus a protected student, in a certain way, without my knowing why. As was the student they introduced to me on the day of my arrival: Loïc Martin. But this advantage that we shared, Loïc and me, had another side to it. Cuvelier had the task of offering us the best teaching, access to the different activities offered by the establishment, and the care necessary to avoid falling ill following maltreatment, as happened to the other children. This limit imposed on his power would also feed his secret, cruel malevolence toward us. He never missed an occasion to set a trap for us, to humiliate us, and, short of making us suffer physically, to inflict on us much psychological baiting. The iniquitous behavior of this terrifying being only reinforced the indissoluble friendship binding me to Loïc.

Loïc was a head taller than me. Malnourished for the long years at the boarding school that had preceded my arrival, he was skinny, which did not prevent his having a cheerful, friendly face. His black eyes were surrounded in fine eyelashes, of a dark chestnut color like his hair, his nose was long and pointed, his lips thin and rosy. Under the piercing gaze of Cuvelier, who stared at us severely, Loïc tapped me on the shoulder in a relaxed way that surprised me. I realized that he was tougher than I was, that he was no longer intimidated at all by the Father Superior. In his nasal voice, Cuvelier ordered: "You have one hour to show our new arrival around our establishment. Show him the chapel path first of all. That is where your first mass will be, tomorrow morning at six-thirty, as it will be every other day."

Loïc had impressed me from the very first moment, as soon as I had seen him enter the Father's office with a decisive, firm step. He had no history, had not known his parents, was afraid of nothing. He sped me through the labyrinths of La Mennais, took me to the places to piss in secret when you couldn't hold it any longer and access to the toilets was prohibited outside of set hours, showed me hiding places for chocolate and other sweets, as well as the spots where it was possible to camouflage yourself in order to smoke when someone had managed to get cigarettes into the school. Then I followed him to go to afternoon classes, two hours of Latin and catechism. Right away, I amazed the teacher, who interrogated me about declensions of the third group, but I filled Father François with consternation when he realized that I knew nothing of the Holy Trinity or of transubstantiation: I hardly knew that Christ was born of a still-virgin Mary and that he had died on the cross to save the world from original sin, almost two thousand years ago. At six in the evening, we were lined up in front of our respective beds for the barrack room review by Father Cuvelier. When the priest approached me and was able to see to what degree I had failed in my attempt at arranging my sheets, his face bore an expression of vicious satisfaction. I prepared to undergo my first punishment. That very evening, after supper, while the other students had time for rest or reading, I had to copy out one hundred times: "I beg pardon from my Fathers and from God for having, out of laziness, neglected the task that was given to me." These punishments were carried out at a desk in a room kept for this purpose and which had the particularity of not being heated at all. Your fingers gradually became swollen. That is where I spent my first evening in boarding school.

After that, the episodes of baiting followed one another, at a more or less regular pace, which did not prevent me from remaining the diligent student that I had always been, graduating with honors, and finally going to university. It is true that, for three and a half years at La Mennais, Loïc and I had nothing else to distract us. We never left each other since we had no family to receive us during vacations. Psychologically, of course, that was difficult to live through, especially when the others left joyously, and then returned to tell about their trips, their escapades, their walks in the forest, their trips in sailing dinghies, or even their winter sports trips for the wealthiest among them, as well as their first surprise parties somewhat later. Loïc and I knew nothing of all that. But, when the establishment was emptied of its students and of a large part of its overseers and teachers, we took advantage of the moment to explore all its nooks and crannies, to find all the ways out, to study the observation posts and the spots where you could enter and exit without getting caught. We were somehow the masters of the house and that gave us a certain advantage over our classmates as well as over the older students. Father Cuvelier would be gone sometimes for several days, or even an entire week, which gave us the chance to break into his office and to rummage around his personal effects. Great was our surprise when we discovered in one of his drawers several photos of a student in our class, a boy blond as wheat, with a reedy voice and diaphanous skin, of whom Father Cuvelier was obviously fond. The young man was named Erwan. On the back of each of these photos, Cuvelier had written a poem.

Erwan your hair of gold,
Without you is my flesh cold,
Erwan oh heaven's child
Your skin so sweet and mild.

That's all I remember.

In January 1963, a bit over two years since my arrival in Ploërmel, Loïc and I decided to take revenge for yet another unjust punishment. We managed, thanks to our perfect knowledge of the place, to sneak out of the dormitory in the middle of the night and to wait in the classroom where Cuvelier would, the next day first thing in the morning, give us a math class. On the blackboard, I copied out the poem in question, which I had learned by heart, without too much effort, I must admit. I added my own line: *Oh! What beauty, his hairy ass!* (the moniker sounding in French like his name, Cuvelier). Then, as we left, Loïc locked the door and broke the lock so that the next day, while we were all waiting in line in the hallway, Father Cuvelier could not open it. Uproar, annoyance, shouting, complaints, threats. If it was someone among us who had done it, he would see what he had coming, he would not get away, they would launch an investigation and he would be administered a corrective punishment he would remember. A collective punishment was also promised to us all. Loïc and I did not protest. Cuvelier called the handyman of the establishment, who came to open the lock. But the Father had made such a racket that other teachers came running at the same time to find out what was happening and causing this sudden and unusual din. Once the door was opened, the students rushed, shoving one another, into the classroom following the adults. When everyone discovered the writing on the blackboard, there was a deathly silence. Everyone religiously took note of the pretty quatrain and of my charming addition. The headmaster attentively scrutinized Cuvelier, who struggled to catch his breath. Poor Erwan was peony-red, but that could not be compared with the scarlet blush burning on the priest's face. Chance would have it that the headmaster chose Loïc to erase the culpable lines that we had written overnight. My best friend walked up to Cuvelier, who was standing in front of the platform, and forced him to step aside to allow him to reach the blackboard. He took his time passing the sponge over the shameful words that I had traced while concealing my handwriting as best as I could, thus making disappear forever the proof of our guilt. Then he returned to his place, smiling with an air of satisfaction. The incident was never brought up again, neither officially nor unofficially, nor even by the students. A graphological analysis could not be done, and Cuvelier of course did not wish to go further into the subject nor to open himself up to dangerous comments. No investigation was carried out. Nobody questioned Erwan, but he was freed of the "interviews" that he had had to undergo regularly in the gloomy office of Father Cuvelier. In everyone's eyes, Loïc was behind this incredible stunt, as shown by the insolent and provocative slowness with which he had erased the blackboard. He earned from that the boundless admiration of his classmates and the at least equal hatred of the teachers. He never denied nor confirmed his responsibility to anybody. He put nobody on my scent. I never spoke, for my part, about the subject and I avoided referring to that episode. That secret definitively sealed our unwavering friendship.

I cannot admit that he who is for me a blood-brother, this companion, this friend with whom I have pulled off so many stunts, has fomented a conspiracy against me. Loïc, solid as a rock and who never ceased being on my side, this same Loïc has abused my trust to trick me and provoke my fall. Why? I refuse to imagine a hypothesis as absurd as it is repugnant.

In the setting sun of Casablanca, the woman in black that Roucaud and I glimpse in the distance approaches as she walks along the dock. She stops when she reaches us. We do not move. She raises her veil: Noura, at last! It's her!

Her face is backlit. She gazes at me and smiles. Unable to react, I remain silent, my voice caught in my throat. Since the first thing that morning when I snuck out of our bed, crept into the hallway and fled our soft nest without leaving a word of explanation, I have thought of her every day. In the hideouts before my arrest, in the boarding line at Le Bourget Airport, in the macabre basement of the powerplant, in the shantytown of Aïn Sebaâ as well as in the bed at Marthe's home, her image follows me everywhere. And here she is in front of me, radiant despite the veil and the twilight. I would like to touch her, to take her in my arms, eat her skin, devour her lips and her breasts, hold her against me, slide my hands along her hips, lay her down without letting go of her, role on the ground with her. I know that is impossible. I cannot even brush her cheek delicately. Time is suspended. All three of us remain immobile and in silence until Roucaud finally interrupts this moment of ecstasy.
"Well! I suppose you are Noura. I have a hard time recognizing you from the photos, but, I believe it based on both of your reactions, there's no doubt."
Without paying any attention to the gendarme, she draws closer to me, without parting with her angelic smile. She bends down facing me and murmurs in a severe tone, a tone of reproach and bitterness:
"I missed you so much."
"Noura, I… I'm sorry, I couldn't warn you. I didn't want to risk worrying you. I would have liked to explain it to you, but it was too dangerous. It was better, for you, not to know anything, including where I was."
Roucaud stands up and says impatiently:

"Alright, turtledoves, this reunion is extremely touching, but we have work to do and very little time! So, let's get to work before Madame has to leave, if you will."
Still ignoring the gendarme, as though he did not exist and as though the sound of his voice did not reach her, Noura asks me:
"What are you doing in Morocco? How did you find Marthe, whom I never spoke of to you?"
"It's a very long story, Noura. I hope that one day I'll have the time to tell you. But there something really urgent. Noura, I need you."
She raises an eyebrow. She waits for what comes next.
"Madame," Roucaud continues, "we think that Loïc Martin, the friend, partner, and confident of Rodrigo Ganos, has information of the highest importance that would allow both advancing various investigations and exculpating Monsieur."
He puts a hand on my shoulder to indicate me. For the first time, Noura turns toward him and seems to discover his presence.
"Who are you?" she asks coldly.
Roucaud is wearing a beige shirt of doubtful cleanliness, jeans, and worn moccasins. He does not look like a classic sub-officer. He is not here on official duty, cannot present his card in this country that it not his own. He inclines his head and, in a solemn voice, responds:
"I am Major Roucaud. I belong to the French gendarmerie. I am in search of the killers of the rue des Rosiers attack, which you have surely heard of…"
He interrupts himself and waits for a confirmation from his interlocutor. Noura does not react. The major continues:
"Well, who cares! It happens that Monsieur Ganos, here present, was suspected of being indirectly implicated in this ignominy. Personally, I do not think that is the case. In my opinion, your fiancé is innocent."

On hearing the word "fiancé," Noura is flinches, and glances quickly in my direction, before being frozen in place once again. Roucaud adds:
"I think that you can help us to prove it by getting in touch with Martin to get information from him that we need. We will guide you from behind the scenes."
She closes her eyes, hesitates, then readjusts her burka that hides her once again. She speaks from behind her veil:
"Help you? Help you!"
She turns towards me:
"That's what you dare to ask of me, you too? A year ago, you abandon me. You give me no sign of life – in fact, I thought you were dead – you give me no news, you do not try to find out mine and you arrive here to ask for me help. Do you even know why I have come back to Morocco? Have I ever spoken to you of returning to live here when we were together? Never, no, never, because I never intended to. You don't wonder why I came back finally?"

Her voice expresses cold anger. My heart is beating like crazy, I feel that I am losing her for good. But I don't manage to reflect fast enough to answer her, to try to calm her, to move her.

"My love, I…"
"My love? Enough of your smooth talking! I returned to Casablanca, because I didn't know where else to go, that's why! You left me alone without a penny while I was pregnant. If I had not looked after myself, I could have given birth in the gutter. And now you want me to abandon my little six-month old baby to throw myself into a counter-espionage career by attacking Loïc? You're joking, both of you!"

I have a hard time focusing on our affair. Addressing this reproach to me, Noura reveals to me that she was expecting a child when I left her and thus that I am very likely the father of the infant I glimpsed yesterday at the bar of the Hôtel Suisse.

"What is his name?"
"Who?"
"Your son, what is his name?"
Noura shrugs her shoulders.
"It's a girl. Her name is Anissa."

After this dry declaration, Noura turned on her heels and walked away quickly. In an instant, her image had faded away in the setting sun. I have remained there, frozen in place, trying vainly to see where she is going. She has gone back to the child, indifferent to my fate and doubtless even more so to that of the rue des Rosiers investigation. Who knows if she has also returned to the arms of that man who was with her yesterday? I realize, only too late, how naïve I was. What an illusion to believe, while I betrayed her trust by abandoning her with no explanation, that she would succumb once again to my charm right away and would let everything else go to help me! How could Roucaud and Rosenberg have thought so too?

We left the Jardins de l'Hermitage around three hours ago. Night has nearly fallen and the wind is nearly gone. The docks and the cargo ships have been emptied of their dockworkers. The port is troublingly calm, as though every life had disappeared with Noura. The heavy silence is suddenly broken by the supernatural psalmody of the muezzin who, from the top of a minaret which I couldn't say is in the north or the south, calls, for the second-to-last time in the day, the believers to give glory to their God in the twilight. He makes me forget Noura, for an instant. The long vibrato of his vocal cords, the modulations of the last *a* in *Allah,* send shivers through me and put me into a brief meditation, or rather a reflection. I think of the three religions of the Book. I realize that I am the product of two of them, but that, if Anissa is indeed my daughter, she brings together all three, she is the perfect synthesis of them. This idea leaves me pensive. The zippo flame that suddenly shoots up in Roucaud's hand brings me back to reality and to more prosaic concerns.

"Not easy to get along with, your girlfriend," he says as he blows out a cloud of blue smoke.

His expression annoys me. How can he call Noura, my *Immortal Beloved,* like Beethoven's that my grandfather so loved, my goddess, my henceforth unreachable nymph, my "girlfriend"! With the eternal smile in the corner of his mouth, he offers me a cigarette. I dryly refuse, gesturing with the back of my hand. I stand up and start walking in front of him, turning around nervously, my hands in my pockets, my eyes on my shoes. Roucaud smokes as he observes me. The last twenty-four hours have been the source of so much hope! I thought I would be able to rekindle my relationship with my fiancée. I nourished the insane fantasy that we would be able to find a little nest where she would give herself up to me as she used to know how do, unparalleled as she was in her knowledge of matters of love. But now sweet Noura has closed the door on me. So why did she bother meeting with me? Perhaps just to tell me that Anissa is my daughter.

"Alright, don't make that face, buddy. It's like you don't know women! Your Noura is angry, she wanted to show you that. But she is crazy about you, that is certain! You are lucky, buddy. Yes, perfectly lucky! She would eat you with her eyes if she could. Ah! A girl never looked at me like that, I can guarantee you. But with your unkempt hair and wild beard, you look nothing like a Roger Moore, even less like an Alain Delon. Honestly, her reaction is understandable. You disappear without a word a year ago, and you show up here asking her for a favor, without any other explanation! And you want her to welcome you with open arms? Come on, let's be reasonable... So, you knew that she was pregnant when you ran off, yes or no?"

I think that Roucaud is really making fun of me. I didn't ask anything of Noura. I have hardly spoken to her. He is the one, the major, who asked for her help first, in cooperation with David. He bade her return to France and to get in touch with Loïc. It was to his proposition that she reacted so violently. And now he is accusing me of tactlessness! He has got some nerve. I pinch myself to avoid giving him a smack. He crushes his cigarette under his sole, gets up in turn, approaches me and takes me by both of my arms.

"Come on Rodrigo! Keep calm. Noura's reaction is understandable. As they say where I'm from, the sun will come out tomorrow! Come on, let's go have dinner. I'm going to take you to discover a great place, you're my guest!"

It is now completely dark. I have no way of returning to Aïn Sebaâ, other than by hitchhiking. I don't have a single dirham on me. How could I refuse? I resign myself to following the major who is already walking away quickly. It takes us an hour of walking to get to the restaurant, Le Prétexte, which is on Anfa Boulevard. A mustachioed man of around fifty welcomes the gendarme with praise worthy of a president who has just decorated him with a Legion of Honor medal. Then the restauranteur turns towards me and offers me his enormous hand, as he says to me in his singsong accent:

"Welcome to Le Prétexte! Like all those who are recommended by my friend," (he puts a hand on Roucaud the back of his neck), "make yourself at home! We will take care of both of you! What shall I give you to begin? A little Pineau?"

The restaurant is three-quarters full. Many French people have come to relax while tasting plates from Aquitaine, but I also notice locals tasting with curiosity the pâtés, cassoulets, and chestnut blood sausages. However, the specialty of the place, the major explains to me, is duck confit penne and foie gras penne. A recipe perfected by the chef, often copied, never equaled. For years Roucaud planned to come to visit his friend here, in Casablanca, since the opening of the establishment at the end of the seventies, and he always put it off. Now I have given him the occasion. He is really happy to show me Le Prétexte. Without being a palace, it is a quite prosperous place, with a well-off clientele. The carpet is plush, the conversation muted, which is quite unusual in this city. It has been too long since I have frequented this kind of place. I am not in my element here anymore, especially dressed in the rags I am dragging around. A maître d'hôtel pulls back the chairs of a round table and invites us to sit. Surprise, there are four places with four place settings. I look questioningly at the gendarme. He does not respond and he thanks the restauranteur in a knowing way. He checks the time on his watch and says in a would-be reassuring tone:

"We are a bit early, the conversation with Noura was shorter than expected"; "they" won't be long in coming. I down my apértif glass, swallow a few olives and two or three little dry cakes. Roucaud is silent and pensive until the proprietor sits down with us to chew the fat. So what has become of the Major, since they have been waiting for him here in Morocco? He has taken his time to come! And apart from that, what good news does he have to tell? Henriette, how has she been since the divorce? And he, Jacques (that's Roucaud's first name, I discover it at that moment), how is he feeling? The gendarme responds with short explanations, asks his own questions. Is business good? Life in Casablanca? A delight! He will never leave! The people are warm, friendly. People spend time with one another. He is seeing a girl. A Frenchwoman from Marseille, who has lived here for five years. Around thirty, a pretty woman. He, a confirmed bachelor, is starting to wonder if he will finally settle down. She wants a kid. He doesn't really know, he feels too old. Roucaud smiles sadly. He thinks of his own son, crushed against a plane tree on the road in Montech five years ago. The other man realizes he has been maladroit, and tries to change the subject. The glazed door of the restaurant gives him an excellent chance. A bearded man enters walking hesitantly and supporting the arm of an elderly lady with hair white as snow and impeccably permed. So great is my shock that I take a few moments to recognize David Rosenberg, walking behind Marthe. Roucaud, for his part, is not surprised. He stands to welcome them. He shakes the cop's

hand in a knowing way, but seems to be astonished by the woman's presence. David explains:
"Jacques, this is Marthe."
The cop bows before the old lady, who extends her hand to him. He greets her politely, then he stiffens as he turns towards David:
"It's a bit late for introductions, isn't it? When I found Rodrigo this afternoon and he spoke to me of a certain Marthe, I didn't know who he was talking about."
Addressing her, he says:
"Please excuse me, Madame, if I seem cavalier to you, but David had not informed me. And I didn't know that it was you who had set the time of our meeting. That's why I was surprised when Ganos mentioned your name."
In a self-assured manner, David interrupts him:
"Look, Jacques, let's not lie to each other. You know my situation. We help each other up to a certain point, but I am obliged to keep some aces up my sleeve, just in case. I don't tell you everything and I know that you also haven't told me everything. But we are here to complete our information. You're not going to invite us to sit?"
I have also stood up. I cannot stop looking at Marthe, who endures my staring. This woman hypnotizes me. On Roucaud's invitation, all four of us sit down at the table. They serve us three Pineau aperitifs, Marthe prefers whiskey. She caresses the rim of the white porcelain plate. David asks:
"So, how did it go with Noura?"
The major is embarrassed; he doesn't respond. I speak:
"David, what are the three of you up to? Who is lying to who? You had said nothing to the major about Marthe. You, Marthe, claimed to have set an appointment with Noura in the Jardins de l'Hermitage, whereas she met us three hours later at the port. As for you, Major, you knew that Noura would meet us and that there would be four of us at dinner here at just after ten in the evening! What's brewing here?"

The three protagonists observe each other in silence, waiting for the others to respond first. David begins:
"As I just indicated to Jacques, and as I had already explained to you before you left France, we cannot, we must not tell each other everything. The less we know about each other, the better. Especially you, Rodrigo, who are the most fragile one among us, and the most sought-after. I have to hide your tracks. If one of us is arrested, or even if it were Noura, it would be better that we know as little as possible, to be sure not to speak. You got that?"
His explanation only partly convinces me. If his mission is as secret as the gendarme's, if our meetings must be known by no one, how is it that we are meeting here, in this well-known establishment on Boulevard d'Anfa? David is lying, as he is lying to Roucaud, and perhaps to Marthe. He is not at all trying to make us impossible to find. On the contrary.
From the menu, we all choose the chef's specialty, pasta with foie gras and duck confit. David suggests a Médoc to accompany this plate. Roucaud makes a doubtful face, but David's decision is made with no possibility of appeal. We toast as though we were old friends. We don't really know to whom, nor to what. I continue:
"Let's admit that is true. But we still ended up finding Noura at the port. But her reaction was, how can I put it…glacial. She doesn't want to help us."
In her old, tender voice, Marthe reassures us:
"Don't worry about the little one's reaction. I know her. She's impulsive, but she won't let you down. She wanted to make a point. Tomorrow, she will have changed her mind."
They bring us the pasta. David orders a second bottle of wine, while we haven't yet finished the first. Marthe furrows her brow and puts her hand on his:
"Take it easy, David… Don't drink too much."
Surprising familiarity. So they know each other that well? He smiles.
"Ah, Marthe, you're like a mother to me!"

She raises her eyes to the sky:
"Well, I could be your mother!"
David, embarrassed, turns away with an ironic sigh. He looks at me, as though he wanted me as a witness. I don't know what to think. Marthe and David speak to each other in an informal register of language. They are far closer with one another than I had imagined. Roucaud also seems to be intrigued, but he doesn't say a word. He tastes the Bordeaux curiously, and seems finally to like this vintage that he is not used to. David continues while we begin to eat:

"Marthe, I am counting on you to reason with Noura. She is our only hope for catching Loïc."
He is speaking softly, nearly whispering, no doubt fearing being heard by people nearby, even if the tables are quite far from each other. But he doesn't bother with other circumlocutions or allusions. It is no longer about approaching Loïc to obtain useful information for the investigation. Now, the objective is clear: to set a trap for him. Marthe nods in agreement. Noura will help us. David continues, between two mouthfuls of pasta:
"Since all four of us are together, now is the time to take stock and explain to you where we are…"
But he takes his time, finishes everything on his plate, drinks two glasses and concentrates. In the subdued and warm light given off by the lamp at the center of the table, David seems to me like a storyteller preparing a story to put children to sleep. But we are not at all ready to drift off to sleep. We drink his words at least as much as the Médoc.
He tells us first of all that there had always been a file on me in his special unit. Among the generous donators who had contributed to financing my studies was a certain Juvin, a former collaborator well-known in his division, but who escaped the dragnet at Liberation, and who became an industrialist in the private sector. This Juvin, who had worked hand in hand with Bousquet, succeeded, after the

war, in establishing a flourishing machinery and tools business in Brittany, which allowed him to, among other things, help me throughout my studies, until I left the École nationale de chimie and founded Rodrigo Chemicals. It was in looking further into that guy's affairs that David and his team came across my name, as well as Loïc's. But this Juvin died of a heart attack in May 1985. David was about to put the cuffs on him for his clearly established role in the financing of a Neonazi terrorist organization with the evocative name MK21, which stood for "*Mein Kampf* into the 21st century." A few days after Juvin's death, the scandal of my supposed insider trading crime broke. David quickly made the connection: the extreme right wing group was short of financing. I had naturally stepped in to help them. Thanks to inside information provided by Loïc, who thus must also have been in on it, I had been able to generate that significant capital gain on my shares in order to continue to sponsor the group. He was shaken up, and then quickly began following my tracks. But it was not easy for him to apprehend me without tangible proof. It was my attempt to flee to Argentina that gave him the chance not to put the cuffs on me, but to abduct me. And only when he saw me resisting torture did he realize that I had nothing to confess. Given the methods used to make me speak, which it was obviously impossible to allow to be known beyond the walls of Golfech, my interrogation could have only one outcome: my execution and the subsequent disappearance of my corpse. To keep me alive, there was no other choice than to kill his two colleagues, two rough brutes, each in his own way. He does not regret his action. Those guys had been useful, they really did the dirty work that was needed, since you can't make an omelet without breaking a few eggs, but they often performed their task with particular foulness. So, David was convinced of my innocence. Nonetheless, he still had to prove it. First of all, he had to get me to safety. Rescue me from the Beaumont gendarme station and send me here.

Jawad's lips are sealed and will never, under any circumstance, speak a word. David has been in contact with the young Moroccan for several years about other subjects whose substance he cannot reveal here, but there reigns an absolute, and reciprocal, trust between him and the young man who has become my friend, Jawad. Then, he had to continue the investigation.

That is when he came across Roucaud, who was also working on Bousquet, persuaded that that was the best way to follow David's and my tracks. Bingo! The gendarme and the cop ended up finding themselves nose to nose while they were each lurking below Loïc's home. Simply because his father, Michel Martin, was very close to Bousquet during the Occupation years. After a night spent sleeping separately in their respective cars, David, who had noticed Roucaud on the sidewalk across the street, took the initiative to join up with him and to make common cause with him. The gendarme accepted the offer. Together, they came to the conclusion that the only way to get Loïc to speak was to use Noura. David proposed to Roucaud, without telling him too much, to organize to meeting with me, then with my fiancée. That is how we have all gotten here. And what about Marthe in all that?

I don't really manage to take my eyes off her face. There is something familiar in her expression, his gaze. Familiar, no, that's not the word. Not familiar. It is more that I have the impression of having seen this woman, long before yesterday. Or maybe someone who looked like her. Another woman. All of a sudden, it clicks, and it staggers me. That's it! I can see whom Marthe reminds me of! Despite the twenty-five years that have passed, I remember these features exactly, that first smile that appeared to me like a gift from the heavens when I put my feet on firm ground. Anne. Yes, Anne, of course. Marthe strangely resembles the person who had come to pick me up upon my arrival in Brest in 1960 and who drove me to La Mennais in her butter-colored 4 CV.

Marthe is now much older, but the features of her face have maintained their character: an angelic face that has remained deeply engraved in my memory. After all this time, she has reappeared like a curious enchantment. Often, at night, I think of Anne. I wonder who she was, why she was there, who had sent her. Stupefied by this resemblance of Marthe with the woman whose memory has haunted me for so long, I suddenly cry out, almost without realizing it:
"Anne!"
Marthe is given a start. She stares severely at me, as though she were challenging me to repeat myself. David creates a diversion by praising the wine:
"This Médoc is excellent. 1982, a famous year. It's crazy how wine-making techniques have advanced. You drink a four-year old bottle and you have the impression you're tasting something from '71."

Roucaud is listening to David, but Marthe and I pay no attention to his oenological reflections. We remain frozen in place, facing each other. I say again:
"Anne."
Roucaud, surprised finally, says:
"Anne? Why are you repeating that name, Rodrigo?"
My eyes fixed on Marthe who does not move, I respond:
"Marthe looks uncannily like a woman I met once, when I arrived in France. A woman who had been given the task of meeting me when I disembarked at the port in Brest. All that I know of her is that her name was Anne. I never saw her again, but I have not forgotten her."
The gendarme turns towards Marthe and asks her:
"Have you ever heard of this Anne?"
David expresses a doubt about the accuracy of my memory:
"You arrived in 1960, Rodrigo, right? Twenty-six years ago! You have a hell of a good memory!"
Marthe isn't listening, she does not look away from me. She takes a sip of wine before announcing in a hoarse voice:

"Anne was my twin sister."

We did not order dessert. The restaurant ended up emptying out. We were the last customers. The restauranteur refused to give us the bill. Roucaud and Rosenberg insisted, but the fellow remained inflexible. He was so happy to see the major again, his friend Jacques… after waiting so long for him! At the moment we split up on Boulevard d'Anfa, Roucaud and Rosenberg exchanged a virile handshake. David hugged Marthe and the major saluted her with a bow. She said:

"My taxi is here."

A red Peugeot, its motor and headlights illuminated, was indeed waiting next to the sidewalk. The cop responded:

"That is true. Please go ahead, it is starting to get late."

This suddenly formal tone surprised me, until I realized he was addressing both of us, Marthe and me. The old lady took me by the arm. It was indeed the time to go home. The next day would be long and difficult. In the time it takes me to realize this, Marthe has already taken a seat in the taxi. She gives me a signal to get a move on, she wasn't going to sleep there. That's how I found myself on the second floor of 12 Mohamed-V Boulevard, in Marthe's apartment, for the second straight night.

This time, I awaken very early in the morning. I have had a troubled sleep with incessant dreams in which Anne's face from when I arrived in France merges with Marthe's of today. I jump out of bed and rush into the living room, fearing that Marthe has already left, like yesterday. I don't want to be alone and at loose ends, without any news of Noura. When, half-naked, I arrive in the living room, Marthe is sitting at the table. She examines me severely and commands me, furrowing her brows:

"Would you be so kind as to get washed and dressed before appearing like that? After which, I will be delighted to offer you something to eat and drink."

With this, she shrugs her shoulders, and smiles knowingly at me. I realize the incongruity of the situation, the indecency, or even the ridiculousness, of my outfit and my posture. When I return, Marthe is standing in front of a cup:

"Coffee?"
"With pleasure, Marthe, with pleasure, thank you."
"Keep your thanks for what I'm about to tell you."
"What?"
She serves me a large cup. I sit down, take three sips.

Marthe is wearing a blue dress with white flowers, low-cut and revealing the beginnings of her wrinkled breast. She slides down onto her chair in turn:

"I spoke with Noura on the phone…"
She smiles, puts her hand on mine.
"Noura's impulsive. But she's calmed down since yesterday. She's leaving for Paris today. She will help us."
I am happy to know that Noura is on our side but pained that she is leaving me just after having seen her again.
"And… and the child?"
"The little one? Anissa? She is leaving her with us. She will drop her off here soon before going to the airport. We will take care of her until her mama's return."

"We?"
"We, yes. You and me."
You and me. She and me. She, Marthe, and me, Rodrigo. Who is this woman? Yesterday, Marthe told me that her sister had died in the rue des Rosiers attack. I wonder if she

183

was talking about the same sister, if she was talking about Anne. I look at her:

"Marthe…"

She endures my staring. I do not know how to put my question.

"Marthe… how is it possible? How can it be that Anne is your sister and that I have met you both? It can't be a coincidence."

Her nails with their nail polish roll, like a drum, on the waxed tablecloth. Then she readjusts her shoulder straps. She stands up and walks to the window that she opens, as though to catch her breath. The tumult of Mohamed-V Boulevard, its morning humming, pours into the room. Marthe's voice is hardly audible amidst the noise:

"No, of course it isn't a coincidence. No more than Noura, indeed."

I start. I wonder if I have heard right.
"Noura? No more than Noura, that's what you said?"
She nods in silence. I repeat:
"How's that, *no more than Noura*? What is not a coincidence?
Marthe turns around, learns her backside and her hands against the windowsill. She pinches her lips together. Maybe she regrets having spoken too much. Then she turns around again, leans her elbows on the guardrail and mutters something. I don't understand a word of what she says. I suppose that that is on purpose. I don't dare get up to approach and listen carefully. I can guess well enough, without admitting it to myself, the nature of the things that she is preparing to reveal to me. And I'm not sure I really

want to know them. Too many emotions are mixed together. I catch only bits of phrases here and there:

"Yes. Anne died on rue des Rosiers... Murdered on the patio in front of Jo Goldberg... After having escaped from the Nazis long ago, after having been able to avoid the various dangers that have threatened her life, my sister died from vulgar machine-gun fire, blind, on a restaurant patio. She wasn't even the target."

I see once more, on the docks of Brest whose outlines were submerged in fog, Anne's luminous face, her blue scarf contrasting with the gray surrounding everything—the sky, the sidewalks, the men. After days and days spent trying to make out the ocean through a tiny, scratched porthole, made opaque by the accumulation of salt and sometimes struck by waves, sometime by the driving rain, in a cargo ship taking me towards an unknown land. For me, Anne symbolized all of humanity. But she was merely a fleeting apparition, lasting only a few hours. Once the time it took to drive to the boarding school at La Mennais had elapsed, she disappeared forever.

An empty interval. Someone rings the doorbell. Before Marthe even gives me permission, I rush to open the door. My feet get caught in the rug, I trip, fall flat on my face on the tiled floor. I am stunned. The pain is sharp and I take some time to get up. When I finally open the door, Noura has already left. She has left the bassinet on the landing. A little doll hardly six months old is wiggling her little hand in my direction and babbling. An envelope is on her stomach. I pull out a white card on which is written in Noura's handwriting: *My name is Anissa. Take good care of me. Mama will give you news quickly.* I bring the child inside. Marthe nearly throws herself on me, grabs the baby and presses it against her breast. Then she begins rocking her, humming a nursery rhyme that she interrupts occasionally with "my granddaughter, my granddaughter!" which she repeats over and over again.

I will soon learn that it's not just a manner of speaking. Anissa really is Marthe's "granddaughter." Once the baby has fallen asleep on her breast, she puts her gently in her makeshift bed, which she places on the chaise lounge. Then she comes back towards me and, suddenly crossing over the distance that had separated us until now, she draws near and takes my hand. She tells me the story. Marthe and her twin sister Arielle were born on June 16, 1923 in Pantin. Their father and mother were tailors. They were not exactly rolling in money, but Marthe had a happy childhood. A few times, beginning in 1936, she even had the chance to go all the way to the sea with her family. Arielle would have to change her first name later, to Anne. Then a third child was born a few years later, in 1931. It was a boy, Thomas. During the Occupation, all five of them lived in their studio. They were not declared as Jews with the authorities and, until 1943, they had miraculously avoided each control, each roundup. It must be said that they went out as little as possible, they remained basically confined to their studio for over two years. But, one January evening, the Gestapo showed up. The policemen took away the father, the mother, the brother, and Marthe. They did not find Anne – or Arielle – who had had the time to hide inside one of those enormous rolls of fabric. They did not wait long. They were, it seems, ill-informed about the number of people in the household, or they didn't care. They forced their four victims into the back of a truck in which other unfortunates, already piled up, had to press together even more to give them space. But just as the motor started and the vehicle began to move, somebody screamed "Halt!" The truck stopped. A soldier opened the back hatch. A German officer advanced and pointed to Marthe, who was huddled against her mother. She tried to resist, but they pulled her out of the vehicle. Just as quickly, the hatch was closed, the truck left, with its cargo of human beings leaving for hell. Marthe would never see her parents or Thomas again. Drancy, Birkenau, no doubt? Possibly, anyhow. But she had just been saved by this soldier who drove her to the Meurice, on rue de Rivoli. The officer ordered her, in very approximative French, to be silent, to reveal nothing about her identity to anyone, to respond to no question. She must simply follow him and try to be as discreet as possible, as invisible as possible. With him, she traversed the hall packed with soldiers and SS members, then she went through the kitchens. From there, a Frenchman named Marcel took her into a convent. She spent the rest of the war there. Or almost. It happened that a new denunciation – the instigator of which she never knew – obliged her to leave the convent in all haste, to avoid falling into the hands of the Gestapo. It was one of the nuns who warned her and who organized her escape. Hidden under a false floorboard of a plumber's truck, she miraculously managed to cross the country, reaching Spain, and then Morocco, where Jewish people were not hunted down. She joined the orphanage that had been founded by one of her distant aunts, the address of which she had.

Marthe presses my fingers a bit more, her hand becomes damp. In a weak, almost reedy, trembling voice, she avows that it was necessary to force herself to make the most terrible decision that ever had to make in her existence, a choice with which no woman in the world should have to be confronted: separate herself from her baby forever or condemn him to death by keeping him with her. To avoid his falling into the hands of the Nazis, she resolved to abandon her child in Paris. A baby hardly older than the one sleeping beside us, born of her guilty love with the German officer who saved her life.

The soldier was Johann Gantzer, of course. And the child was me. Marthe's real name was Sarah. She is my mother, as she confirms in a sob.

My emotion is profound. Yet David's story comes back to me. He said that my biological mother had been arrested finally in the convent, then deported. But Marthe asserts, on the contrary, that she fled to Morocco. There is something that doesn't add up.

"David assured me that my mother must have wound up at Drancy or at Auschwitz, while you claim to have fled…"

She shrugs her shoulders.

"Yes, the version of my arrest and probable deportation was the one the nuns let be spread. That way, nobody would look for me. The rumor worked marvelously. Nobody ever tried to find me. The Germans, for their part, began to have other worries."

But my doubts do not disappear. I have a hard time believing that I have my biological mother in front of me. But she will give me the uncontestable proof, the same one that convinced David. I had, at my birth, a quite unsightly birthmark on my neck, she tells me. That is correct and it is not possible that she has guessed it. I had the birthmark removed in a clinic fifteen years ago now, which rules out the possibility that a photo of me has circulated from the time the birthmark appeared beneath my left ear; and as there is no scar today, Marthe could only have this information from her memory.

Her eyes have filled with tears, which she lets run down the furrows of her wrinkles, then drip into our interlocked hands. Since last night, I had intuited the revelation that Marthe would have for me, and yet she collides headlong with my certainties. I knew only one mother, and her name was Soledad. She died before my eyes, on a peaceful seaside road, in 1960. A year ago, David told me that I had in fact had another biological mother, whom I hadn't known, named Sarah. I had overcome the news without being troubled excessively by it. That woman remained a concept. She had disappeared. Perhaps she had been deported, or she was dead. She was only a ghost, or the mere invention of the policeman. But here I am in the presence of a woman who has lost her self-confidence and cannot hold back her tears. Trembling against me, she has just confessed to me that she gave life to me and that she had to abandon me to save my life. So this mother invented by David is real, in the flesh. I should take her in my arms, no doubt. I don't manage to. Nor she. We remain immobile like this for an undefined, suspended moment. Then we separate tenderly, we sit down face to face, each of us on our respective side of the table. Suddenly, Marthe pulls herself together, wipes her already almost dry eyes, clears her throat, and asks me:

"A little more coffee?"

I extend my cup to her without responding. I let out, dreamily, without really posing the question, as though I were speaking to myself:

"But then Anne… Anne knew. Was it you who sent her? She cannot have arrived in Brest by chance the moment I disembarked."

Marthe shrugs her shoulders.
"Of course not! Arielle… well, Anne, once she came out of hiding after the 1943 roundup, had no landing place. She had to do what she could to get by…"

By the false grin that Marthe cannot hide, her little brusque and fitful movements, her eyelids that have begun vibrating, I can tell that she is embarrassed. What she has to tell me is particularly delicate, indecent.

"Anne was a very pretty girl… Like me, it seems. Physically, we were similar in every way. We must have had the same survival instinct since in some way we followed…similar paths."

She coughs again, stands up with effort, goes to get a packet of almond cakes that are on a shelf next to the oven, brings it back, offers me a piece, chooses one for herself, then takes another sip of tea, before continuing:

"There were not many things to do for a twenty year-old girl without an identity, who wanted to hide her Jewishness at any cost. She presented herself at Le Chabanais, in Paris. She was immediately accepted."

I don't know what is, or was Le Chabanais, even if I do have an inkling. Marthe tells me that it was a brothel in the 2nd arrondissement in Paris, which operated from 1878 to 1946. During the entire Occupation, the brothel in question was put in the service of the German clientele, which was particularly fond of it. Anne prostituted herself there for some time, but she was quickly noticed by a loyal customer, a Frenchman and unequivocal collaborator, who had the privilege of benefiting from the place's services. He fell in love with the young woman. The man had relations, power, and money. He set Anne up in a two-room apartment at place de la Madeleine, where he could visit her regularly. But at the end of August 1944, a few days after the liberation of the capital, he was arrested by the French Forces of the Interior. He awaited his trial in prison until summer 1946. He escaped, doubtless thanks to this delay, the death penalty, and was sentenced to ten years in prison. For her part, Anne must have experienced a hardly enviable fate: her head shaved in public, she was marched through the streets of the city throughout an entire day. An expiatory victim of an ashamed country seeking to efface from its memory its own turpitudes, she felt the hatred of a whole people pour over her. She was spit on, insulted, and even slapped here and there. Sentenced to five years in exile, she joined Marthe in Casablanca. She had also heard of the orphanage of their old aunt. The two sisters lived together for seven years. In September 1952, Anne received the news, in a telegram from a friend, that her lover from Paris had just been freed, two years early. She jumped in the first boat and returned to France to find him. Anne's heart had remained loyal to that elegant and cultivated man who had taken her out of the brothel and had given her an easy life in occupied Paris. Their relationship had rapidly evolved since her departure from Le Chabanais. To him, she was not merely a sexual distraction. She had become his nymph, his muse. He recited Baudelaire to her, wrote her poems; they listened to Beethoven on a splendid gramophone he had given her. And if her man had chosen to collaborate, she claimed, it was only out of a survival instinct, just as she had chosen to prostitute herself. She did not think of him as a dirty collaborator any more than he thought of her as a whore. Or as a Jew. She had been prompt, no doubt naively, in telling him of her origins and of her birth. He did not take offense, had assured her that he was not at all anti-Semitic, but on the contrary well-meaning toward "Israelites" as he said. He had sworn that his collaboration with the Nazis did not go beyond the financial sphere – her ran a real estate company – that he had not participated in a single arrest. Of course, he had turned a blind eye on some iniquitous confiscations, but did he have a choice? In any case, Anne did not hesitate. As soon as he was freed, she rushed into the arms of her lover, Didier Le Bellec, in whom she had remained madly in love. He was from Concarneau, so they settled in Brittany. It was Anne who informed Marthe that I would arrive in Brest in December 1960. Naturally, Marthe asked her sister to take care of me. Anne came to pick me up and drove me to the boarding school in her incredible Renault 4 CV.

I start.
"How can that be, that 'Anne informed me of your arrival in Brest?'"

In this, there are two pieces of news in one, and I don't know which staggers me more. If it is at least surprising that Anne knew about my arrival, had even heard about my existence, it is even more so that Marthe herself knew of it! I bang my fist on the table. The cups are given a jolt, the coffee and tea overflow onto the waxed tablecloth. I stand up, shouting:

"I am starting to have enough of this! What is all this bullshit? You... you have known for all this time that I had survived? You knew it? First of all, how? What is with these stories?"

I have completely lost my nerves. In a reflex, Marthe recoils, but she shows no sign of fear. But my yelling has awoken the baby, who has started bawling. Her cries make me realize I have gone too far. I rush to rock her, I hum her the melody of an old nursery rhyme that I remember:

"Hamaquita de oro para este chiquito, Hamaquita de oro para mi bebé..."
Anissa wriggles her hands a bit, then falls back asleep as she yawns. I turn back towards Marthe and sit back down sheepishly.

"Sorry, I shouldn't have gotten carried away like that, but after a while..."

Marthe puts a warm and benevolent hand on mine. She explains to me:
"Don't worry about it... Don't worry about it, I understand. It's a lot of things at once. So here's what happened. When he got out of prison, Didier La Bellec quickly got into touch with former collaborators. They helped each other, gave each other tips, organized visits, and had packages brought to those who were still in prison. Anne telephoned me regularly, wrote to me too and, in a coded language that only we knew how to decipher, told me about the activities of the man who had become her husband. And I, egotistically saw in that, on the contrary, the opportunity of my life. I asked her to find the trace of Johann Gantzer and your own. Through many intermediaries, Le Bellec was able to get into touch with Miguel Martinez, you teacher. Thanks to that contact, Anne informed me that your father had become Juan Ganos down there, in Buenos Aires, and that, you had survived. I even managed to find out your first name. Over intervals of a few months, sometimes even only once or twice a year, Anne gave me news of you, which she obtained. Until she told me of the death of Johann and his wife, and announced to me that Michel had sent you to France in that cargo ship..."
Marthe's voice is becoming more and more hoarse.
"It was the chance for me to go and get you..."
My throat tightens also. I think again of my arrival in the Brest fog, of that damp road through the countryside of bare trees, next to Anne, silent, then the discovery of the austere establishment of La Mennais and the glacial and terrifying reception of that fearsome Father Cuvelier. I tell myself that instead of letting me make that sinister voyage in her sister's car, she who today claims to be my mother could have acted like my real mother by coming to meet me and taking me to Morocco, where I could have enjoyed happy days with her.

Marthe lets go of my hand and lowers her head. She turns back towards the table and leans on the back of the chair that

I was just sitting in. In a weak and hoarse voice, she explains to me:

"I would have liked to come take you. I packed my bag. I rushed to the port. I had a ticket, I was ready to board, I would arrive in France two days before you. Anne had planned for me to stay with her. But, once I was there, on the dock of the port of Casablanca, I couldn't. I couldn't…"

She has begun to cry. In the midst of sobbing, she tells me:
"Two months earlier, I had received Noura at the orphanage. I cherished that child as though she were my own. I rocked her day and night, I never took my eyes off her. I would have wanted to take her to France with me to join you. I didn't have the right. When the moment came to get in the boat, I thought of her and of you. I remembered the baby you were, that you wouldn't be anymore, that she still was. You were over sixteen, even if you thought you were fifteen. I realized that I would never be your mother in any case; you didn't know who I was, you might not have believed or accepted me. Here, I had the chance to know the joy of that motherhood that had gotten away from me. By remaining in Morocco, I could finally be the mother I hadn't been, even if I never hid the truth from Noura afterwards…"

Her voice has become choked, almost inaudible. Marthe vacillates an instant. Then, just as before at the mention of my father and my birth, she stiffens and straightens up suddenly, wipes her eyes with the back of her hand and turns toward me. She looks me over coldly like the first time we met the day before yesterday. Furious at having let herself be overcome with emotion and at having shown it to me, she manages to re-establish a distance between us, as though we were two strangers, as though we had never said anything to one another. The baby, in her bassinet, grunts lightly.

Together, we both turn towards her, which dissipates the malaise a bit. The child falls asleep again right away. I ask:

"Noura? And Noura is not a coincidence either, if... It was you who sent her to me?"

Marthe takes the teapot, and more and more embarrassed, goes towards the kitchen. I do not move. I had not, so far, paid much attention to the oil painting and other watercolors covering the living room walls. Most of them represent Eastern landscapes: the desert, oases, a white house in front of the sea. From time to time, an animal appears—a lion or an elephant. A few faces are intermingled with the rest. One of them in particular sparks my interest. It is the portrait of a little girl, with olive skin and green-blue eyes, who could be around ten years old.

"You painted these?"

Delighted with this diversion, Marthe responds to me right away that indeed she found in this art form a way to forget reality while she held the paintbrush, to evacuate bad memories, to get away from the world when it's too ugly. She paints in a studio, a bit down the road on Mohamed-V Boulevard. For her, it is also the occasion for a certain social life. She needs that in order not to feel like a recluse in her narrow lodgings. Is the pretty child posing in front of palm trees in the setting sun Noura? Yes, it is. Marthe painted her portrait from a photo she had kept.

"It is very well done. I congratulate you, Marthe, if you allow me. But you didn't answer my question: You sent Noura? She was remote-controlled to me by you?"

Marthe is given a start, ceases filling the teapot.

195

"No! Remote-controlled, no! Noura knows nothing. She knows nothing of anything I have just told you. And fortunately."

This response, which seems sincere to me, calms me. If it were the case that, in addition to everything else, Noura would have been acting since the beginning, I could not have borne it. Marthe continues:
"But of course, your meeting… was not pure chance. Yes, I managed for your paths to cross. I thought, I hoped, that you would hit it off. And I imagined that if you got together, well… that would bring me closer to you too."

Thus, since I had acquired some renown, thanks to Rodrigo Chemicals, Marthe could follow the evolution of my career and my private life through the newspapers. She did not want to reveal herself, but she dreamed of knowing more about me. Having read about a competition I had organized on behalf of Rodrigo Chemicals, she convinced Noura to participate. It was a musical composition competition, which Rodrigo Chemicals had established as a community engagement initiative. Rodrigo Chemicals intended to produce an album with 12 original songs whose theme would be childhood. The profits would go towards research on childhood leukemia. Participants had to compose and perform joyous and tender songs, which would please children. It was the occasion for the firm to show its social engagement and to improve its brand image with the public. The success of this initiative vastly exceeded expectations, and a blessed period for Rodrigo Chemicals followed. The awards ceremony allowed me to meet Noura, who had come in third place for an Oriental melody sung in French, entitled *Terre de sable*, land of sand. Marthe's plan had worked. The meeting between the woman she had raised and the man she knew was her son happened as she had hoped. I was immediately hypnotized by the flamboyant gaze of the beautiful Moroccan. For a reason I don't understand, she was also seduced, it seems. Two days after having given her a kiss on the stage as I bestowed her medal under the hot light of projectors, I devoured the sweet skin of her entire body in a room in the Crillon, the preferred hotel of her king, Hassan II. Three months later, we were living together. Apparently, Noura had a more pronounced taste for eating and drinking well, lounging, the good life, than for artistic creation. She quickly gave up her musical ambitions to content herself with a sumptuous and peaceful existence with me, which fulfilled me, too. We loved each other. Her adoptive mother was my biological mother and we had no idea. Marthe knew it. Every time Noura called her, wrote her to give her an update, she spoke of me, of our life as a couple and that of the firm. Marthe was with us by proxy. If there had not been the suspicion of insider trading around the AIDOS study, the years could have gone by without Marthe, whom I would have met eventually, ever having to tell me the truth. The rue des Rosiers attack, David's investigation, and that false accusation of insider trading would decide things otherwise.

Here I am in Marthe's living room, the sun now in my eyes, already covered in sweat in this mid-morning. The little girl wakes up for good this time, she needs water. Marthe was warned. In this heat, Anissa has to be hydrated regularly. The grandmother goes to fill a bottle with cool, but not too cold, water, then walks towards the child, takes her in her arms and gives her the bottle to drink. Her movements are precise and confident. This is not her first try. I observe her without moving. The baby purrs as she swallows. I become lost in thought.

I don't know how much time I spend thinking dreamily of all I have learned, musing, recalling the happy days interspersed with moments of doubt, but suddenly, I return to reality. What is Noura doing? When will we hear from her? Will she manage to gain Loïc's trust, or will he, on the contrary, manage to trick her? And what murky role did he really play in this affair? I think out loud:

"Since taking our revenge on Cuvelier, Loïc and I have been inseparable. I am not naturally very sociable, very engaging, and even if, by necessity, I have developed relations in society, they have hardly ever turned into a real friendship. I think I can say that, until I met Jawad, Loïc was my only friend. Our closeness was extraordinary. It's impossible that he wove such a plot against me. I can't imagine it."

Marthe, as she continues to give the baby water to drink, observes me during my tirade. She seems sorry for me.
A week has passed since Noura left us the baby. Marthe and I take turns taking care of her, giving her food and cuddles. A little awkward in the first three days, I already feel more adept. I am feeding the baby when the telephone rings. Marthe, who had been drinking tea and munching on *cornes de gazelle* that Ahmed, her favorite grocer, affectionately made for her, springs up. I accompanied Marthe to Ahmed's store two or three times. The man is not exactly young, but dynamic, warm, charming. He has an immaculately white mustache, always has a smile which reveals gold crowns covering two incisor teeth, and is always wearing his blue coat ornamented with many pens and pencils stuck in a pocket like so many decorations on his chest. He offers multiple friendly words to Marthe, in French, in Arab, sometimes even mixing in a few words in Hebrew or Yiddish. Marthe blushes, simpers, tell him to be quiet, not to say so many silly things, and to serve her, for goodness' sake! Then she eggs him on, bursts out laughing, takes a pack of salt, a bottle of olive oil, always forgets the flour or the eggs that she will return for the next day. Ahmed is a single man. He traveled around a bit in Morocco and North Africa, in Spain, and even in France, before settling in Casablanca a

few years ago. With his voice, his accent from everywhere and nowhere at once, his expressive gestures, he amuses the crowd and seduces Marthe. She who has not known love for a long time, perhaps since the adventure with my father, would indeed be tempted by a last idyll before the coming arrival of old age. But time is passing, everything rushed, she is busy with her wish to find out who her sister's assassins were, and preoccupied with my fate. She will probably not have the time to frolic around with Ahmed. So she contents herself with imagining herself strolling with him hand in hand, gazing at the sea, taking pleasure in the flattering attention her grocer gives her on her daily trip to his store.

While Anissa suckles avidly, Marthe rushes to the phone. Noura is on the line, I hear her voice, from afar, through the receiver. Despite her emotion, my mother listens to Noura and responds to her calmly and assuredly. The conversation is quite long, maybe fifteen minutes, and dense. After hanging up, Marthe explains the situation to me. Noura has gotten in touch with Loïc. She was even surprised by his warm reception. He seemed happy to hear her voice on the phone, and spontaneously proposed to her to meet him at his house. She went to meet him in his apartment on avenue Mozart, in the 16th arrondissement, on the fifth floor of a superb Haussmannian building in stone, in which the verdure of plane trees seems to come in through all the windows. Loïc lives comfortably in this enchanting place with his wife and their two sons, ten and eight years old. The older son practices piano two hours a day on a Bösendorfer baby grand piano with a delicate yet powerful sound. It would seem that the neighbors don't complain, since the kid is endowed with exceptional talent. He charmed Noura with his interpretation of Mozart's variations on *Ah! Vous dirais-je, maman.* And his mother swooned over him. Blond with very blue eyes and diaphanous skin, the little musician's physique corresponds in every point to the old ideal of the Reich. It could be that

Noura made this observation because she knew Loïc's origins and my story. She had never had such thoughts before on meeting blond, blue-eyed children. But the young prodigy also has a brother with 'mongolism,' or Down syndrome as one says nowadays, a very cute boy as it happens, but whose parents are embarrassed to introduce to visitors. He has a special nanny: she keeps watch to contain his uncontrolled affective excesses, which could bother strangers. After Loïc grilled Noura for two whole hours about what she might know about me, he let her leave, but invited her to dinner the next day. He is burning to know what happened to me, how I finally escaped from the police, if I am still alive, where I am. He has become interim CEO of Rodrigo Chemicals, and he feigns to be waiting impatiently for my return to head of the company. Noura thinks he is lying. Loïc is no doubt very worried by the idea that I could come back and talk. She returned the following day. It was not really a dinner, but rather a society cocktail party bringing together around twenty people. Two or three senior executives from Rodrigo Chemicals, two politicians, a writer, two bankers, three lawyers, doctors... It was difficult to tell what brought this Areopagus together, and how Loïc had, over time, become close with them. Noura had the surprise of running into a dignitary of the Moroccan monarchy, on vacation in Paris. He told her that he had studied in France, at Polytechnique, as he deemed it necessary to specify. An oil specialist, he explained to her in detail the reasons for the spectacular fall in the barrel since the beginning of the year. According to him, the price drop literally dried out the USSR, which is short of foreign currency, with the result that Mikhail Gorbachev was obligated to launch his ambitious reform program called Perestroika. The Soviet Union no longer resembles its former self. The secretary general of the Party grants liberties the population never even suspected could exist. The consequences of the Chernobyl disaster, last April, also played a role. The country needs international aide and transparency. That's the famous Glasnost.

I wonder if we are not departing a bit from the subject at hand. Marthe rebuffs me dryly. Noura is precise. She leaves nothing to chance. And when she wants something, she gets it. She does not neglect a single detail, that is how she always arrives at her purpose. If I have not always understood that, then I don't know her. And if I hope to arrive at results thanks to her intervention, I have to trust her.

The Noura I loved was not this resolute, willful, and persevering woman whom Marthe describes to me. I visualize again our happy days, our languid afternoons, our long nights of love, our carless trips, our vacations spent half-naked under palm trees. Noura was nothing but lightness and insouciance, and that is what made her so seductive. Marthe continues:

"Noura is friends with this Moroccan who also has connections with French senior civil servants, his former classmates. Through him, she hopes to find out a bit more about the investigation about you and about Loïc's real role."

I am not convinced. I ponder.

"So Loïc still lives on avenue Mozart... I remember the day we visited the apartment together. That was almost ten years ago. Rodrigo Chemicals began to make serious profits. We had developed a new product, a sleeping pill with a quite short half-life in the organism so that the soporific effects dissipated completely on awakening. The miracle pill saw worldwide success. Money was flowing in, we were hardly thirty years old and we were already becoming very rich. Loïc was a womanizer. His physique and his wallet opened the doors to numerous bedrooms. He wound up becoming infatuated with a woman a bit older than him, who worked for a prestigious real estate agency. She decided to get him to buy this exceptional property. Loïc had consulted me, as was his wont before making a major decision. I had accompanied him for the visit and I confirmed his choice. He had barely signed when the girl packed her bags and left, and we never saw her again…"

Having emptied her bottle, Anissa has fallen asleep in my arms while Marthe and I chat. I put her back in her bassinet. As I do so, I suddenly understand what I knew already but had never fully realized. This is my child. Will I be able to see her again when it's all over? Will I be able to raise her serenely one day? And if I cannot prove my innocence, if I am accused finally of the murder of the two cops in Golfech, if I have to spend twenty years in prison, then she will grow up far from her father… she will never know me. Does Noura herself now wish to live with another man?

"Do you know who was with Noura the other day, at the Hôtel Suisse bar?"

Marthe smiles at me, approaches, and takes my hand again.

"Don't worry… That was her brother. Well, her half-brother, the one Azis M'Barek had officially with his first wife. Noura has not gotten together with another man since you fled. She still loves you, like the first day. She is very mad at you, that's certain, but you will get her back."

At this promise, I break out in joy and grasp Marthe in my arms. But I will quickly be disillusioned. Marthe pulls away and says:

"That's not the problem, Rodrigo. You will win your fiancée back in good time if you manage to get yourself out of this tight spot. I spoke with David on the telephone last night, while you were out getting milk. I was very afraid that you wouldn't come back... I didn't say anything to you in order to avoid worrying you, but..."

"Why?"

"I feared that you had already been arrested. David told me that the French police had figured out, no one knows how, that you had managed to flee to Morocco. The authorities here have promised France their entire cooperation, in other words to use all means possible to find you and to extradite you. You are now in danger the moment you stick your nose out the door. They have dozens of photos of you, of Noura, and your fingerprints. Luckily, you are still more or less unrecognizable with you hair and your beard. I am going to get you clothes, a white djellaba and a chechia to cover your head. But you must now be very careful whenever you are in public. The best thing is not to go out at all. I don't trust my neighbors either. They've noticed that I'm hosting someone and they are gossiping, I can tell. They will certainly mull it over and they will suspect that you're not in an ordinary situation. If just one of them chats with a cop, we're screwed. You're screwed. I'm sorry, Rodrigo, but..."

She's sorry. Not as much as I am! I get it. I leap up, as though there weren't a minute to lose, as though I had to leave this place immediately. Marthe stops me.

"You have to leave, okay. But wait until I have the time to bring you your Moroccan clothing. In traditional dress and a cap, you will be unrecognizable. I will not be long, I will be back in less than an hour with what you need."

When the door shuts as Marthe says "Be right back," I know already that I will not see her again soon. Perhaps never. I don't intend to wait until her return, contrary to her recommendations. I would rather get going without any delay, to avoid the torture of goodbyes. In just a few days I have become attached to Marthe, and if I cannot say that I have a son's feelings for her, I know that, for her part, she now loves me like a mother. The rites of separation would be heartbreaking for her, which she would try as she could to hide, but which I would sense. And I would leave her with, in my mind, the image of her despair, of that old hand that would be shaking sadly. I do not want to go through that moment. I am leaving. I go towards the baby. She is sleeping with her fists clenched, moving a leg or a hand, suddenly now and then, in a reflex. I hesitate to take her, to bring her with me, for I may never see her again either. What if I took her away with me? I believe that I began moving towards her. I readied myself to grab the baby, before reconsidering. Am I a monster?

How could I have dreamed of tearing this child from her grandmother's arms and especially from her mother's, when she returns?

I quickly chase these black ideas from my mind and I flee, abandoning the baby. Marthe will not take long to return and to take care of her, in any case.

At times on foot, at times hitchhiking, traveling between the chickens and the sheep, at times standing next to the detached pieces of a motor or the carcass of a washing machine, I return to Aïn Sebaâ. Fatima and Jawad, at the threshold of their house, welcome me with cries of joy that draw the whole neighborhood. The locals, my pals for the most part, gather around us. We hug, each giving a bigger hug than the other, and then we share a giant couscous.

A week has passed since I have returned to the village. I asked Jawad to alert David that I was back in Aïn Sabaâ. That way, the cop will be able to find me if something new comes up and... I really hope that it will. He will also tell Marthe and Roucaud that my hideout is secure, without telling them exactly where I am, of course. Jawad sent my message and brought me one back in return. Noura seems to have obtained information, both from Loïc and from the Moroccan dignitary with whom she has struck up a bit of a friendship. The high-ranking civil servant was able to obtain access to part of my file thanks to the minister of the Interior, a personal friend. From the beginning, there was some doubt about my real guilt in the insider trading scandal. However, all the pieces of information that could exonerate me were ruled out, with the result that the investigation was conducted exclusively against me. I was the ideal guilty person. In naming me, they would offer to France the expiatory sacrifice for astronomical unemployment and for the fact that "cash is king," at the same time that they put the cuffs on a guy suspected, for a long time, of far-right activism. A way to advance on the rue des Rosiers investigation, which had been spinning its wheels for too long. The government spooks assumed that I financed tons of not very frequentable people, from former collaborators hiding out here and there, to obscure Neo-Nazi and terrorist groups. Apparently, the minister of the Interior gives out information with relative ease, content as he is to undermine his predecessor's work. Whatever the case may be, the police as well as the other services did not look into the past of Loïc, whom nobody was interested in. They were beclouded by Rodrigo Ganos, even though passing time and the change in government put distance between that file and the most urgent concerns.

That is not the case for Loïc, who went into action! Convinced, with reason, that Noura has kept in touch with me this year, and that she might know where I am, he saw her again several times, hoping to extract new information and trying to convince her of my guilt. Doing so, he set a trap for himself: he revealed the troubling ambiguity of his role. He told her that he had alerted me about the cardiac sign that had appeared in the AIDOS study, which had led me to sell my shares before that information was official and widely known. Noura listened to his story attentively and did not contradict him. Loïc got mixed up in his lamentations, regrets, and tears. He was sorry to have to tell her about the blameworthy behavior of her fiancé, but he unfortunately had to tell her the truth, just as he had been obligated to tell the Stock Markets Commission when the investigator had interrogated him, then the police.

What should be done? He would never have believed that I would react in that way when he called me to tell me about the problem. Moreover, he couldn't understand how a guy as rich as me could have yielded to that kind of temptation, for a trifling amount of money, ultimately, what you think about it, compared to my total financial worth. I was his only friend and I would remain so forever, He did not feel he had betrayed me, but had only told the truth, which was both somber and simple. However, if they found me, he would testify to my probity up until that sad event and he would try to burnish my image as favorably as possible in order to attenuate, to the greatest possible extent, the judiciary sanctions threatening me. He hoped, in any case, that I was innocent of the murder of the two cops in Golfech and of the third, who had disappeared also.

Luckily for me, Noura didn't believe a word of this bilious and hypocritical tale, which even, on the contrary, reinforced her trust in me. She knew that Loïc was lying, because he made at least two mistakes. First, he forgot that at the moment of the AIDOS affair, Noura and I were living together. Perhaps he doesn't suspect that she has the memory of an elephant and that she retains dates and times with the precision of the director of a Swiss train station. She very well remembers the call from Loïc telling me the bad news, she remembers my discomfited face. In fact, just as she remembers the evening of the telephone call, she knows very well that Loïc's announcement had followed several days when I was selling my Rodrigo shares. I had indeed informed him of the sale of a part of my capital, showing him the catalogue of Riva boats that we could now order thanks to this little influx of fresh liquidity. We had also spent a long while speaking about the beachside villas I could buy. Noura was exulting in joy. She had flown into my arms, we had emptied a bottle of champagne while watching the sun set on Trocadéro, and then we slipped under our sheets. We then had a candlelit dinner and knocked back, this time, a bottle of Mersault. Still quite tipsy, we had jumped into the convertible and drove with the top down along the Seine. We braked at the approach of flashing lights, which ultimately didn't stop behind us. Drunk with wine and happiness, we had lied down again naked, side by side, and we had slept until the middle of the following day. Noura would remember forever the date of this memory, and she can have no doubt about it: these events preceded by several days the terrible call from Loïc, since, after the news, I no longer had the heart to laugh, nor to dream, nor to act crazy at the wheel of my sports car. So she knows that Loïc is lying on this first point. Next, regarding Golfech, Loïc can only have made the connection with me thanks to confidential information. For since the sudden disappearance of the two policemen started making noise, the nuclear power station has never been mentioned in the press. The location of my torture was not made known, and only the cops, only certain cops to tell the truth, know those sinister basements where no one leaves on their own two feet, where the only right you have is to die to shorten your suffering. If Loïc has heard of this place, that means he is informed, very well-informed even, by somebody. There's a rat on the inside, with whom he is in cahoots and who is giving him information.

We are making progress. We can now be certain that Loïc is working against me, and no doubt has been since the beginning. Who knows if he even set up the whole affair as a trap for me? But we are missing concrete elements that could exonerate me. We are merely convinced that Loïc is indeed the Judas. But we cannot prove it. Loïc! What could have happened? I recall our youth in La Mennais, our first loves, our car jaunts, – we would sometimes find ourselves behind the wheel of patched-up cars on country roads – the beginning of Rodrigo Chemicals, the first medical and commercial successes, the mornings on the golf course speaking about nothing but putts, the green and drills, and also, from time to time, girls' asses. Between Loïc and me, it was more than friendship, it was a brotherhood that bordered on love. I loved him. "Because it was him, because it was me," as Montaigne said. And even if the abundant dividends that we received from the firm eventually gave my associate a nouveau riche air – an attitude that more than one person found exasperating and that made him seem haughty for some people, conceited for the more severe – our relationship, simple and strong, never suffered from that, our bond was never undermined in the least. Between us, we always shared the same schoolboy jokes, the same winks, the same secrets, and the same trust. Loïc cannot have betrayed me out of mere jealousy or greed. He has to have another motive. That's the motive that must be discovered.

The weeks pass and no acceptable hypothesis occurs to me. Every day, Jawad brings me French newspapers, which I dissect conscientiously. There are many articles about Coluche's death in a motorcycle accident. I read them with a certain chagrin. I really liked that comedian. Noura and I had gone to one of his shows. In my exile last winter, I had also heard of the creation of the food charity *Restaurants du Coeur,* and I had found the idea both kindhearted and compelling. On the pages devoted to the economy, they mentioned the continuation of the vertiginous drop of the oil barrel price, which went below the ten dollar mark in July. August is very calm. Debates about nuclear energy are intensifying following the Chernobyl catastrophe. Italy plans to organize a referendum on the issue. I regularly ask Jawad for news of David, but he tells me he hasn't heard from him either. A dull fear sets in gradually in me. Am I condemned to spend the rest of my life here in hiding, without being able to return one day to France, nor even to Argentina, without seeing Noura again, without having the means to defend myself and to prove my innocence? Even if Fatima does not speak my language, she guesses at my worries. She increases her thoughtful gestures for me. She who lives here in the most total destitution bends over backwards to relieve my suffering, makes me pastries, prepares me mint tea, instructs Jawad to fetch me cigarettes even before I fear being short of them. This woman dotes on me. Before, one day or another, my eyelids are closed for me and my body is thrown in a common grave or in a princely vault, before I leave this world for eternal rest, my last thoughts will be, I am sure of it, of this veiled, wrinkled, toothless woman of limitless devotion, this woman whose natural goodness bursts forth on her face marked by the years. In my heart, she will forever incarnate the symbol of charity, of self-sacrifice, of selflessness. For the moment, her presence at my side helps me to overcome my impatience and melancholy.

The summer is hot, but thanks to the ocean breeze, the atmosphere in Aïn Sebaâ remains breathable. When September comes, there is still no news. Suddenly, astonishment. On the 18th, I discover in the newspapers that, the day before, a new attack was committed in Paris, on rue de Rennes in the 6th arrondissement. A bomb exploded at

5:20pm in front of the Tati store. For the moment, the most likely lead is the Revolutionary Lebanese Armed Forces, a communist organization. I am, shockingly, relieved that people are not talking about the far right for once, nor of fascist groups. Whenever tragedy strikes, I now worry I will be accused. In reality, the press is not interested in me at all. A few days later, though, I read a short piece about me: the board of directors of Rodrigo Chemicals has officially taken cognizance of the death of its CEO and founder, Rodrigo Ganos, and has elected the co-founder, Loïc Martin, his right hand man since the beginning, to replace him. My heart skips a beat. I ask Jawad to do whatever he can to get in touch with David. This time, the joke has gone on for long enough, I want to return to France. Impressed by my determination, my young friend does everything possible to help me and brings me a telephone number that very evening. The next day at exactly one p.m., I will be able to call David. Jawad tells me the name and the address of a telephone booth at the entrance to an old, closed down French movie theater, which was called Le Beaulieu, a concrete building, whose pediment covered in electric blue paint seems to have survived a devastating war.

Vegetation has grown around it, but I easily find the telephone. I dial the number. Before the end of the first ring, David picks up. Jawad told me that I would have to prove my identity by completing a phrase the first words of which the inspector would say, but which Jawad himself does not know. Rosenberg begins straightaway:
"You are the accumulating…?"
"Present."
I respond without missing a beat.
In a serious tone, David informs me that Marthe was arrested last week. She was right to mistrust her neighbors. Some of them noticed my presence in her home. One of them thought there was a remarkable resemblance of the hirsute tramp I

was with the shadowy Rodrigo Ganos. Marthe was taken away. David, embarrassed, adds:

"After what happened in Golfech, I am probably in no position to denounce the quite... muscular... methods of the cops from here... I am rather worried, but I trust Marthe. She will not have admitted to anything. Moreover, and that's all the better, she doesn't know where you are. We will organize your getaway. Roucaud is in the loop, that should help us. I will send someone to you, be ready."

"Tomorrow?"

"Yes, wait at Fatima's at eight pm. But you won't leave until a bit later, around ten at night. In the meantime, you're going to get a new look. They're looking for you with your beard and long hair. We're going to make you up and give you a new appearance before your departure."

David's voice is serious, calm, authoritative. Dripping with sweat in the booth heated by the still intense late summer sun, I feel that I don't have a say, don't have the freedom to change the plan concocted for me by the cop. Had I an objection, he wouldn't give me permission to formulate it. As it happens, I don't have one. I want to return to France, clear my name, get back what belongs to me and take my revenge on those who fomented this plot against me. I will miss Fatima and Jawad immensely, as well as the five calls to prayer of the muezzin, the mint tea, the couscous, the pastilla and... above all, Marthe. It is to be feared that I will never be able to hug my real mother again. I regret that, but, contrary to what she doubtless feels for me, I do not yet have a filial feeling for her. I have a hard time forgiving her for not having come to meet me in Brest, despite her explanations. Try as I might to be reasonable, to dwell on her justification, I cannot accept that she abandoned me a second time, that

211

she left me defenseless in the hands of Father Cuvelier. I can feel that, once I am back in Paris, I will miss her. I will miss her tender voice, but I also believe that I will never completely forgive her. Maybe, after all, it is better that we never see each other again. What I am above all worried about is Noura's reaction. Will she agree to come back to me with our daughter Anissa and to start up again where we left off? I do not contradict David, who asks me finally:

"Is everything clear for you? You have any questions?"
"I have several, yes…"
"You can ask two. I will hang up in a little over a minute."

In the rush he imposes on me, I stammer:
"What is the guy's name who will come tomorrow, how will I recognize him? And where I am going in France?"

"Good questions! The person coming tomorrow is easy to recognize, you will have no doubt. It's Roucaud himself, simply. As for the return trip… it will be faster than the departure. You will not go back through Bordeaux, you are taking the plane to Toulouse. The Major will accompany you and will give you your false papers. Your flight is the day after tomorrow at ten in the morning. The night before, you will spend a short night of rest in a little hotel on the airport road. You don't need to know any more at this stage."

"Thanks, David. And…and you? Where are you? What will become of you?"
"If anyone asks you, you can tell them that you haven't the slightest idea."

And he hangs up. I rush outside for a breath of somewhat fresher air. I breathe the aroma of jasmine, I hear the echo of the surf in the distance, I admire one last time the azure sky veiled by the hot haze. I love this country that welcomed me in my exile. The summer months enveloped in damp heat reminded me of the happy days of Buenos Aires. On the other hand, the brotherhood of those who supported me brings to mind no memory. I hadn't known that before, this simple brotherhood. And I am already aware that I will never have it again. Tomorrow evening, I will leave Aïn Sebaâ with a heavy heart.

Major Roucaud arrives at Fatima's home at exactly eight p.m., and enters our abode with his usual cowboy saunter. He greets my hosts with a nod and a barely audible "good evening." He addresses me only with onomatopoeia or short commands: "Sit down! Get undressed! Put on these clothes! Bend your head back, bend it forward!" He shaves my beard and my head and decks me out in a wavy, ash blond wig. He colors my eyebrows and makes my nose broader. He takes a photo of me with a Polaroid camera, cuts the picture into the required format, and inserts it with confounding dexterity into the notches of a passport in the name of Bruno Cochet, born on August 24, 1946, in Barcelona, in case the slight Spanish accent I still have raises the suspicions of a too-scrupulous border agent. It is time to go. Jawad hugs me, squeezes the breath out of me. His eyes are red. He doesn't say a word. I don't have the strength to speak, either. In the corner, Fatima waves goodbye. We have always maintained physical distance, she and I, out of a sense of decency. We are not going to change that today. I answer her with a similar gesture. I know that I will probably never see these two beings again, whom I have cherished so much, and who have given me so much. All the thanks I leave them is my unwavering affection. The gendarme in civilian clothes has already put away his materials and is impatient:

"We have to go, Bruno."
I am not used to the name yet. I look around the room for a moment before realizing that he is speaking to me. I resign myself to it:
"Let's go."
I turn my back on Fatima, on Jawad, on Aïn Sebaâ, forever. A sand-colored Mercedes 280 SE is waiting for us at the entrance to the shantytown. We drive calmly towards the Mohamed-V Airport, the windows open. Roucaud does not say a word on the drive. We don't run into the law, and we stop for the night in a little run-down hotel, just next to the

airport. We don't run into anyone. My guardian angel authorizes me to take off my wig and my artificial nose. He will put them back in place when we wake up, at six in the morning.

I have a terribly hard time finding troubled sleep. I manage to dose off only for an hour or two. I am ready before the major even knocks on my door. He puts my makeup on again and we leave. The police checks upon boarding are a mere formality. A quick glance by the guy examining my passport and his coworker, and here we are seated in row 2, seats A and C, in the Boeing 737 that will bring us back to France. Already, the hostess is offering me a glass of champagne. Decidedly, David has connections, I tell myself, while the gendarme refuses all alcohol and opts for a Perrier. Less than three hours later, we land with no problem on the Toulouse-Blagnac runway. Roucaud's car awaits us in the parking lot. We don't have any baggage, and leave the airport of *la ville Rose,* to go to Beaumont-de-Lomagne. On the second floor of a building with a view of the central market is a small lodging in which some clothes to change into have been left. Roucaud tells me to go into this little apartment that he puts at my disposal and not to move until he gives me a sign, in a few days at the most, he promises. The place, a cramped two-room apartment, is not totally charmless, despite its minimal furnishings.

A room facing the inner courtyard is equipped with a single bed. The kitchen-living room overlooks the square through a large multi-paned window. The exposed beams of the ceiling, which is hardly more than six feet high, confer to the space a certain cachet that the gray Formica cabinet does not completely ruin. The kitchenette is composed of an aluminum sink, a small refrigerator, and a small stove with an oven and two electric burners. On the wall, there are two cabinets holding some dishes and a few pots. It's not enormous luxury, but not misery either. I have been left pasta, meat, rice, several tins of vegetables, milk and fruit in the fridge. I am in need of almost nothing, if not company. But from an alimentary point of view, I can hold out one or two weeks without needing to go out for any reason. I also notice, near the cabinet, a television sitting on a pedestal table. That will help me to kill time and to stay up to date with world news.

I did not yet imagine how many long months I would spend stuck in here, confined between these walls, waiting, but waiting for what?

The major did not keep his word. More than a week after arriving, he has still not given me a sign of life. An unknown person knocked on my door, on the sixth day, to resupply me. He brought me a variety of provisions and was not very talkative. He left as he came. A dial phone sits on top of the tv. It taunts me all day. I have made sure that it is indeed connected to the network and that you hear a tone in the earpiece when you pick up. No doubt that this telephone would ring if I had a call. Yet it, too, remains silent. Neither Roucaud, nor David, nor even Noura try to reach me. On the fifteenth day, I am like a lion in a cage. I have seen all the tv programs, the shows, the music variety show *La Chance aux Chansons,* the tv series, the 1 o'clock and 8 o'clock news, on TF1 and Antenne 2, sometimes even a clear program on Canal+, like the *Top 50*. While listening to the hit of the moment, I almost forget my sad fate.

Almost two months pass in this way. They no longer speak about me on tv or on the radio, nor of the rue des Rosiers, never of Rodrigo Chemicals, until November 7th, twenty-six years to the day after the death of my parents in Argentina. On this evening, one scoop follows another: the German intelligence service is said to have informed Chirac that an attempted attack on an Israeli plane was not committed by Syria, but rather by the Israeli intelligence service itself. It makes no sense. Georges Ibrahim Abdallah, the Lebanese

Communist militant, defended by Jacques Vergès, is reported to have been sent to a special assize court. They move on with no transition to progress in medicine: it is now possible to insert a vascular endoprosthesis into the coronary arteries of patients at risk for a heart attack, a sort of metallic spring making it possible to avoid stenosis. The journalist is astonished. But just as I am about to change the channel, the presenter says suddenly, just before signing off:

"We have just learned of the arrest of Loïc Martin at his home, in the 16th arrondissement in Paris. The current CEO of the pharmaceutical company Rodrigo Chemicals had replaced the founder, Rodrigo Ganos, last September. We don't have any details for the time being on the reasons for the possible charges against Martin. But right away, the weather…"

My mouth is wide open. I go through the five television channels, in search of further information, a commentary, an allusion, but nothing. They speak about nothing but the relations of England with Israel, about stability in the region, about the expected reaction of François Mitterand. I turn on the radio: Europe 1, RTL, the free radio stations… Nothing. Loïc's arrest hardly interests the public. It is not taken up again. I eat a bite, without any appetite. After another troubled night, I turn back on the tv and radio. I do not yet dare to go into the street, complying with the instructions of the gendarme who has still not given me a sign of life; nor has David or anyone else for that matter. I am starting to wonder if they've imposed on me a kind of mental torture, condemning me not only to remained confined *ad nutum* in this small apartment, but also – and this is far worse – making me my own jailer. There are no chains, no locks, no barriers between the outside world and me. I am the only one standing in the way, held fast by my voluntary servitude. I have neither the audacity nor the unconscious courage of

Monsieur Seguin's goat, I am afraid of the wolves waiting for me outside. I remain here, shut away, attentive to the slightest sound, a step in the stairway, a sound of footsteps, the humming of a motor in the street, hoping that Roucaud, or the cop, will finally come knocking on my door. A new day thus comes to a close in the most complete silence. At eight p.m., I put on channel five. The star journalist discusses current events in the Middle East, but all of a sudden, after ten minutes of the news, he continues:

"Let's return now to a mysterious affair: the disappearance, in Paris, over a month ago, of a young Moroccan woman whose trace has been completely lost. Noura M'Barek has given no sign of life to her loved ones since October 6th. The investigation begun several weeks ago led to a surprising and stunning arrest yesterday morning. The police came to the very chic avenue Mozart, in the 16th arrondissement in the capital, to arrest Loïc Martin, the CEO of Rodrigo Chemicals, that pharmaceutical company that was widely talked about eighteen months ago, you'll recall, when its founder Rodrigo Ganos was accused of insider trading, before disappearing. Ganos has still not been found to this day. Considered to be gone forever by the board of directors of Rodrigo Chemicals, he was replaced by Loïc Martin at the head of the business, but, of course, without the consent of the founder himself! So, what happened between Martin and Noura M'Barek, the latter being no other than the former partner of Rodrigo Ganos? That is what our investigators have tried to find out."

There follows a long report retracing my trajectory to the head of Rodrigo Chemicals: from its first successes, through magazine covers, the articles in *Paris Match* showing me at the wheel of a sports car, or in a white lab coat, hygiene cap on my head, in one of my factories, all interspersed with short extracts of interviews given to newspapers or short tv appearances. Filmed images, of a rather low quality, show me giving the award to Noura for her single *Terre de Sable*. The story ends with a close-up shot of the face of the woman who has disappeared. On the set, the presenter then mentions again that I am still at large, and the possible – probable – link between the two affairs, the charge against me and the disappearance of the girl eighteen months later.

I didn't expect that! So Noura has been missing for thirty days and no one told me anything. I think again of Marthe, fallen into the clutches of the police in Casablanca. What is happening to Anissa? Who has taken care of the baby since Marthe has been locked in a secret place from which no one knows if she will ever get out? Why didn't David or Roucaud inform me, why did they hide Noura's worrying disappearance from me? Short of breath, I pace back and forth. I cannot stay here, quiet, immobile, inactive. I can no longer continue to wait. I must react. I can no longer allow myself to be carried along by events, like a dead leaf floating on the surface of a river, tossed about by the waves, following the course of the water, unable to move on its own. I must take back control over my destiny. It is already ten at night and fog envelopes the Beaumont night in opaque gray. All is calm and perfectly quiet. It's perhaps an opportune moment to leave, to slip away without being recognized, find a train station, somewhere, take a train for Paris, go into the Rodrigo offices, try to glean information, indications, go back to my apartment, too, if possible, without being able to say what I could find there. The ideas jostle around incoherently in my head. I refuse to believe in Noura's disappearance. She must be hiding somewhere. I will find her. In a cabinet, I grab a bag. I throw in the few clothes I have, a razor, a toothbrush. My makeshift bundle is ready when, the moment I am about to leave, I hope for forever, the telephone rings, for the first time in the fifty days I have spent in this hole. I hesitate. Pick up or leave before Roucaud or Rosenberg can convince me to stay? But what if it is neither of them? What if, on the line, someone had crucial information to give me? My curiosity wins out: I retrace my steps and pick up the phone.

"You are the accumulating present."

It is a woman's voice, perhaps deformed or camouflaged by a handkerchief, but which I recognize right away: it's Marthe. The coded message that she enunciated confirms it. I am happy to know she is free and alive! Expressing herself in a discreet language, she continues:

"The little one is well. She's returned to her grandfather and is in good hands."

"Very good. I was worried. And her mother?"

"I have no news."

She observes a short silence, which I do not break." In a serious voice, she adds:

"Ultimately, when you think about it: August or November, what does it matter? Anne died on that day. I will be there, at the hour of her death."

She hangs up. Our conversation lasted hardly thirty seconds, not long enough to locate the call. I repeat to myself her last words, trying to decipher their meaning. "August or November, what does it matter? Anne died on that day." Anne, her sister, was shot on rue des Rosiers, during a terror attack. The murder took place on August 9th, at one fifteen in the afternoon. "August or November, what does it matter?" Marthe could be referring to November 9th. "At the hour of her death": so she will be there at one fifteen in the afternoon. November 9th, the day after tomorrow, at one-fifteen in the afternoon, she will be waiting for me in the Jo Goldenberg restaurant in Paris. That is what I believe I understand. All I have to do is find a way to return to the capital. I open the wallet that Roucaud left me. It is full of false papers in the name of Bruno Cochet: identity card, driver's license, and even a voter's card. Not having used it until now, it hadn't occurred to me to look through the wallet. It has over five hundred francs, in small bills. Divine surprise. I begin to explain to myself the behavior of the cop and the gendarme: if they haven't given me a sign of life, that is because they expected me to decide to run away on my own. Without encouraging me to do so, they gave me the means. I rush outside. When I come hurtling into the street, I breathe in with all my strength. I haven't gone outside in over a month and a half. I walk randomly and find a bus stop. A little poster indicates the schedule. Tomorrow morning at seven fifty, a bus can take me to Montauban in forty-five minutes. From there, I will take a train to Paris. It's much easier than I had thought, after all. I realize all of a sudden that I have forgotten to put on my wig and my false nose. I go home as quickly as possible. After a few short hours of sleep, I disguise myself again and leave in the early morning.

The trip takes place without any difficulty, without any identity-check, without any problem. At the Montauban train station, I calmly bought a second-class ticket in a Corail train that took me to Gare d'Austerlitz in Paris, in an incalculable number of hours, which I spent combing through the many newspapers I bought before my departure. On Rodrigo Chemicals, on me, on Loïc, on Noura, I read only banalities, summaries of summaries. Here and there, there is an error about dates, places, or names. Nothing essential, nothing interesting, no element that could help me untangle the threads of the plot against me since the beginning, nor to guess why Noura has suddenly disappeared. Except perhaps one piece of information. A paraphrase in an article, which drew my attention, and which I re-read several times without, however, realizing in the moment its importance. I put the rag down and I put my nose against the window. For a long time, I watched the landscapes of the French heartland pass by, which in reality I barely knew. I had not left La Mennais very much; I did not often frequent the Breton woods or the beech tree forests that surrounded us. Then, studying and rare nighttime trips to the capital with Loïc were my only occupations. Then the rise of Rodrigo Chemicals, the lightning trips to our labs in the countryside, didn't give me the time to stop for long in Sologne, Berry, or in Beauce. I did not have the chance, nor, really, the desire, to see the Dordogne valleys, or the Northern plains, or the volcanoes in Auvergne. So yesterday, I took my time observing, with interest, the rural and varied panorama that this train ride offered me, the belabored and smoking fields surrounded with heath, the little hamlets lost in fog, the Scots firs, still green and competing with the orange of the few leaves left on the birch and oak trees. I started daydreaming before these colorful and picturesque tableaus, when there ripened in my mind that strange notation in a little sidebar in *Le Monde:* "the police also searched Loïc Martin's luxurious property in the Chevreuse Valley, not far from Rambouillet…" Loïc had never spoken to me of this famous "property." He had never expressed the intention of acquiring a secondary residence, nor had he mentioned any inheritance. We spent our Sunday mornings playing golf, sometimes Saturdays too. If he had a country house, I would have known! Is it possible that he bought this place after my departure from France a little over a year ago? That's not impossible, but what is most likely is that he hid from me the existence of this property. Throughout the end of the ride, I asked myself why. I could find the answer neither in the rush of prairies, trees, and villages, nor that of the low-income housing blocks in the suburbs outside the city, nor in the sinister faces of my neighbors in the train car, nor in the orange imitation leather of the SNCF.

Once in Paris, I had enough left to pay for a room in a simple but comfortable-enough hotel. As this room had a view of the inner courtyard, there was no unpleasant noise and, against all expectations, the multiple torments from which I suffered did not prevent me from falling asleep. After a large dinner – an entrecote accompanied by scalloped potatoes, followed by an apple pie, all washed down with a modest but very drinkable Beaujolais – I slept eight hours straight, peacefully. At one in the afternoon, I sit down in the Jo Goldenberg restaurant. I wait. A little early, Marthe enters and heads straight to my table, as though she already knew where I was sitting. I am hungry again, but I don't know what to choose from the menu. I don't know the Jewish cuisine of Central Europe at all; I am not even sure I understand the description of the plates. Marthe is dressed up. She is wearing a long-sleeved navy blue dress, decorated with a brooch. Her foundation makeup gives her a rather good complexion, and partly hides her wrinkles. I regret her slightly gaudy red lipstick, but admire the way her hair is set. She has perhaps just left the hairdresser. She orders for both of us fish balls with farfel. I ask her about what I am dying to know:
"So they let you go?"

She shrugs her shoulders.

"I have been through a lot more than that, little dear. It wasn't very pleasant in the Moroccan jails, that's for sure, but I didn't speak. The cops who interrogated me had, how can I put it, persuasive methods! But I did not yield a single inch. They came to doubt that I know anything, I think. For whatever reason, they were finally obliged to free me. I think my phone is being tapped, I have maybe even been watched by the police since I arrived on French territory, but I am capable of losing them. Here, we are okay. I completely trust the staff, they won't denounce us."

"Let's hope so… Where is Noura?"

"What I told you on the telephone is true, I haven't heard from her. But I am certain she is alive."

Marthe's gaze loses itself in the restaurant's window. Outside, on the sidewalk, the tables and chairs are stored for the winter, carefully aligned and piled up along the wall. This is the sidewalk where Anne was killed. I respect Marthe's contemplation. She adds:

"When Anne died, I felt it. I did not need to turn on the radio. I did not know there was a terror attack. But at the exact hour of her death, the hour when those monsters short a burst of bullets, I felt a crushing tightness in my chest. The image of my sister came to me. I knew that it was over, that I would never see her again. Over the rest of the day, I spoke to no one, I did not want to have a confirmation of what was more than a feeling. Towards evening, the telephone rang for a long time; on the twentieth ring, I resigned myself to pick up. It was Didier Le Bellec, her husband, on the line, who unfortunately confirmed my intuition."

A veil of infinite sadness traverses her face and disappears just as quickly. A ray of sunlight now illuminates Marthe, which leads her to pull herself together and to return to our subject.

"If Noura were also lost, I believe I would have felt it in the same way. But it's not that impression that's the source of my certainty."
That reassures me. If I only had to trust the more or less magical instincts of Marthe to be sure Noura is alive, I would only have limited confidence. Fortunately, Marthe has other elements of information.

"Noura's disappearance was organized by David, with the goal of setting a trap for Loïc. And the poor devil jumped right into the trap!"
She smiles. I notice for the first time that, an upper molar is covered in a silver crown and that below, she is missing one. That observation leads me to think that Marthe had never really smiled at me during the brief periods when we have lived together. We have been traversed by many emotions in little time: hope, vexation, anger, worry, and regret. But we have never really laughed.

There was no reason to. This time, she seemed satisfied, as though fulfilled, happy, close to an ending that she had been waiting for, for a long time. She explains to me the plan that Rosenberg had imagined to trick Loïc and that worked better than expected. Noura continued the relation she had begun with Loïc, meeting, speaking, and having lunch together many times. Little by little, and with her characteristic finesse and subtlety, she led Loïc to believe that she knew where I was. She led him to believe that, lying low somewhere in the capital, I was preparing my return and my revenge. Soon, the past of Loïc's father would be brought to light and the parallel activities of the new CEO of Rodrigo would be revealed. Making herself more and more threatening, she finally insinuated that she was on my side. He went into a rage, protested against the slander, asserted that he had no kind of parallel activity. She referred to the financing of secret organizations and far right groups. He belched insults, was prepared to strike her. She fled under the stunned gaze of his wife, purposefully letting drop a piece of torn paper on which a Paris address was scribbled, including the floor and door number. It was the little room Noura was staying in. Loïc rushed there that very night with the intention of making her talk, and forced his way in. Noura had taken care to run off and disappear, of course. Loïc turned the place upside down, in search of a detail that would allow him to find me and no doubt to eliminate me, but he left emptyhanded. While Noura had already been gone for two weeks, David arranged for the police to learn of the existence of this place and about this visit. There were still clothes and personal effects of Noura's. But the cops also discovered Loïc's fingerprints, which he had left everywhere. A neighbor also told the police that he had seen a strange person enter the building, climb the stairs, and break his way into Noura's apartment. The silhouette he described corresponded indeed to Martin's. That is how Loïc stupidly fell into the trap and found himself accused of having kidnapped Noura.

Now, the question is where Noura is. Marthe doesn't have the slightest idea, but David assures her that she has not really disappeared. She is hiding somewhere. Loïc was freed after being held in custody. He is under house arrest, but in the absence of irrefutable proof, no charge has been placed against him and he was not held in preventative detention. However, in his rash act, he acknowledged his guilt. Yes, he plotted a blow against me to eliminate me; yes, he deliberately led people to believe that I had committed insider trading, and, yes, he organized secret financing. It's my turn, now. Shut up in his home, he must be in total panic. This is the moment to catch him.

A waiter brings us our steaming plates. He is wearing a kippa and offers me one, advising me to put it on. As I put it on

towards back of my head, Marthe breaks out in laughter. She stands up, making fun of me:
"Look at you, it's completely crooked!"
She walks behind me, readjusts it as best as possible, and sits down again, satisfied:
"There, you're less ridiculous. Now eat quickly, you don't have a moment to lose. Martin is backed into a corner."

But I feel like taking my time, savoring this moment as much as the farfel. I ask for wine. It is brought to me. We toast. Loïc, up against the wall, will be forced to admit his plotting to me. My reputation will soon be restored. The government will have to offer me its apologies, as will the media, the board of Rodrigo Chemicals, and all the people who turned their back on me, pretended not to know me, who had claimed to be my friends but who doubted my probity and proclaimed their constant mistrust. My revenge will be terrible. Then, Noura will come back. We will raise our daughter Anissa together, we will have other children. We will buy a house beside the sea, in Casablanca maybe. My joy is immense. I feel like taking Marthe in my arms, hugging her tightly... I hold myself back. I enjoy my fish balls without taking my eyes off of the woman who has proved to be my mother. If I listened to myself, I would almost forgive her the unpardonable, this deep wound that being abandoned by her left me. But time is of the essence, it is vital to force fate by confronting Loïc. I don't have any money to pay for my lunch. I pretend to look for bills in my pockets, standing up. Marthe grabs my arm.
"Let it go. Quick, get going, hurry."
I leave the restaurant without saying goodbye and I rush towards the Saint-Paul metro. Thirty minutes later, I am at Avenue Mozart, beneath the windows of Loïc's luxurious apartment. There is an entry code, which I don't know. I wait fifteen minutes before an old lady, a gray scarf on her head and Burberry's raincoat on her back, opens the door and lets

me into the building warily, even trying vainly to shut the door on me behind her. I pass in front of her, climb the majestic, red velvet-covered steps four at a time. Loïc will pay! When I reach the fourth floor landing and prepare to enter this apartment where I came to have dinner a few times when we were friends, I am full of a formidable energy, I am ready to move mountains: I will make Loïc give in, I will force him to admit his dastardly plan. He will not take to paradise the torture I underwent at Golfech because of him, the weeks of wandering before my arrest and the exile that followed, the months of solitude, and my infamy.

The door is wide open. There is a strange odor. I take a step in the vestibule. The hardwood floor creaks, breaking the deathly silence that seems to reign in all the rooms. Another step. The hallway opens onto the large living room. I see the low table on the Persian rug and, in the background, the pompous, forsaken Bösendorfer. I walk forward a little. I already feel less self-assured than a few seconds ago. In a voice that I wish were firmer, I call:
"Loïc? Loïc, it's me! I have to speak to you!"
Nothing. No response, not a sound. The living room is empty. I see an upturned lamp, magazines scattered near the piano. The stool is knocked over too. I turn towards the bedroom. I push open the door. Loïc's wife is lying on the bead.
"Oh, sorry, Nathalie! I… wanted to see Loïc."
I did not notice her total immobility. I did not noticed that her lungs did not rise. I did not notice the puddle of blood in which her neck lay. Only as I approached did I discover the sad reality: Nathalie, the traitor's wife, has just been killed. The odor of gunpower is still floating in the room. Behind me, a voice I know well says in a gloomy tone:
"It was Loïc who killed her. It is nearly certain. I arrived too late."

I turn around: David Rosenberg, his hands in his jean pockets, is holding his head sorrowfully.

David recommends I return to Beaumont right away. I protest. He insists: I should flee before I am investigated. I exclaim:

"Why would I be accused? I hardly knew Nathalie; we met at most on a few occasions, dinners at each other's homes, or cocktail parties in the city, before my escape. We had nothing to do with one another, we didn't really spend time together. Since my return to France, I haven't had the least contact with her. What's more, officially, I have not even returned. In any case, I had no reason to hold anything against her, even less to kill her. It's ridiculous."

"It's more complicated than you think. You are here, in front of her body, and you very well could have murdered her, who knows? As for me, I am not even capable of exonerating you. And I don't have any legal existence anymore, either. Take my advice: return to Beaumont for the moment. Loïc will not look for you there, for now, at least."

"Loïc? But I am looking for him!"

"I know. But for now, you are in danger. Go hide out, I'm telling you. You see what he's capable of?"

He nods at the lifeless body of the poor woman. The argument is not unconvincing, I have to admit. But I had not planned to return so quickly to the little hideout I had left to meet Marthe. I don't have a cent, I can't buy a train ticket. I tell David. He can't help me out, he doesn't have anything on him either. I would like to follow his advice, but before that, I have another question to ask him: what does this home in the Chevreuse Valley look like? I wonder if it's where we will find the missing piece in our puzzle. Does David now the address? Of course, he knows exactly where Loïc's property is. He has always known. He has known of its existence since Loïc acquired it over five years ago. Only now the area is full of police, it is almost impossible to access the house. In any case, we wouldn't discover anything interesting. When David became convinced that I was not involved in the rue des Rosiers affair, nor in insider trading, his suspicions were shifted onto Loïc and he investigated him. Did he maintain relations with former collaborators or partisans of sulfurous ideologies and Neo-Nazi networks like those who could be behind the attack? He searched meticulously. He found nothing. This home never hosted any terrorist. It never served as a secret command center, never facilitated the development of clandestine networks. No. It is much simpler than all that. Loïc used this country house to receive… his numerous mistresses!"

I am stupefied. Loïc? Mistresses? But who, how? And I, his best friend, I never suspected anything! I can't get over it. I wonder if David is playing another trick on me. He continues:
"That discovery is secondary. The more important one is this: the rue des Rosiers attack can certainly not be attributed to far-right cells, I have the strongest conviction of this. I have good reasons to believe that it was an action by the revolutionary Fatah-council, a radical Palestinian group seeking to destabilize Arafat. Thus, the Nazis couldn't have anything to do with it, no more than you, or even Loïc."
I'd like to believe it. But then what?
"Loïc isn't an ideologue. Not at all! You know him, you should know that. If he maintained contact with clandestine collaborators, it was out of thanks for what they did for him, out of loyalty to his father. Period. He is neither for nor against the Jews. Same for the communists, Arabs, or freemasons, he doesn't care! But he does have it out for you, on the contrary. Yes, he's the one who got you mixed up in that, he's the one who made up the false insider trading crime, he's the one who did everything so that you would be

suspected of financing terrorist groups, hoping that you would be liquidated. And he almost succeeded, I have to admit."

We are speaking, David and I, in the sinister gathering dusk, beside the remains of poor Nathalie, without paying the least attention to her. When I entered the room, I crossed myself, out of an old reflex from La Mennais. It is the only tribute we will have paid to the dead woman. Neither David nor I have the time or the intention to cede to emotion. I must admit that I don't really feel sorrow before the bloody corpse of this woman whom I don't know very well after all. I don't feel sadness. A malaise, rather, disgust, disquiet, but grief, not really. David, who has seen much else, is even more indifferent than I am.

"What you're telling me is that Loïc conspired against me, as we have imagined for a long time already, but that this affair ultimately has nothing to do with his past, nor with mine, nor even with unavowable friendships."

David takes me by the arm, and leads me out of the apartment.

"Come on, let's go, let's not stay here. The colleagues won't be long to show up. The shot must have been heard in the whole neighborhood."

I follow him docilely, annoyed. I would like to get to the end of the story of the affair.

"Huh? But why did he stab me in the back? Out of jealousy, is that it? Because he wanted to be head of Rodrigo Chemicals?"

David stares at me as though taken aback. If Roucaud had hypothesized this during my first interrogation, Rosenberg does not seem to have considered it at all. No, of course not, it has nothing to do with the flourishing company that Loïc and I founded and of which I held the reins. Loïc had a perfect niche, freed from the troubles tied to the responsibilities of being boss, and satisfied by our large dividends. He never envied my fate, and it was only begrudgingly that he accepted the position of president after my departure, on the insistence of the board. He could have done without that! No, he eliminated me for an entirely different reason, which David tells me he discovered, sort of by chance. We have now left the apartment and we are tiptoeing down the stairs, watching out for any inopportune visitors, before slipping away. We walk a few dozen yards on the sidewalk to reach David's car, an ordinary gray-green Golf, parked in front of the police station. Lighting a Gitane, he starts the car and says:

"I'll bring you back to Beaumont. We will have the whole ride to talk. I'll explain."

We go back up Avenue Mozart until La Muette. While Avenue Ingres would have taken us straight to the beltway boulevard, then to the A10 highway that would need to take to reach Bordeaux and finally Tarn-et-Garonne, David turns right onto Avenue Raphaël. At number 34, he stops in front of a modern and fancy building. Pointing up at the sixth floor, he says:

"Up there is where René Bousquet lives, you see. In a certain way, he's the one responsible for a portion of your misfortune. He worked for your father during the war, and Loïc's father worked for him. For a long time, I believed that I could connect both of them to this guy and to the rue des Rosiers. But I was wrong. You have nothing to do with either of them, and Bousquet has no link to the attack. Still, I am sure I will put my hand on him one of these days, to make him pay for his past."

I am ashamed. Ashamed of being born, ashamed of being here, alive while the Vél'd'Hiv children are dead. Ashamed of having loved my father, of loving him still beyond the grave, despite myself, despite everything I have learned. Seeking to relieve my conscience, I let my indignation explode:

"That bastard, Bousquet! How could humanity create such monsters? I ask myself that every day. Especially since I know that my father…"

My voice has stopped working. I don't manage to finish my sentence. I swallow in order to avoid making myself ridiculous in front of David. The cop, weary, shakes his head. Clearly, I have understood nothing. He takes out another cigarette from the pocket in his leather jacket, and offers me the pack. I refuse, waving it away with my hand. It is almost night now. David cuts off the engine and cracks open the window to let out the smoke.

"Bousquet?" he asks me, blowing out a mouthful of smoke. "A bastard? A monster? No, but have you seen Bousquet? Do you know what he looks like? That's what you call a monster? I will tell you something, Rodrigo. Bousquet has nothing ferociously villainous about him. I have already met him several times, I will tell you what I think and it will surprise you: that fellow is a regular guy. He was an ambitious civil servant, of course. Gifted, intelligent, efficient. That's what he still brags about. Efficient, that's his favorite word."

I don't understand what David is getting at. I lose my temper: "Efficient? Efficient for deporting innocent men, women, and children to the camps? Oh yes, efficiency is necessary for that! But what are you telling me?"

I have grabbed his jacket collar. He frees himself brusquely, throwing me against the door.

"Calm down, please! Let me speak. René Bousquet was a good Marne region prefect, a zealous and conscientious civil servant. He was twice offered ministerial positions; he refused both times, because he preferred to pursue the task he was given as best as he could. When he finally becomes secretary general of the police in April '42, he negotiates with the Germans, cajoles them. He organizes deportations, he even anticipates orders. Why, in your opinion?"

"Because he was an anti-Semite!"

234

"Anti-Semite... that's possible. But he has always defended himself against that accusation. Even today, he claims that he had nothing at all against the Jews. And you know what? I believe Bousquet!"

Hearing David speaking in this way, I wonder if I am dreaming, or having a nightmare. He continues his argument without paying the least attention to my astonishment.

"In the thirties, all of Europe was anti-Semitic, convinced that the international Jewish conspiracy was at work sucking the blood of the children of the homeland. That was the common belief. Bousquet shared it neither less nor more than any other. I will surprise you even more: I have rarely seen a gaze as frank as his. He is convinced that he did his best. He has not had an ounce of remorse, you see. How many thousands of people died in the camps because of him, he doesn't know. He only recalled those whom his collaborationist zeal could save. And it is true that some were spared thanks to him, thanks to his action... To begin with Mitterrand, would perhaps not be in this world anymore without his intervention. Yes, that's doubtless what explains the strange, politically risky, loyalty of the president to the former prefect. He owes his life to him, simply."

"But Bousquet is responsible for the crimes against humanity that the round-up of Vél-d-Hiv and of Marseille are! The scandal is that he was not punished and that he could have a brilliant career in the private sector, keeping friends in high places. It's revolting!"

David looks me over with a certain benevolence mixed with a form of condescension.

"Oh, of course, you are right. Let's even add that all this upper crust is not the least troubled by having to do with this gruesome person. But it is undeniable that nobody, or almost nobody, at the time, considered him to be a monster. They wanted to see in him a disciplined civil servant, the methodical executor of Laval's policy. And that is no doubt what he was: a cogwheel of horror. And Bousquet himself, in his innermost being, believes himself to be innocent. He can be tried and sentenced a hundred more times, but there is something that nobody will ever be able to do, even with all threats, courts, and prisons on the planet, and that is to shake his conscience or provoke his remorse. He will die with his soul at peace, convinced that his action was well-founded. The worst abuses are not committed by abominable, bloodthirsty criminals, but by normal, enthusiastic guys, devoted by vocation to the authorities deemed legitimate. That's what I think."

He raises his nose pensively towards the balcony on the sixth floor, then he throws his cigarette through top of the cracked-open window and starts the car. We are on the way to Beaumont for good this time. I think that, if he insisted on making this speech to me before our paths separate probably forever, it was not to hold forth on René Bousquet's psychology, for which I have no cure, and even less so to give me a lesson on general psycho-sociology. No, I think that David wanted to help me to accept myself, to take on the only role that I will never be able to renounce, which consists in being the son of Juan, of John, of Johann. That good man, that nice husband, sweet and thoughtful, that modest waiter in the Argentinian restaurant, that loving father was also one of the artificers of the final solution and, at the same time, the savior of Sarah, my mother, pulled from the claws of the Milice that was taking her to a certain death. I am the product of this ambivalence and, whether or not I want to, I am condemned to live with that.

We have been sitting in silence for over an hour in traffic jams when, finally, the circulation becomes a bit more fluid. David hits the gas. He likes to drive fast, he explains with a smile. I ask him:

"Where is Noura?"

He blinks and knits his brows, shuts off the radio softly playing *L'Aziza,* by Daniel Balavoine, a song that reminds me of my own Oriental woman. We hear nothing but the humming of the four-cylinders pushed to five thousand rotations per minute, despite being in fifth gear. The speedometer flirts merrily with 200 kilometers per hour. I have the impression that David continues to accelerate, perhaps to draw my attention to the road, to provoke my anxiety, or to change the subject. He postpones the moment when he will have to tell me the truth. But I do not allow myself to be distracted, I do not stop looking at him until he responds:

"Noura... Noura is in Loïc's house, in the Chevreuse Valley. That's where she took refuge a month ago."

Have I heard that right? Have I gone completely mad? Am I the suffering from improbable auditory hallucinations? Noura, who was supposed to lay a trap for Loïc, disappeared several weeks ago. Loïc was accused by the police of having kidnapped her. Marthe claimed that these maneuvers were part of the strategy decided by David. But now Rosenberg is telling me that Loïc has hosted her throughout this entire period, and still is as we speak. After having caught my breath and gotten hold of myself, I ask:

"How's that, 'that's where she took refuge'? You mean that he really did kidnap her?"

"No, I said, 'took refuge.' Hid, if you prefer..."

"I don't understand."

"Or rather, you don't want to understand..."

He clears his throat. Holding the wheel in one hand, he reaches for his cigarettes with the other, pulls out his Zippo, and lights one, keeping an occasional eye on the road, whose guardrails are flying by. We are surrounded by blue smoke that serves him as a protective veil. I can see his embarrassment less.

"Fine, if you prefer, I will spell things out for you! Loïc and Noura are lovers! The disappearance of Noura, contrary to what Marthe thinks, is not part of my plan, but theirs. They managed to engage in double dealing with remarkable skill, and I was fooled like a rookie."

He takes a long drag and puts the pedal to the metal as he puts out his cigarette, doubtless to contain his wrath. He is full of shame. The fable of the little piece of paper with Noura's address, left on purpose at Loïc's home, the history of Loïc's break-in at Noura's apartment, the fingerprints he left leading to his arrest, that whole well-oiled scenario that Marthe told me about in detail and in which the poor woman believes completely, all that is totally false. The real truth, which no one had considered, is that Nathalie, Loïc's wife, found them together. She was quickly rewarded for that with a bullet in the head. David eases off the pedal, leans back, and drives at a more reasonable speed. He continues his explanation:

"The authentic version is this. It might be hard to swallow, but I have to tell you. Loïc and Noura have been lovers for a long time. Among the mistresses marching through the Chevreuse Valley, one of them left her suitcases and her toothbrush: Noura."

I'm not sure I want to hear the rest, but David will not stop. He continues:

"Let's say that starting at the end of '84, she definitively chased away the other women, and she became, in a way, his favorite. The turtledoves were very smart and very discreet. They avoided seeing each other over weekends, preserving your morning golf with Loïc, your amorous escapades in Noura's arms, and the piano afternoons with the young Martin. They behaved with all the prudence necessary to never awaken your suspicions nor Nathalie's. They favored afternoons during the week. You were at the company headquarters. Loïc claimed he had to visit a factory, or had meetings in the countryside. Noura didn't have to justify herself. According to what I know, you never asked her, in any case, what she spent her days doing while you worked tirelessly for the company. When you traveled for a few days, Noura never accompanied you, and Loïc did so rarely: it was the occasion for them to spend several nights in a row together in Rambouillet. Nathalie allowed herself to be fooled by any old tale. She didn't know your schedule and didn't notice the conjunction of your trips with her husband's absences."

David looks furtively at me. I must look like a goldfish, my jaw falling and my eyes globular. He deals a final blow:

"There is no one blinder than the person who doesn't want to see, Rodrigo. You loved that woman and you were convinced that she felt the same passion for you. It didn't occur to you that your friend Loïc, your right-hand man, could have been seduced like you by this fatal beauty. Nathalie didn't have the least suspicion either. Until then."

"Until when? When happened?"

"Until the day Noura come back into their life. It's funny. After having kept up a secret relationship in the most perfect discretion for months, the lovers ended up being caught like kids when she returned to Paris."

It has begun drizzling. The windshield is blurred by drops that the windshield wipers efface with their characteristic squeaking. David, holding onto the wheel, paying attention to the traffic and the signs, continues his story without turning towards me, not noticing my distress. Over a year ago, already, my whole life collapsed, everything that gave it its savor and its pleasure. In a few days, I lost my status, my fortune, my company, my friends and, finally, in the Golfech basement, my human dignity. Then I learned about the shameful past of my father and, at the same time, I found out that my mother was not my mother. When I arrived in Morocco, all I had left was the memory of Noura and the marvelous perspective of seeing her again. Since then, I wander around, waiting for our definitive reunion. This last hope, this last thread connecting me to existence, has just been cut. My mind wanders. I hear the rest of the cop's explanations merely distantly. I have made my decision. As soon as he has left me in the Beaumont apartment, I will find a way to put my days to an end. Take revenge on Noura and

239

on Loïc? For what? As I loved them both so much, it's not crazy, at the end of the day, that they fell for each other. I could throw a stone at them, give them sermons, reproach them for their lies and disloyalty. But I will never be able to break what unites them. Noura got away from me a long time ago, without my even noticing. I have nothing left. I now hold it against David that he didn't let fate take its course, that he prevented his colleagues from shooting me. I would have preferred to stay there rather than having to go through this drama.

As I ruminate over these macabre thoughts, David continues his story. So Noura went to Loïc's home! They must not have seen each other for a while. Their reunion must have been electric. Nathalie noticed right away that something was happening between them, especially as she had rarely seen them together. Her intuition as a woman did not fool her this time. She began spying on them, listening to their conversations, looking for signs. She sometimes followed them. She ended up discovering the Chevreuse Valley house. All this time, Noura was double dealing and giving Marthe, Roucaud, and David more or less real or distorted information. They galloped like idiots until one day David gets a call from Nathalie that unravels everything. He can't believe his ears. He advises her to keep quiet for as long as possible, glean as much information as she can. Thus, Noura and Loïc have been lovers for a long time, she tells him. But starting in spring 1985, their relationship became more and more difficult to keep secret. They decided to collude to get rid of me. With Noura's cooperation, Loïc sought a way to bury me. Learning of my stock sale, he had the idea of fabricating the insider trading scandal. At the Ministry of the Interior, where he had connections, he spread the rumor that I could be involved in the financing of clandestine groups organizing terror attacks, including that of the rue des Rosiers. That is how he believed he got rid of me for good, until I reappeared in Casablanca. In the meantime, Noura had given birth to a child that was not mine, but his. The plan, it seems, was to get rid of Nathalie in turn. But Loïc procrastinated. For the many months that Noura spent in Morocco, with child, then taking care of the baby, he didn't have the heart to do away with his wife. His reunion with the beautiful Moroccan was ceaselessly postponed. Finally, Noura decided to return to Paris.

Only then did he have the courage and the will to eliminate Nathalie too, all the more so since his wife had worked to have her husband accused of Noura's kidnapping, as revenge. That's the anonymous denunciation that led to Loïc's arrest. Realizing the danger that his wife represented for him, the recently named CEO of Rodrigo Chemicals decided to murder her. He knew I was on my way to Avenue Mozart, through Noura, who had been informed by Marthe. I would be the ideal guilty person when they found me with the body. Luckily, David arrived in time to get me away! Proud of having foiled the murderer's skillful move, he turns towards me, looking away from the road for a moment, and smiles at me.

Thus, my sad fate has nothing to do with the machinations of the former prefect Bousquet, nor with the shameful past of my father, nor of Michel Martin's father, and even less with the lugubrious rue des Rosiers: it is nothing but the disastrous consequence of banal adultery. The two people I loved most in the world joined forces against me. David accelerates again. The speedometer needle rises and leans right, to the maximum. We are speeding towards the last stop, towards my one and only goal: death, eternal night, at last.

David dropped me off at Beaumont, promising, like last time, to visit me soon. That was eight months ago. He never returned. Major Roucaud hasn't given me a sign of life, either. I have at times noticed Deputy Mollard spying on me, pretending to walk through the market. But he has never showed up at my apartment. In the formica cabinet, I found wads of bills, giving me something to survive on and meet my modest needs for over a year. I don't know who left them. On the television and in the newspapers, I learn that I am sought for the murder of Nathalie Martin. Loïc played the role of a widower in mourning. Noura reappeared in Morocco and was sure to exonerate her lover. Loïc was never officially investigated, neither for kidnapping nor for the murder of his wife. In March, I read, in a short article, that David had been reinstated in the national police. Yet the Ganos case is not closed. The supposed murderer of Nathalie Martin and the two police officers is still at large. From time to time, I disguise myself and go shopping in the supermarket at the edge of the city, on the Auch road, ten minutes on foot from my apartment. Before entering the store, I walk around for an hour near the Gimone River. I have thought of jumping in, but the current is not strong enough and the water too lukewarm. I have no chance of being carried away. I recall the accusations against Rodrigo Chemicals: our painkillers were regularly used by suicidal people. A large enough overdose would cause a certain death, quick and painless. So it was often said that the prescription of our products had to be regulated more strictly. We fought against that and always achieved our objective. So in the pharmacy across the street is the key to my deliverance. A box full of pills from Rodrigo Chemicals would allow me to quit this world. Alas, I have no means to procure a prescription. Despite myself, I am still alive. The days pass and lengthen progressively. Now it is springtime, with its buds, birdsong, blackbirds, starlings. I even have my habits. Eat, walk, sleep. Seem to live. Do not love. Do not hate either. Think no more.

Remember. In January, I began writing this autobiography. July has arrived. Intense, dry heatwaves alternate with the Tramontane and the eastern wind, which brings merciful downpours. I finish my account today; I have reached the end of my story.

I count up what I have left in my moneybox. Three hundred fifty-two francs. I can hold out a month or two, not much more. Then I won't have anything else to live on. Will I have the mettle to succumb to famine? I pray to heaven to give me the strength. Since La Mennais and its forced genuflections, I have not addressed the All-Powerful. I beg him today to give me the courage to join him. I will put this manuscript in the cabinet. After my death, someone will find it eventually.

To the possible reader of these lines, I have only one request: convey to Marthe my affection and my forgiveness. Tell Jawad and Fatima how much I loved them and how much I miss them. Tell Noura and Loïc where my grave is. Ask them to bring flowers on All Saints' Day.

Henriette called an ambulance, which came for the body. After having aired out the room, Roucaud asked his deputy Mollard to return to the station in order to remain on call. The major had many hours of reading in front of him, he explained. David and Henriette sat down in front of him. And they read aloud, taking turns, Rodrigo Ganos' story, stopping only to drink a glass of water and stretch their legs. Six hours later, they arrived at the end of Ganos' text. Henriette, who had followed the affair only from afar, exclaims:
"So, my Jacques, you've been keeping secrets from me the past two years! You didn't consider telling me about all that?"
Roucaud responds with irony:
"You only need to call more often, my dear. You haven't given me much news these days. It's like you are only

interested in your corpses. But they must not occupy you with their chattering…"

She shrugs her shoulders and takes a cigarette from the pack David left on the table.

"I thought you smoked Gauloises?" says Rosenberg.

"Gitanes will do the trick for this evening. I finished my pack, I can make the most of yours… You don't seem to want to share! You're not going to finish it yourself, like a 'Jew' are you?"

David is given a start. Roucaud yells:

"Henriette!"

"Oh, come on, Jacques, I'm kidding… We can still joke a little, can't we?"

And she gives the cop's back a good smack as she lights her "ciggie" as she calls it.

"So, kids, speaking of corpses, you told me that it was the Martin's body that we found here and sent to the morgue this afternoon?"

David and Roucaud seem to suddenly realize it, as though they awoke from a dream. It's true, they found Loïc Martin in the middle of the garret where Ganos was living! And the person who killed him can only be Rodrigo. Roucaud gets up and prepares a coffee pensively. The night will be long. The sun is beginning to set, and a certain welcome freshness enters the cramped room. Henriette tenderly observes the man she loved for thirty years, whom she still loves. She recalls their years of happiness. She sees their son's accident again, the heartbreak. For some time, she is overcome with grief. David allows her to forget her melancholy:

"Jacques, make us some strong coffee, we're going to have to stay up all night. We have only one thing to do, but it will have to wait for the early morning."

"What is it?"

"We'll go to the airport."

"How's that?" exclaims Roucaud.

"It's very simple. Only four of us know that hideout. You, Marthe, me, and Noura. I suppose that it wasn't you who gave Loïc the address. Nor Marthe, whom I spoke with on the telephone yesterday and who has not heard from Noura. She picked up little Anissa from her father and disappeared. There is only one other person who could have told Loïc about that address: Noura. She guided him, even encouraged him to come here and get rid of the only remaining witness to their misdeeds, who could have compromised them. Only, it was a trap. She sent her lover to his death, deliberately. She warned Ganos by telephone. So he was ready and waiting for the felon. He let him in, indicated the manuscript to him. Martin, his curiosity piqued, approached in order to find out what he had returned from. Ganos took advantage of that to attack him. Then he left in a hurry, without thinking to bring his text with him."

Henriette and the gendarme listen to David circumspectly.

"But why the hell would Noura ambush the father of little Anissa?" Roucaud asks.

David stands up, lights a cigarette and leans against the windowsill. He lets the suspense build, takes his time to take two or three drags, and says contemptuously:

"Out of jealousy!"

The two others are thunderstruck. They wait for an explanation. David gives it. While he was working to be reinstated in the police thanks to a credible fable about the Golfech events, which nobody at the ministry wanted to touch in any case, he continued spying on Loïc, was sure he would be able to trap him and bring him down for the murder of his wife. What he discovered then surprised him as much as it excited him. Hardly had he officially moved into a new apartment with Noura did Loïc Martin begin to chase after women, like in the good old days. His relationship with Noura had doubtless interested him only when it was secret. The daily grind got the better of passion. Loïc went in search of a new thrill. The meetings could not take place in his bachelor pad; Noura would have noticed them too quickly. So Loïc contented himself with early evening rendezvous in Paris hotels. From time to time, he made up a trip to Switzerland or Italy, claiming that he would meet up with friends, or colleagues. In fact, he bought a ticket for his mistresses and took them with him. David conscientiously took notes and photos. Then he got in touch with Noura and revealed everything to her. She was stunned! A case of the biter being bit, in some way. Furious, full of regret and shame, she accepts delivering Loïc to Rodrigo on a plate. But now Rodrigo and Noura are thus both complicit and guilty. They have only one choice: to flee the country, together. They have only one possible refuge: Argentina. Noura's papers are in order, Anissa's too. Rodrigo's false passport, under the name of Bruno Cochet, will do the trick."

David straightens up, looks at his watch, and declares:

"There is only one flight per week for Buenos Aires from Toulouse. And it is leaving tomorrow morning at seven."

Roucaud is surprised:

"You want to go there to arrest them"'"

David guffaws:

"Arrest them? No, of course not! I want to make sure they get into the plane!"

The years passed. René Bousquet was assassinated in June 1993. In one of history's ironies, he was buried in Larrazet, that village in Tarn-et-Garonne where David and Rodrigo had stopped to have lunch, after having left Golfech, in the little hamlet where Roucaud had gotten his hands on Ganos for the first time, letting David escape. Klaus Barbie, who had been sentenced in 1987, died in 1991. Maurice Papon, much later, in 2007. David unofficially participated in all of these consequential matters. He postponed his retirement as long as possible, but one day, he was forced to leave the police. He continued to pursue former and neo-Nazis, on his own. Over time, they became rarer. Ten years ago, he definitively gave up his quest. He devoted himself to the study of the works of Edmond Rostand, the dramatist his father liked so much. He wrote an essay on the great poet. Henriette was struck by a heart attack in 2005. He went to her funeral. She is buried a stone's throw away from René Bousquet, in the cemetery in the hills above Larrazet. Roucaud was there, dignified, impassive. In the vault, there remained a spot for him. He moved in there at the end of winter in 2011. Marthe left this world in 2013. She had just turned ninety. She stopped breathing, her glasses pushed on up her forehead, her photo album in her hands.

David moved into a little two-room apartment in the 14th arrondissement, in Paris. He likes to take his coffee every morning in the betting bar next to his building. But since it is not permitted to smoke at the bar, this November 19, 2018, he goes out to smoke the first Gitane of the day. Sixty-five years of tobacco consumption has still not done him in. A woman stops in front of him. With her curly hair, her blue-green eyes, and olive skin, she is diabolically beautiful. She is around thirty years old. She is a little taller than him: he has lost height with the years.
"My name is Anissa and I have a message for you. My parents send you a hug. If you feel so inclined, they would be

delighted to welcome you in their home. Here is their address."

She gives him business card, then kisses him tenderly on the cheek. She looks him over for a moment with a smile, before turning on her heels and disappearing in the morning sunlight.

I would like to express my gratitude to Jason Kavett for his excellent work translating a book originally written in French into English.

Thanks to my parents, tireless readers, advisers and proofreaders.

Thanks as well to James and Emmanuel who acted as proofreaders of that novel written in their mother-tongue.

Thanks to all my family and friends, who have followed me, read me, encouraged me and given me advice for so many years.

Printed by Amazon Italia Logistica S.r.l.
Torrazza Piemonte (TO), Italy